FEVER

WAYNE SIMMONS

Proudly Published by Snowbooks in 2012

Snowbooks Ltd.
Tel: 0207 837 6482
email: info@snowbooks.com

www.snowbooks.com

British Library Cataloguing in Publication Data
A catalogue record for this book is available from the
British Library.

ISBN 978-1-907777-52-3

For George A. Romero

PROLOGUE

The grey-haired man sat on his chair, one bloodied hand hanging over the armrest.

The dog watched from across the room, reading the man's mood: the low-hanging head, the gritted teeth. A sense of dread hung in the air like muggy heat, like a sound the dog couldn't quite hear or a scent that wasn't strong enough to trail.

The dog moved towards the man, sniffed his hand, and licked it, enjoying the salty taste of the blood. The dog's stomach began to growl. It was hungry, ravenous.

The man spoke: "I have to do this," he said, tears filling his eyes. "It's for the best." He pulled his hand away from the dog's mouth, stroked its head, tickling behind its ears. "You have to understand that, pup."

The man pulled himself up from the chair and walked to the table where the shotgun lay. He lifted the gun. Traced his fingers along the barrel. He pulled back the hammer, turned, then aimed at the dog.

The dog froze. It feared the gun, knew what it was capable of. The dog wanted to run, wanted to hide, but there was nowhere to go.

A sudden noise interrupted them. Like the sound of a car starting, only faster, stronger.

The man lowered the gun.

He looked quickly to the dog, listening intently to the sound.

"My God..." he breathed.

He bolted for the stairs.

The dog followed, ears straining to trace the sound.

As they moved upstairs, the sound got louder, more defined.

They reached the landing. There was blood on the landing carpet. Its scent was familiar, and the whiskers on the dog's nose danced. For a moment, the dog forgot about the sound. It sniffed the blood, tracking its smell. The trail led towards the bathroom.

The bathroom door was ajar. The dog dipped its head through, sniffing. Body parts filled the bath. They were coated in plastic, like the rump steaks the man used to bring home every weekend. The dog's mouth watered.

The man was shouting.

The dog's ears pricked up. It left the bathroom. Followed the man's voice into the bedroom.

The man stood by the window.

A woman lay on the bed, shaking and struggling against the bonds around her hands and feet. Her mouth was taped, her eyes bulging. The dog recognised the woman's smell. It jumped on the bed to greet her.

The window was open. A blast of wind blew in, caressing the dog's fur. The dog looked away from the woman, followed the man's gaze out the window.

The dog moved off the bed, climbed onto a nearby chest of drawers. Leaned its front paws onto the windowsill to look out.

The light was dazzling at first, revealing a spectacular view across the fields.

Countless bodies lingered outside, surrounding the house like a drunken army. Their coughs and wheezes faded into the new mechanical sound. Their smells were dense and putrid, mixing with the summer air like freshly-made silage.

The sound from before was stronger now, almost deafening. It filled the whole house, drowning out everything else.

And then the dog spotted it – the thing making the sound. The thing the man was so excited about. Was calling for, waving to.

There was a helicopter in the air.

And it was coming straight for them.

PART ONE

THE DAY IT STARTED

ONE

He switched the light off, reached for her.

"No," Ellis said, pushing him away forcefully.

"Why not?" Blake said.

"Because I said so. I told you: I want to talk not – "

"Not fuck?"

"Blake!" She hated him being crass. He was an HSO, for God's sake. Men like Dr Blake Farrow shouldn't talk cheap. Ellis wanted to bring him home to Derry one day, show him off to her family, but Mother hated a potty mouth.

"Okay, okay," he said. He sat down on a nearby stool. "What is it, babe?" he said.

His voice gave her goose pimples. It was one of the things that had attracted Ellis in the first place. Being an American company, Alturn had migrated some of its most experienced staff when setting up the Belfast lab, their investment welcomed by Stormont. But Ellis was invested in other ways: there was something about Blake Farrow's Southern-fried drawl that stood out from the crowd. It reminded her of Sawyer from the TV show, *LOST*. The accent worked for her, and Blake Farrow knew it.

Ellis sighed. "This," she said. "Meeting in your storeroom. Hiding our…" She checked herself, chose her words carefully, "Hiding *whatever-this-is-we-do* from everyone else in the lab. I just can't do it anymore, Blake, I – "

She stopped talking. In the poor light she watched Blake rub his eyes with a forefinger and thumb. She knew what that meant. She'd seen him do similar after looking through a microscope for too long or coming out from a meeting with Johnson. *She was boring him.*

Ellis reached for her lab coat, pulled one arm into it.

Blake went to touch her, but she tore away from him. "Don't!" she said firmly.

"Come on, Ellie," he said, "I was listening. Really."

She went to leave but then stalled by the storeroom door. She froze. Waited.

"Ellie?" Blake pried.

She stepped back from the storeroom's small glass pane. Looked to Blake, her eyes wide.

"What is it?" he asked, but she placed a finger over her lips.

"Kill the light," she said. "Someone's coming."

Blake fumbled for the nearby torch, switched it off.

Ellis returned to the glass pane, watched as someone entered Blake's office, flicked the light switch then looked nervously around.

"Who is it?" Blake said, peering over her shoulder.

"Shush!"

The intruder was at Blake's desk, opening and ruffling through each drawer. He stopped, looked around for a moment, said, "Come on, come on, where are you?" He reached for a line of files on a shelf, pulled each down separately, flicked through them.

"It's Chris Lennon," Blake whispered. "One of the reps."

Ellis shushed him again.

Lennon looked towards the storeroom, and Ellis froze, but something in the corridor outside disturbed the rep. He swore under his breath, replaced the file in his hand, and then quickly left the office.

Ellis opened the storeroom door.

Blake pushed past her. He reached towards the line of files, picking one from the shelf just as Lennon had done.

"What was he looking for?" Ellis said.

Blake didn't answer. Ellis watched him flick through the file. It didn't look like anything special: experiment checklists, health and safety memos. The kind of paperwork she would see in the lab every day.

"Blake?" she pressed.

He looked up, met her gaze. "No idea," he said. But the expression on his face seemed guilty, like he knew *exactly* what Lennon had been after.

"Come on, Blake," Ellis said, "He was looking for *something*. I'm not stupid."

"Call security," Blake said. He retrieved the phone from the wall and handed it to her, but Ellis replaced it, folded her arms and continued to stare at him. "Look, I don't know any more than you do!" Blake protested. "Johnson handles all the contract stuff. I just do what I'm told."

"And what *have* you been told?" Ellis countered. "Blake, you're an HSO. You've been told a hell of a lot more than the rest of us."

Blake went to move, but Ellis blocked him. She wasn't going to let this go. He knew something, and she wanted to hear it. Damn it, she deserved more than this!

"Come on, Blake, talk to me!" she pressed.

Still Blake said nothing.

Ellis threw her hands into the air, deflated. This wasn't how it used to be between them.

When they had first started seeing each other, they'd talked a lot. There were stories from Blake's years of working as a surgeon, prior to joining Alturn. Stories about Johnson and other characters they both knew within the lab. He talked of how Alturn had lured him away from a career in medicine to work as consultant on a range of anti-viral drugs. But once Blake took over as head of Project QT, a new contract that made lab monkeys like Ellis very uncomfortable, the talking stopped.

And now some rep was digging around his office…

Blake threw his hands up in the air. "You see, this is the problem," he said.

"What do you mean?"

"You want to know why we can't be more than," he searched, finding similar words to those she used, "*whatever-it-is-we-are*. Well, *this* is why. There's stuff I'm not allowed to tell you. Stuff I'm not allowed to tell *anyone*, even my –" He stopped short, looked at her. His face fell.

"Your *wife*," Ellis finished for him bitterly.

"Ellie, I –"

"Forget it, Blake. I've had enough of this. We're finished."

Ellis slammed the door as she left. She stood for a moment, seething. *The using bastard*, she fumed, and then marched quickly down the corridor.

Ellis used her pass on the security door, moving into the lab's second admin block. She turned a corner then stopped dead in her tracks.

In the distance she noticed Chris Lennon. This time the rep was heading for Johnson's office.

Ellis decided to follow him.

TWO

Ellis didn't know Lennon. She knew some of the other reps. They came into the lab frequently: selling equipment; giving demos on whatever product they were peddling; littering the place with catalogues. But this Chris Lennon guy was new to Alturn. He didn't look like a sales rep. His bleached-blond hair and perma-tan lent him the appearance of an ageing boy band wannabe. Not great for cloak-and-dagger stuff; the poor beggar stood out like a sore thumb.

Ellis watched as he slid his card onto Johnson's office door reader and entered.

She had always questioned the security clearance for reps. They weren't meant to have their own access cards, but lab assistants would often lend them out, saving the bother of having to babysit all morning. With their own cards, the reps would have access to almost everywhere.

Everywhere apart from the QT labs, of course...

Ellis slipped out from behind the corner of Corridor B4 and moved down B1. She reached Johnson's office, took a cursory glance through the door's glass pane. She could see Lennon, going through Johnson's desk the same way he'd gone through Blake's.

What was he looking for?

He lifted his head, looked towards the door.

Ellis pulled away from the glass. She stood for a moment, her back leaning against the wall. Gingerly, she returned to the window.

Lennon mustn't have seen her. His face was turned away again, nose buried in some files.

Ellis checked both sides of the corridor. Still empty.

She took a deep breath, swiped her card to open the door, slipped inside the room, and then closed the door behind her.

Lennon looked up, face like a deer caught in headlights.

"You're one of the sales reps, right?" Ellis asked.

Lennon swallowed. "Y-yes," he said.

"So what are you doing in here?"

"Looking for Mr Johnson. I-I need to talk to him about an order he put in last week."

"Order for what?"

Lennon thought for a moment. "Ethanol," he said.

"I don't believe you," Ellis said. Her voice was firm, confident. "We've a storeroom full of ethanol. And it comes straight from the suppliers. You should know that."

Lennon didn't move. He stared at Ellis for a second, the corner of his mouth upturned like he was either going to start laughing or crying.

"So, what are you *really* doing here?" Ellis pressed.

"Sorry?"

"You overturned Farrow's office. Now you're in here. What are you looking for?"

Lennon still held the file in his hands. He set it down, stepped away from it. He smiled uncomfortably. Sweat broke across his orange face. "Nothing," he said. "I'm looking for nothing."

"You're lying. Look, I'm going to have to call security."

"Please don't."

"Sorry," Ellis said, reaching for the phone on the wall. "I have to."

She rang through to the front desk. A voice answered. It was Abe, the lab's head of security.

Ellis opened her mouth to speak, looking at Lennon. But the words didn't come.

Lennon held a revolver in his hand, aimed right at her.

"I – er – punched the wrong number in," Ellis said down the phone.

"That you, Ellie?" Abe said, laughing.

"Sure is, Abe," she said. "I'll be up to see you later. Need some coffee?"

"That would be great. You're an angel," Abe said.

"You better believe it," Ellis said then replaced the receiver.

Her hands were shaking. Her eyes remained fixed on the revolver. "You know, Farrow's probably called them anyway," she said to Lennon.

"Doesn't sound like that to me," the salesman replied.

They stood in silence for a moment. Ellis could hear a clock ticking, keeping time. It seemed slow. Her heart was beating twice as fast.

Lennon turned his attention to another set of drawers. They were locked, but he fumbled in his pocket, pulling out a small, thin wire. He glanced back at Ellis and then leaned down, still holding the gun, his free hand working the lock with the pick.

Once in, he ruffled through each of the drawers. He seemed to find what he was looking for: a set of papers, some memos. He slid them into the inside pocket of his jacket.

"What *is* that?" Ellis dared to ask.

He stood up, looked Ellis in the eye. His face was strained. "I'm sorry," he said. "I didn't mean to scare you. Please don't call security when I go." He held her gaze for a moment and then quietly slipped out the door.

Ellis reached immediately for the phone.

Do it! her head said.

But her gut told her something different.

She placed the phone back on its receiver then sat down in the nearby office chair, her body shaking.

"Oh boy," she said.

THREE

Ellis grabbed a coffee and took it up to Abe as promised, but she told him nothing about the incident. Abe noticed she wasn't herself and commented on it, but she fobbed him off with talk of not sleeping well, made her excuses then left.

Her belly was full of nerves. She went to the toilet, threw up, flushed, then lowered the seat and sat for a while.

"Come on," she whispered to herself. "Keep it together."

She kept it together. Worked her shift as normal, heading next to the lab's Animal House. It stood one block over from Admin.

Health and safety was stringent when working with the animals. Ellis needed to dress head-to-toe in protective clothing before she could enter the storage rooms. As ASO, it was part of her job to inject the animals. Monitor the effect of various dosages of SAMPLE A on them. But it killed Ellis to hurt the little darlings. She loved these creatures; the rabbits, the mice - even the rats.

She particularly loved the cats.

"There you go, beautiful," she said, lowering one of the kittens back into its home.

The cage was labelled C75, but Ellis called the kitten Ginger, due to the auburn fur that covered its small body. Ginger was purring. Despite all the needles Ellis inserted through its skin, the wee kitten still seemed to like her.

She placed the cap back over the syringe, removed the needle and dropped it into the nearby yellow box labelled CONTAMINATED SHARPS. She ditched the syringe into a separate waste bin, also yellow, with the familiar Biohazard sign on its front.

Her eyes fell upon the little bottle on the bench. SAMPLE A19. It came from E Block, Project QT's restricted area. From the symptoms the animals would present, Ellis guessed the bottles contained various dosages of some sort of flu virus.

Ellis wrote the time and date of Ginger's injection into the relevant folder, adding some brief notes indicating the kitten was healthy when she'd injected it. She signed her name beside the entry.

Ellis moved along the line of similar-looking cages, going through the same process with each of the other kittens. They were all part of Project QT. And looking at the little beggars, Ellis knew *exactly* why she hadn't reported Lennon...

In her ASO persona, Ellis was good at following orders. She did what she was told to do. Injected the kittens with SAMPLE A. Some of them died. Others developed sniffles and sticky eyes and then died. A few lived through it, got better. And these were the ones Blake Farrow was interested in. These were the ones that were taken to the restricted area over in E Block..

It wasn't her business what happened after that.

Only it *was* her business...

Ellis was feeling more and more guilty these days. She couldn't just say she was following orders. She needed to take responsibility. After all, it was her that was stabbing the poor things with those goddamn needles. Sure, she found it eased her conscience a little when she spent some quality time afterwards with the little moggys, rubbing their legs where she'd injected them, petting them. But God forgive her, some of them wouldn't see another week, never mind another year…

Damn you, Blake, Ellis mused. *Damn you for all of this.*

She entered the next room. This one also had cages, but where the previous room's occupants were feline, there were only birds here. Chickens, to be precise. Ellis nodded a quick hello to the two men attending the cages as she passed. She wouldn't bother them. Birds spooked her. Always had.

As a child, she remembered one day being surrounded by pigeons, her mother running to her aid, shooing them away. Ellis reckoned the incident hadn't been quite as horrific in reality as it was in her mind. Probably just some people feeding pigeons in the park. But that's the problem with the things that frightened you as a child: over time, after years of nightmares and phobias, they became something completely different. Something otherworldly.

She left the animal storage rooms, using her card to enter Corridor C1. It ran long and straight, connecting to the next corridor that looked exactly the same, with its pale, metallic walls, the fluorescent lighting along each side and ceiling, reminding Ellis of those little 'cat's eyes' lights she would see on motorways and country roads. The corridors of C Block formed a grid pattern, connected to A, B and D by security doors. *A for Admin. B for Blake. C for Cats*, Ellis thought, remembering the mnemonic she'd taught herself.

Blake again! Ellis couldn't get him out of her head.

She knew her relationship with him, this thing they had together, was going nowhere. He had no intention of leaving his wife. Ellis was just a plaything to him. She needed to ditch him for good and move on. Get out of this godforsaken place. Get another job, a job she didn't feel guilty doing, and put all this behind her.

But she couldn't help herself. When it came to Blake Farrow, Ellis was like a moth around light.

She remembered the day she'd first met him. Ellis had walked through the glass-fronted entrance of Alturn for her interview. Blake was the first to greet her; he was on the panel. He was older than Ellis, almost twice her age, but the young ASO had been immediately attracted to him.

A lot had happened since then. The girl Ellis used to be all but disappeared. The friends she used to love spending time with, the music she used to listen to, all part of her old life.

She even *looked* different: her once short, spiky hair was now grown out, fashioned into a bob. She dressed differently, more business-like. Worse still, Ellis felt comfortable in these clothes now. She couldn't see herself wearing what she used to wear. And that scared her. This place: these grey, metallic walls, the needles, the cats, Blake and his storeroom – it had consumed her. It was her whole world.

Ellis entered the washing room in Corridor C3. She pulled the surgical mask from her face, peeled off the cover-all and popped it into the large washer in the middle of the room. She picked up the wooden stick leaning against the washer, using it to dunk her gear firmly into the soapy water. Along the walls, three large dryers spun merrily, humming like drunken old sailors.

Ellis stopped at the mirror on the way out, checking her reflection.

Sex hair.

It was something Blake would say that always made her laugh. *You've got sex hair*, he would whisper, pulling her back into his arms. And on retreating to the ladies' room, Ellis would find out why: her naturally curly hair would be frizzy, standing on end as if she'd been electrocuted.

Ellis tried to flatten the hair as best she could before leaving the wash room. She removed her shoe covers and placed them in the waste disposal by the door. She used her card, leaving the Animal House and entering D Block.

She thought of going home, of taking the lift from D up to the surface, getting in her car and driving away.

Never coming back.

She called the lift.

The lab area itself ran underground, with only a basic shop-front reception and some meeting rooms up top. The lift came three stories down to a fully air-conditioned research area. This was deemed safest for viral work; any of the labs could be contained at the flick of a switch, something the staff tried not to think too much about.

Ellis waited, drumming her fingers on the wall impatiently.

She was disturbed by a clatter of footsteps. Fellow lab workers hurried up the corridor.

Something was happening.

FOUR

Ellis spotted Dave Lightfoot, a fellow ASO amongst the crowd, and grabbed him.

"What's going on?" she asked.

Dave didn't reply, instead taking her by the arm, dragging her along with him.

Ellis couldn't help but notice the grave look on his face. Dave was normally the lab joker, and Ellis might have thought whatever happening now to be part of some elaborate ruse he'd concocted. But his eyes said otherwise.

She followed him along Corridor D3, towards the security door leading to E, where Blake's Project QT was based.

Someone produced a card and ran it through the reader.

They were in.

E Block was like Pandora's Box to those who didn't work there. Ellis felt her heart skip as she followed the others, finding even more people on the other side, gathered around the small glass pane looking in on room E21.

"Dave, tell me what's going on," Ellis said again.

Dave shook his head. "You wouldn't believe it."

"Try me," she said.

"They've been experimenting on *people*, Ellis."

"What?!"

"Farrow's project, QT. It's not just those fucking cats. He's been doing something to people. Injecting them with the same shit."

"You're not making sense," Ellis said. "That's not allowed and you know it."

"Some bloke called Jenkins showed up around lunchtime, started kicking off at reception. They called security. I was with Abe in the canteen, so I went along for the hell of it." Dave shook his head. "I wish I hadn't, Ellie. Jesus, that Jenkins guy was a real fucking mess. Claimed Farrow had done something to him, injected him with some shit. Then Farrow weighed in and took him away. And now –" Dave's voice suddenly failed him.

"And now *what*?!" Ellis pressed.

Excited voices filled the corridor. Someone shushed them.

Ellis fought for a good vantage point at E21's door, cursing her small stature. She heard a sharp intake of air: one of the lab assistants pulled away, hand over her mouth, gagging. Ellis fought to take their place. She reached the glass pane, peered through.

It was a typical holding room, but the equipment inside was different to what Ellis would normally see in a lab. It looked more like a hospital, with drips in holders and heart monitors next to gurneys. One of the gurneys was pulled out of its place, now in the middle of the room next to a metal trolley, and it was to here that Ellis' eye was drawn.

A naked man stood by the gurney. He turned towards the door and Ellis could see immediately what all the fuss was about.

"Christ," she whispered, her throat suddenly dry.

She stepped away from the door, looked at Dave.

"Where's Farrow?" she said.

"Gone."

"What about Johnson, then? Anyone told him about this?"

"Not yet," Dave said, staring at her invitingly.

…

"What!" Johnson barked, minimising his screen. He looked up from his desk, "This had better be–"

His voice trailed off.

A young woman stood by his chair. Although Johnson recognised her, he didn't know her name. He was terrible with names, much better with faces. Especially a face like hers.

She leaned in close, and he could smell her perfume. It was very different to the perfume his wife would wear; hers was floral, musky, saccharine, like dried up flowers wilting in the sun. But this young girl reminded him of youth, of vitality and colour. Of nice things, like dessert and chocolate and sweet ale – things Johnson longed for but, since his operation, could no longer have.

"Sir," she said, and her voice was as pleasant as her perfume, "I need to show you something."

"What is it?"

"Please sir," she said. "Probably best you see it firsthand…"

She looked nervous. A red blush, starting around her cheeks, was spreading down her neck.

Johnson sighed. He turned back to his computer, called up the user menu, typed in his password to lock the screen. He got up, stood for a moment then retrieved a pen from the holder by his monitor. He tucked the pen into the front pocket of his lab coat.

"Okay," he said to her, "Lead the way."

He followed the girl out of the admin block, down Corridor B4 towards the labs. His eyes were drawn to her lab coat fluttering in front of him, offering a glimpse of her shapely legs.

She used her card to exit B Block. They continued through the complex, passing through C and D Blocks. Johnson noticed very few people on his travels. When they reached the security door to E Block, he realised why he hadn't spotted anyone: through the heavy door's strengthened glass, he could see most of his staff team filling the corridor.

Johnson looked suspiciously at the girl. This was out of bounds. Only the Contract Boys were allowed in here, a term used to describe staff with the highest level of security clearance.

The girl ran her card through the reader. Its light turned green.

Johnson's eyes narrowed, "Wait a minute. Who gave you that card?"

"Room E21, sir," the girl said.

She stood aside to let Johnson enter first.

At the other side of the door, a middle-aged black man in security uniform nodded gravely at Johnson then moved to let him pass. Johnson recognised the man as Abe, head of security.

The corridor was blocked by an excited gaggle of lab workers.

"Step aside, please," Johnson said abruptly, wondering why Abe hadn't removed them already.

The crowd parted, and Johnson approached the door, drawing his own card from a lab coat pocket. But the young woman placed a hand on his shoulder. "Sir, I'm not sure it's safe to go in."

Johnson fixed her with a quizzical look. He slid the card back into the pocket of his lab coat. He sighed, cupping his hands to look through the glass pane on the door.

Behind the glass, Johnson found a gurney in the middle of the floor. Standing by the gurney was a man. His back was turned, so it was hard to tell what age he was. The man was naked, his back, legs and buttocks exposed. He looked unhealthy; his skin had a distinctly grey pallor about it.

Johnson turned back to the others. "Okay, someone talk to me. What have we got here?"

An older woman cleared her throat. She looked to the others, but they avoided her gaze. She took a breath then referred to her clipboard, flicking through the attached notes.

"This is Mr Alan Jenkins," she began. "Forty nine years old. One of the test subjects for Project QT. Injected along with all the others twelve weeks ago."

The woman paused. She looked up, found the others staring back at her.

Johnson frowned impatiently.

The woman continued, "Jenkins showed standard symptoms of flu three days after contracting the virus but then proceeded to make a full recovery. Responded positively to all tests. Released from quarantine four weeks –"

"We don't need the finer details," Johnson interrupted. "These people don't have clearance!"

The older woman looked up from her notes. She cleared her throat, began reading again.

"No reports of ill health until yesterday, when he left work early, complaining of migraines. Chronic flu symptoms presented as the day continued. Jenkins showed up at the lab around lunchtime today, and Dr Farrow took him in, commenced tests at –"

"Can you *please* get to the point?!" Johnson barked.

The woman jumped at his voice. She looked up then adjusted her glasses.

"Sir," she began, and her voice was very small and faint as if carried to Johnson's ears from far away, "Mr Jenkins passed away this afternoon, time of death just past three o'clock. The virus consumed him. There was absolutely nothing that could be done…"

FIVE

Johnson stared at them each in turn, his face incredulous. "I'm sorry," he said, "But *this* is Mr Jenkins we're watching now, yes? *So how can...*"

"It's impossible," the woman cut in. "I know that."

Johnson grabbed the clipboard from her, flicked through the notes. He removed the pen from the breast pocket of his lab coat, tapped it against the clipboard as he read.

Ellis cupped her hands, peering once more through the glass pane on E21's door. She watched carefully as the dead man investigated his surroundings. It was like the poor sod had just woken, finding himself somewhere he didn't expect to be.

He looked up, then began to stumble towards her. As he edged closer, Ellis could see his wounds more clearly. Both lungs and heart were missing, his chest all but hollowed out.

Ellis raised a hand to her mouth, feeling distinctly queasy.

Jenkins continued towards her. His movements were slow and deliberate, and it took much longer than it should for him to reach the door. His head fell to one side as he drew closer, both eyes on hers. Ellis fought the urge to back away, but a very wrong part of her remained deeply intrigued by Jenkins.

A constant string of drool hung from the dead man's mouth. One side of his bottom lip hung lower than the other. Yellow, tobacco-stained teeth were locked in a permanent grimace. His eyes were bloodshot. They sat like two rubber balls, cocooned within the pale, blotchy skin of his face.

Jenkins came right up to the door's window, as if about to kiss it. Were he breathing, his breath would have steamed up the glass.

But dead men don't breathe…

He pulled away, stumbling back towards his gurney.

Ellis strained to see what had distracted him, eyes widening at the revelation.

She could hear Johnson in the background. "Where's Farrow?" he barked. "I want to speak to Farrow!"

"No one's seen him," Dave Lightfoot answered.

"He vanished," the woman with the clipboard added. "We think he left the complex."

But Ellis turned, fixed all three of them with a look. "I know where he is," she said. "He's behind this door. Blake's still in there."

…

For a moment, no one spoke. The silence was painful.

Ellis felt sick again.

Dave went to E21's glass pane, cupped his hands and stared in. "She's right – he's in the room," he said. "I can see him now."

"We can't leave him there," Ellis said.

"What else can we do?" Dave countered. "No one's mad enough to open that door!"

Ellis rubbed her mouth, thought for a moment.

She pushed Dave aside, ran her card through the reader. It beeped, allowing her access through the door.

She looked pointedly at Johnson, expecting him to say something, to try and stop her, but he didn't say a word.

Ellis reached for the door handle and began to turn it.

It was Abe who intervened.

"Ellie," he said quietly, placing his big hand over hers, "we don't know what's happening in there. Farrow could be infected with…" he thought for a moment then continued, "With whatever Jenkins has got."

"Please," Ellis said, "Take your hand away." But she didn't really want him to. She wanted Abe to stop her. To drag her away and lock her in some room until all this was sorted out. Instead, Abe smiled thinly, released his hand and backed away.

Ellis swallowed hard.

She opened the door and stepped inside.

SIX

Dr Blake Farrow was curled up in the corner of E21. He didn't know how long he'd been there.

He was in shock, his breathing laboured. His chest thundered, as if his heart were about to explode. But Blake knew that wouldn't happen. He was a doctor, for Christ's sake. Hearts didn't just explode, no matter how nervous a man got. There were rules to medicine. Things didn't just happen without a logical reason…

Except this. There was no logic to this.

Blake watched the man he'd known as Alan Jenkins amble towards him, blood flowing freely from huge gaping wounds in his chest. No man could function without the use of his heart or lungs. Yet here Blake was, staring into the eyes of what was essentially a dead man walking.

Blake pulled himself slowly to his feet; eyes still fixed on Jenkins as if expecting the dead man to suddenly charge.

An idea struck the doctor.

He looked towards the trolley in the centre of the room, next to the gurney. He moved towards it, reaching for the box of needles. Blake retrieved a needle, snapping the first protective cap away before grabbing a syringe from another box. He inserted the needle to the syringe, glancing quickly at the shambling corpse moving towards him.

Jenkins was almost upon him.

Blake scrambled for the small bottle of sedative on the trolley. He shook it vigorously and then, after snapping the second protective cap from the business end of the needle, pierced the bottle's cap, sucking up a healthy dose of sedative. He released the air from the syringe, watching as a little of the liquid seeped from the needle.

A sound at the door. Blake stared towards it, distracted from the task at hand and the creature drawing towards him.

It was Ellis.

"Jesus, Ellie," he shouted at her, "Get the hell out!"

But she cut him off, screaming, "Blake, look out!"

He turned to find Jenkins lunging forward, the dead man's arms outstretched, clammy hands finding his throat. There was strength in the attack. Inexplicable strength. Blake dropped the needle as he fell to the floor, fighting for breath as Jenkins' grip tightened.

He could still hear Ellis screaming at him. There were other sounds too. Commotion from outside, heightened voices, as if a crowd were gathered at the door, watching him struggle like some hapless cage fighter.

His right hand found the needle again, gripping it tight.

Blake held Jenkins' chin with his other hand then attacked with the needle. He found Jenkins' left eye, teeth gritted as he forced the point through, digging more than injecting. A small jet of yellowish water spurted into the doctor's face as he forced the needle deeper.

But Jenkins didn't even flinch, his grip like a vice.

The needle broke, part of it still jammed in the dead man's eye, the syringe tumbling to the floor.

"Fuck!" Blake croaked as the cold hand tightened around his throat.

...

Ellis hadn't planned this.

She wasn't quite sure what she thought would happen when she entered E21. Maybe she would fall dead right there, succumb to whatever mutated virus was in the air. Maybe Jenkins would turn, growl, then chase her around the room like some kind of B-Movie monster. But instead the dead man had lunged at Blake, the doctor distracted by her entrance.

Blake was going to die, and it was her fault.

Ellis hurried to the trolley, a scalpel the first thing she saw. She made a grab for it then rushed to Blake's aid.

She grabbed Jenkins by the hair, stabbing the infected man's neck, blood splashing across the room as the scalpel's razor-like blade cut into his flesh.

A low moan escaped from Jenkins' lips, the infected man releasing Blake in order to reach behind his head. His hands groped for Ellis, but still she persisted, tearing through his dead skin.

Blake slid himself away, coughing as his lungs refilled with air.

But still Ellis hacked, screeching as blood soaked her face, spraying from the wounds as she ripped deeper into the flesh and cartilage, the dead man's head almost removed from his body.

Finally, Jenkins stopped moving, his body slipping from Ellis' grip.

Ellis fell to the floor beside him, Jenkins' head still in her hands, attached only by the bloated veins running down the remainder of his neck.

SEVEN

While none of the other witnesses doubted the authenticity of what Blake Farrow relayed, Johnson remained sceptical. He wanted further proof, and he wanted it in the comfort of his own office. And so Abe was forced to link the security camera of E21 to Johnson's PC. A video recording of the whole terrifying ordeal, from Jenkins' admission to Ellis' brutal confrontation, seemed the only way to convince the old fool once and for all.

Blake stood behind Johnson as the older man worked the mouse on his PC.

They started with footage from earlier in the day, when Alan Jenkins was first brought in. They watched as Jenkins was led into Room E21 and then prepped for a variety of standard tests, the infected man dealing with several ASOs as well as Blake himself.

Johnson grew bored, hit FORWARD on his media player.

"I would have called you," Blake said, as they watched the footage speed up on screen. "But you never seem too interested in the affairs of the lab at the best of times. Always wrapped up in your paperwork."

Johnson shot an acidic glance at his colleague then returned to his PC, clicking the footage back to NORMAL speed.

He clicked on PLAY, leaning closer to the screen as Jenkins took his last dying gasps. There was no sound on the recording, but Johnson could see the infected man's face change, the laboured coughing and wheezing giving way to stillness.

An ASO hurried into the room, checking Jenkins' pulse. Blake was then called to confirm the infected man's death. In the recording, Blake looked at his watch and called time, then left the room. Johnson looked to the timer on the screen, checking it against the notes from his clipboard..

More time passed, the body lying perfectly still on the gurney. Johnson clicked on FORWARD again, speeding the video footage until he saw Blake Farrow return to the room, this time readied for autopsy. He watched as, onscreen, his colleague made the first incision into Jenkins' chest.

"You're in trouble," Johnson said to Blake.

"What do you mean, in trouble?"

"Dammit, man, you opened his body up! You're not a surgeon here! That is *not* the protocol, and you know it!"

"Fuck protocol!"

Johnson sighed, rubbed his eyes.

As the footage continued to play, Blake leaned in closer. "Watch this bit," he said to Johnson, pointing to the screen. "His eyes open. Just as I remove the heart, his goddamn eyes open. Can't you see that?!"

Johnson said nothing.

Onscreen, Blake was backing away from the gurney where Jenkins lay. Soon the dead man had pulled himself upright and was clambering onto his feet. He stumbled, fell clumsily to the floor like some old drunk.

Johnson laughed humourlessly. "This can't be happening," he said. "It makes no sense!"

"Of course it makes no sense," Blake said, his face deadly serious. "Dead men don't open their eyes. Dead men don't stand up and walk around the room and attack you. It's nonsense! But you can see it as clearly as I can, Johnson. The video doesn't lie. This happened just as I'm telling you it happened. And you know it!"

"M-maybe it's some sort of joke," Johnson barked, furiously pointing his finger at Blake. "Maybe you're trying to make a fool out of me. You and the rest of them!"

"Why the hell would I do a thing like that!?" Blake yelled. He strode across the office, his face tight with anger. "You're impossible!" he said to Johnson. "You were there, right outside the door. You saw it, just like everyone else."

"I'll tell you what's impossible; all of this," Johnson said.

He fiddled with his pen nervously. The pen slipped from his hand, colliding with the picture of his wife and kids, knocking it over. Johnson immediately righted the photo.

"Well it happened. Bottom line," Blake said. "And you have to –"

"I have to do what?" Johnson cut in. "Report it to the funders?"

"Yes," came another voice. Both men looked in its direction.

Ellis stood by the door to Johnson's office. She wore clean scrubs. Her face was dry and sore from rubbing so hard with a cloth that the skin had peeled away. But she needed to get every trace of Alan Jenkins from her body. God knows, there was enough of the dead man left imprinted in her mind...

"Damn it!" Johnson fumed, slamming his fist on the desk. He glared at Ellis. "Do you know how vital this contract is to us?"

"Sir," she began, coming through the door, "I hardly think that's —"

"All of our jobs are on the line here," Johnson cut in.

Ellis fixed him with a cold, hard stare, "This is a lot more serious than jobs," she said. "We had a dead man walking around the room where his autopsy was held, for God's sake!"

"The cadaver was mobile, but we can't be sure it was alive in any other sense," Johnson countered.

"You've got to be kidding me," Blake protested.

But Johnson ignored the other man, rising up from his seat to confront Ellis. "You're right," he said. "It isn't *just* our jobs we're talking about; it's much more serious than that. Each and every one of us will be dragged through the courts for this, hung drawn and quartered! Those of us lucky enough not to do jail will never work again."

Ellis felt her eyes water. She blinked, but Johnson had noticed. He drew closer to her, right up to her face. She could smell his sweat amongst the expensive aftershave; could see the short white chest hairs under his thick gold necklace.

"What age are you?" he asked, and a faint smile crossed his lips. "Twenty? Twenty-one? Barely out of college, all excited about your new career in research." He straightened, clicked his fingers. "A career that could be snuffed out like a fading match."

"Stop it," Ellis said, pulling away.

Her eyes were drawn to Johnson's PC screen. She watched herself come into Room E21, searching for the scalpel and attacking Jenkins, hacking at the man's throat until his head all but cut away from his body.

She watched herself scream silently, the blood from the wounds she inflicted on Jenkins showering her, soaking her clothes, her skin, her hair.

She looked to Blake, tears breaking across her face.

Blake's eyes lit up in anger. He lunged for Johnson, grabbing the older man by the collar.

"No, Blake," Ellis said. "Leave him! He isn't worth it."

Blake released Johnson, turned away and leaned against the door. His shoulders were shaking, and Ellis could see that he was tired, emotional.

She went to comfort him, but he resisted.

"Blake, please –" she said but he opened the door and left.

She looked back to Johnson. "I should have let him rip your head off."

"L-like *you* did to Mr Jenkins?" Johnson laughed, straightening his tie.

Ellis seethed, went to follow Blake out of the office.

"That's right," Johnson chided. "Run along after your boyfriend."

Ellis paused, looked back.

"Yes, I know all about that," Johnson said. "The sordid little affair you're having." He smiled piously. "Have you met Mrs Farrow?" he said, reaching again for the photo of his own family. "A very pleasant lady. Sophisticated. Elegant…" He raised an eyebrow. "All the things you aren't, dear child."

Ellis grabbed the door handle angrily, intent on leaving before she *did* rip the old codger's head off. But the door held firm. She tugged it again to no avail.

She looked to Johnson quizzically.

He pushed past her, tried the door, pulling it hard. But still it held. They were both somehow locked in.

Johnson returned to his computer. He swore and then began feverishly punching at the keys, all the while looking nervously to the screen.

"What's happening?" Ellis asked.

He ignored her.

She drew closer to him, standing by his side as he continued to bang the keyboard. The company logo receded from the screen, basic white lettering taking its place, reading: QT SHUTDOWN.

"What is this?" Ellis pressed.

But Johnson didn't look at her, still hammering the keys uselessly. "This isn't right," he said, more to himself than to Ellis. "This shouldn't be happening without my authorisation." He pulled away from the computer. "It's Farrow," he said. "It must be. He's shutting us down!"

"What!" Ellis cried.

She ran back to the door, tried her card. It was useless, not even registering. She tried the handle, desperately trying to pull it open. Beat her hands upon the glass, calling Blake's name.

The lights went down.

Ellis startled, feeling around in the dark, finding the edge of a desk. She clutched it as if expecting the floor to give way next.

EIGHT

Like a dream. Like a nightmare. Like some sort of hallucination. That's how Ellis saw the world now, her mind's eye filling the dark with its own creations, dancing to the steady beat of Johnson's fevered breathing.

Time passed. She didn't know how long. Hours? Days? A week?

She found a torch, clicking it on and off to save the batteries. Darkness or partial darkness.

She huddled in the corner.

Johnson remained on the other side of the room.

He'd been coughing, wheezing. Crying out for help.

The storeroom door hung open nearby, its contents strewn across the floor, Johnson no doubt trying to find something that would help him escape.

But there was no escape, their only exit still locked tight.

Ellis would have called for help, phoned someone, but everything was dead. The power was gone, the phones cut off. Their access cards were useless. No computer or internet. She'd left her mobile phone in her car. Not that it mattered: she couldn't get a signal down here even at the best of times.

Sleep finally came. And with sleep came dreams. Ellis dreamed of monsters. She dreamed of Jenkins.

She dreamed of her school days, of exams she hadn't worked for, formulas she couldn't understand, biology terms she no longer remembered.

But then the lights came back on.

The air was misty around her, but she could see.

Ellis looked over to Johnson, but he wasn't on the floor. Instead, she found him floating in the air, his nails scratching into the wall, blood flowing down like thick red paint.

He turned to look at her, and his eyes were hollowed out, worms crawling through.

And then he said her name.

...

Ellis woke with a start, eyes flicking open to find darkness again. Her hands fumbled along the floor for the torch. Ellis switched it on, gripping the damn thing tightly, searching the room with its narrow beam. She aimed at each wall, then towards the door.

She reached her free hand to her mouth, gasping.

The door was open.

Johnson?!

She shone the torch around the room again, finding him on his chair by the computer. His body was still. His hands were hanging off his gold chain. Scratch marks ran up his neck. His eyes rolled back into his head. Ellis knew that he was dead. She didn't have to examine the body to know that.

But dead men sometimes move again...

Ellis slid up against the nearest wall. She shifted away, still keeping her back against the wall, torch fixed firmly on Johnson's body. She inched towards the door, her foot colliding with something on the ground, kicking it across the floor. Her beam followed the hurtling object. It was just a cup.

A shuffling sound.

Ellis whirled around, the torch's beam finding Johnson's chair. He was still there.

She found the open door with her beam, made her way carefully to the exit. She paused before leaving. Shone the torch back towards Johnson.

He was gone.

Ellis gasped, a cold sweat breaking across her back.

She searched the room frantically, finding Johnson on his feet, creeping towards the storeroom. He stopped. Turned. Looked to the light.

Ellis backed out of the doorway, into Corridor A1.

Johnson began his slow and steady pursuit, his movements encumbered.

"Johnson?" she said, her voice but a rasp.

He didn't answer. Nor would he ever answer. Johnson was dead. Dead like Jenkins, the man Blake had called time on. The man with no heart or lungs but eyes that flicked open. The man who lunged for the doctor even though it was physically impossible for a dead man to move, let alone attack with such aggression.

Ellis tried to flee, but her legs seized up, her joints stiff.

She reached forward, pushing Johnson away with as much strength as her worn-out body could muster.

He fell backwards, tripping clumsily on the clutter strewn across the floor. He hit the ground and lay there for a moment before pulling himself up.

He came towards her again.

"Jesus," Ellis whispered, "Jesus, Jesus, Jesus…"

She looked around for something to use.

A trolley stood parked in the corridor. A flask and some cups rested upon it.

Ellis sat her torch on the trolley, careful to aim its light towards Johnson, then took the flask in both hands and waited.

Johnson reached for her, but she stood aside, the dead man tripping again, this time over her outstretched foot. He hit the floor hard and Ellis followed through, bringing the flask down hard on his head. She hammered again and again, Johnson's skull caving in, blood and brain seeping out onto the tiled floor.

Ellis dropped the flask and grabbed the torch. She fell back against the corridor wall, allowing herself to slide down against it.

She took deep breaths. Felt herself gag. Dipped her head between her knees and threw up.

And then she was still, her heavy breathing the only sound within the empty corridor.

But then…

A sudden screeching noise. It seemed to be coming from C Block, the next block across.

That's where the animals lived…

NINE

There was no sign of life in A Block.

With the exception of Johnson's mutilated corpse, there was no sign of death either.

In the cold silence, even her flat shoes pounded hard against the tiled floor as Ellis moved down the corridor. Every step she took seemed to echo.

Another screeching sound. Definitely coming from the Animal House in C Block.

Ellis wondered just how long the poor little things had been left alone.

She thought of little Ginger, so young and innocent. She wanted to hold him, pull him close. In the icy chill of the powered down lab, Ginger's warmth would be very welcome.

Ellis reached the adjoining door to C Block. It was hanging open. Yet other doors along the corridor remained closed tight, their readers non-functioning with the loss of power. Ellis wondered for a second why some doors just fell open, while others remained closed.

She was reminded of Chris Lennon, the sales rep. She'd forgotten about him with all that happened, but the man had broken in and taken something from Johnson's office. He'd pulled a gun on her. Begged her not to squeal on him. And, God help her, Ellis hadn't squealed. What was Lennon's part in all of this? Was he responsible for the shutdown?

She pushed through the access door, leaving A Block and entering C.

More screeching. Louder now.

She searched Corridor C1 with her torch, finding the storage room where the cats lived.

Ellis pushed the door. It gave easily, allowing her access.

Inside, the place was deathly quiet. She pointed the torch to the centre of the room, finding the cages. Ellis squinted against the light's glare, but she couldn't see Ginger. She couldn't see *any* of the cats.

She walked over to the cages, giving them closer examination. They were open, like someone had hacked their way through the little door catches.

Ellis swept the entire room with the torch. Nothing.

"Ginger?" she called.

The screeching noise again.

It was coming from the next room, where the birds lived.

Ellis pushed the door to the bird's house, peering in.

She was scared. God, that was ridiculous when she thought about it. She'd tackled Dead Jenkins (hell, she'd tackled Johnson both alive *and* dead!). Hardly much to fear from a few chickens. Still Ellis held back, her torch doing a cursory sweep of the room before she stepped inside.

The room was a mess. There was chicken feed everywhere. The remains of its packaging lay strewn across the floor, like someone had ransacked the place.

Ellis felt her grip on the torch tighten.

She moved towards the middle of the room. Her eyes narrowed, struggling against the glare of the torch as she leaned in closer to the cages. Seemed like there was something inside.

Her hand rose to her mouth as she realised what she was looking at. Chicken skeletons, flesh cleaned from their bones, littered each cage. Ellis looked back to the floor, this time noticing feathers, caught up within the birdseed and ripped packaging.

"Oh God…" she whispered.

There was movement everywhere. Black shadows bled out from the walls and ceiling, falling upon her.

Ellis dropped to the floor, losing hold of the torch. She could feel what seemed like a hundred claws and teeth ripping and tearing at her skin, the screeching noise from before now deafening. She couldn't move, completely overwhelmed by her attackers, pain surging through her body.

Something grabbed her, started to pull her away. Ellis struggled against it, still screaming, still hurting as those little teeth continued to tear at her flesh.

She found herself in the corridor.

"Get up!" she heard a voice cry. "You have to move!"

Ellis allowed her eyes to open, finding the corridor filled with small, dark creatures.

Were those things… cats?!

The figure of a tall man wearing a yellow suit and mask stood over her, tearing the cats from her body. She heard some shots as her suited saviour disposed of the damn things with his handgun.

"Run!" he shouted.

They retreated down the corridor.

Her bones and muscles ached, but Ellis kept going, bounding down C2 and along C3, a torch on the suited man's headgear pouring out light.

There was a sign dead ahead. The masked figure turned, taking the walkway that led out of the research area towards the canteen.

They both tumbled through the double doors in front of them. Once in, the suited man pushed a long, sturdy table up against the unsecured entrance.

Ellis watched in fear as the cats leapt at the glass, desperate to get in, but the blockade held tight.

She had petted those things, fed them from her hand, given them names. Now they were feral killers.

No, more than that…

Ellis looked again at their eyes. Those were dead eyes. She knew what dead eyes looked like, and that's what was staring at her through the canteen door window.

The masked figure stood opposite her, blocking her view.

"Are you hurt?" he said. It was a gruff voice, muffled through the breathing apparatus.

Ellis looked down at her arms. She hadn't thought about it until now but as she looked at the long bloody scratches, they started to smart. She ran her fingers across her face, finding more painful lacerations.

She looked at her hands, which were covered in blood.

She started laughing. At first it was nervous laughter, but then came full-blown mania.

The masked stranger seemed baffled.

"Bloody cats!" was all she could manage, looking once more to the simple-minded, dead, furry faces on the other side of the glass, glaring back at her.

And then the stranger joined in, his large, heavy-set body shaking inside the yellow suit. It was then that Ellis knew her saviour's identity: his laugh was legendary, definitive even through the mask.

TEN

He pulled the light from his headgear, set it on the centre table. He changed the setting, creating a makeshift lamp.

"Looks good on you, Abe," Ellis said, pointing at the suit.

Abe looked Ellis up and down. "There's a locker room full of them near the doors to E Block. But I'm guessing you're more of a scrubs kind of girl."

Ellis smiled faintly. Dropped her head, ran her hands through her hair. Even if she could get over to that locker, it would be pointless to don a suit now, after she'd been exposed to the infection. And the scratches from those animals…

When she looked up, she saw that Abe was perhaps thinking similarly: Ellis no longer looked into a visor; Abe's face smiled back at her, the mask in his hands.

"Fuck it," he said.

He made a face at the cats through the glass.

Ellis laughed so hard she thought she might burst.

The laughter gave way to sobbing.

…

Abe held her as she cried. Ellis curled into his broad shoulders and sturdy chest like a little doll. She could feel the warmth of his body even through the yellow plastic. Even his smell, that 'sweaty man' odour, was welcome. This was exactly what she needed: comfort and security. Safety.

"Where were you when they sealed the lab?" she asked him, tears still trickling down her face.

"E Block," he said. The accent was American but milder than Blake's Southern drawl. "When the lights went down and they locked the doors," he continued, "it got pretty crazy down there. There were people screaming at me. Begging me to open the lab room doors, but I couldn't. They were locked tight and my card wasn't working." Abe looked away. "I just had to leave them."

Ellis reached forward, touched his arm. "Abe, there was nothing you could do for them."

"Really, Ellie?" He seemed angry. "I work security. I should have stayed, found some way through. Done my job *right*." He lowered his face into his hands. "God, their eyes staring back at me through that glass…"

Ellis squeezed his shoulder.

"What about the others?" she asked cautiously.

Abe looked up. "Ellie, you saw what happened to that Jenkins guy. And those animals… whatever infection got them is spreading fast. There's a lot of those… *things* roaming the corridors now."

"Is there *anyone* left?"

"Only us."

"What about… Blake?" Ellis had to ask.

Abe couldn't look her in the face. "I met him outside E Block. He was hurt but still alive. We tried to find a way out, but it was no use. My card wasn't working on any of the doors we needed. One of the airways looked promising. There was a gap, and I thought I could crawl in, somehow. Make my way through the system, climb to the top, and get help. But that shit's easier to do in the movies.

"In the end, Blake got sick." Abe sighed, looked at his gun. "Ellie, he went the same way as Jenkins. I had no choice…"

Ellis swallowed hard.

Abe continued: "I was here in the canteen when I heard you."

Ellis looked at the cats again, scraping at the glass.

"Sorry," she said.

"It's okay," Abe said. "Kinda nice, getting a chance to do my job right."

ELEVEN

Ellis was hungry. Ravenous. Even with all that happened – that was still happening – she was famished.

Maybe it was the scientist in her, thinking through the consequences of not eating. Her body would become malnourished. Exhaust its fat reserves, move onto muscle mass. She'd get weaker, suffer vitamin deficiency. She *needed* to eat.

Abe was sleeping.

She thought back to all the things he'd told her. The people in E Block. Blake. They'd been *murdered*. That was the long and short of it.

Someone had let the cat out of the bag (so to speak) when the Jenkins thing went down. And the funders, the government or whoever was behind Project QT, responded by sealing everyone into the labs. After all she'd seen, Ellis could only suspect the worst. They'd contained the virus, buried their dirty little secret. It was only a matter of time before they sent some clean-up team in.

Her stomach rumbled.

Ellis slid open a few cabinets. Her mouth watered with the thought of eating. She moved through to the kitchen area, checking the various cupboards and cabinets there, finding nothing, save shining pots and pans all neatly stacked, awaiting the attention of chefs and catering staff that would never again use them.

Ellis reached a door at the back. She read the sign STORE and went to open it.

A hand reached to stop her. Ellis pulled away, startled. It was only Abe.

"Sorry, Ellie. You don't want to open that…"

"Why not?"

"When I was here , before I met you, there were a few of those things lurking around. I took care of them. Put their bodies in that store. The place is going to stink."

"But that's just… *stupid*." Ellis complained. "You could have put them in the maintenance cupboard. We *need* this food, Abe!"

Abe looked embarrassed. "I… er…" His head dropped and he started playing with his hands.

Ellis swore under her breath. She remembered how the seniors would sometimes talk to Abe. People like Johnson weren't shy of belittling the security guard in front of other staff when something went wrong. Ellis would feel pity for Abe when they were mean like that, but he'd always just laugh it off. Deep down, it was bound to hurt.

"I'm sorry," Ellis said now. "That was rude."

"It's okay. You're right; it *was* a stupid thing to do." He smiled meekly. "But I'm just the dopey security guard, after all…"

Ellis blushed. She felt terrible.

Abe pointed to a few boxes stacked by the fridge. "Look, it's not much," he said. "But I noticed those earlier."

Ellis investigated, finding the boxes filled with tinned foods and cans of drink. She looked up, smiled.

"I think they were to be thrown out," Abe said. "Most of them are close to their use-by date, but they should keep us right for a while."

"Thanks," Ellis said, cradling a tin of canned tuna to her chest. "For everything, I mean. You saved my life back there, and…" She looked down at the tuna. "Well, I just don't know how I can ever repay you."

"You don't need to," Abe said. "I'm just doing my job. Dopey security guard. Remember?"

Ellis smiled.

"Seriously," he said. "I'm going to take care of you now. It's going to be alright."

Ellis wished she could believe that.

TWELVE

Days passed. Maybe a week. It was hard to tell. The clock in the canteen had stopped. Neither of them wore a watch. *When you're standing in the same position for eight to ten hours a day*, Abe had told her, *the last thing you need is a damn watch.*

They remained in the canteen. They waited for something to happen, someone to come.

They ate sparingly. Occasionally they slept.

They talked.

Ellis wept sometimes, her sobs echoing like breaking plates throughout the empty canteen. Abe would try to comfort her but then get embarrassed, look away or stare down at those big hands of his.

With the complex located underground, there was no natural light. No windows to look out or call for help from. They saved the batteries on Abe's headgear light by using candles. Sometimes the candlelight preyed on their minds, throwing shadows across doors, suggesting movement where there was no movement.

There was noise.

The quiet murmur of the air con; still working despite their fears to the contrary. The lazy scraping on the glass from those infernal cats, grating like nails across chalkboard until Abe pinned some more buffers against the door, obscuring the view and dulling the sound to a faint, yet still annoying, whisper.

Sometimes, they heard commotion from deeper within the complex. Ellis could only imagine what further horrors lurked down the corridors, deep in the labs at E Block, where the others were trapped, falling prey to infection, one by one.

She wondered how long the two of them had left. They didn't talk about it. They talked about everything *but* that; everything that didn't matter; everything that might distract them from the reality of being trapped in an underground facility with nothing but an airborne virus and the infected majority for company. But the thought of death was never far. How it would happen, how it would feel. What the infection would do to their bodies…

Another sound, this time a scream. It made Ellis jump.

Abe looked up from his nap. "What is it?" he said. "Are you okay?"

Ellis snapped. "Abe, how *could* I be okay?!"

Her eyes were starting to itch and she rubbed them, wondering if it could be the first signs of infection setting in. God knows, with those scratches all over her body, it didn't look good for her.

"Look, we've got to get out of here," she said. "I can't stand it any more."

Abe looked around the room. He lifted his hands, palms upwards. "How, Ellie? You've seen what's out there."

"And what's in *here*, Abe? Certain death, that's what! We've almost run out of food and drink."

"You have to be patient, Ellie. It's only a matter of time before help arrives."

"Really? Who's going to help us? The people who fund us? They'll *kill* us before they help us."

His eyes fell to the floor.

"Come on, Abe. We have to try something. *Anything* to get out of here. It's our only hope!"

"I'm not opening those doors."

"And you think *I* want to?! Jesus, Abe, we *have* to. Otherwise we'll end up no different to those bloody cats out there."

Abe looked very serious for a moment. Then he started to smirk.

Soon Ellis was smiling with him.

No matter how grim things looked, the cats would always raise a smile.

"Look, little lady," Abe said in his calmest voice, "you just have to trust me,"

Ellis dipped her eyes, smiled. "I like it when you call me that," she said. "It's very American. And then there's *Ma'am*. That makes me feel all important. I remember feeling wound up one day after a rollicking from one of the HSOs. But then you came over, asked, *Is everything okay, Ma'am?*" Ellis looked up. "It meant a lot."

Abe looked uncomfortable. Ellis thought he might be blushing.

"Please," she said, feeling him soften to her idea. "Let's at least *look* for a way out."

Abe fixed his eyes on her. He seemed tired beyond belief, like even if the will were there, the body might be too weak. To Ellis it looked like the security guard had just given up without telling her.

She reached a hand, touched his face. "Come on, Abe. I need your help. I'm not strong enough to do this on my own."

"Okay," he said, taking her hand and squeezing it. "Let's do it."

"That way is definitely a no-go," Abe said, pointing to the boarded up doors to the south, where they'd come in. "So this," he said, pointing to the north door, "is the only other way in or out."

Ellis lifted a candle, tried to shed some light on the corridor behind the glass of the north door. It was too dark, and the glare of the flame against the window meant she couldn't see too clearly. But there was nothing leaping up at her, scraping the glass or peering through with misty-eyed, empty gazes. And that was good enough for Ellis.

She looked to Abe, nodded.

"Are you sure about this?" he asked.

"No," she said, flatly. "But what choice do we have?"

"We could stay here. Wait."

"We've been through this, Abe."

He smiled. "Okay then. Stand back."

He'd checked when they'd entered the canteen, finding the northern doors padlocked manually. They couldn't find the key, but in his hands, Abe held a crowbar. He jammed it into the gap between the double doors and pulled hard against the chain. He put his back into it, the effort lining his bearded face. Ellis could see the veins building on his bald head as he worked the bar.

He relaxed, stepped away. Exhaled.

"Can I help?" Ellis asked.

Abe looked her up and down, allowed himself a chuckle. He returned to the task at hand.

This was man's work, Ellis realised. Not for the likes of a scrawny *little lady* like her. That's the way men like Abe thought, and, to be honest, Ellis welcomed it right now. She hadn't much fight left in her. She needed a hero.

Blake...

Ellis wondered whether Abe had glossed over what happened to Blake to make it easier for her to deal with. The infection was vicious. She'd watched it consume Johnson. Ellis was comforted in knowing that Blake would at least *stay* dead now: Abe had seen to that.

Yet a part of her wished she could have been with Blake when he died. At least that way, she could mourn him. Instead, Ellis' mind played tricks on her: perhaps Abe got it wrong; perhaps in the darkness and insanity he had mixed Blake up with someone else. It was madness to think like that, but these were the thoughts eating away at her.

A snapping sound.

Ellis was brought back to reality.

"Got it!" Abe said to her, the padlock's chain giving against the crowbar.

He looked to Ellis, breathing heavily. "Okay, ready?"

Ellis nodded.

Abe pulled the doors open.

THIRTEEN

Abe went out first.

He wore the light around his head, his gun gripped in both hands. He checked both directions of the corridor he found himself in.

Empty.

Ellis didn't have to ask if it was safe to move; she knew by the relief on Abe's face.

It was dark. Darker than the canteen where they'd set up candles on tables, where they'd created a routine of sorts over the last few days, week or whatever.

That mirage was gone now. And a mirage was all it was; it didn't take a university education for Ellis to realise that they would have died in that canteen. It may have been a slow death, but death was death. And Ellis wanted to *live*.

She'd packed some rations into an old gym bag she found in the kitchen: a few cans of Coke, some tinned foods, and batteries for Abe's light. They'd even found a handheld torch in one of the cabinets.

Ellis carried the handheld. With two sources of light in the corridor, it became less dark, less foreboding.

But they still had every reason to expect only the worst.

In the canteen, Abe had spoken of the horrors down in the labs. He mentioned names, sometimes. People Ellis knew and worked with every day. People Abe was forced to kill as they changed into something altogether monstrous.

They turned a corner.

Noise. Dead ahead.

Abe stopped. His gun was still outstretched, both hands shaking.

Abe searched the corridor with his light.

Ellis followed with her torch, noting six doors, three on each side facing each other. A set of double doors stood waiting at the end, beckoning them.

Abe found a sign on the wall and read it out loud. 'Corridor B3', it said. But Ellis knew where they were, even in the dark. She suspected Abe knew too, that the checking and confirming was born of nerves, to confirm some sort of order to what now seemed a place without order, a place where even *natural* order was no more.

They began to move down the corridor.

A sudden bang startled them.

Ellis stopped dead, shone her light on Abe. His eyes were wide with fear.

Again the sound. And again, as if hammering out a beat to some inaudible tune. It was coming from one of the doors ahead. A thudding sound. Then a crack like glass breaking.

Abe's light searched every inch of the corridor.

The noise struck again, and Abe found its source. The second door along on the right hand side. Someone… *something*… was behind that door.

Ellis could taste the bile as it rose up her throat. She wanted to go back to the canteen and hide. She didn't care, now; she'd take the slow death over this any day.

"Keep going," Abe said, as if reading her mind. "It looks like those doors are locked. We'll be okay."

Ellis swallowed hard. They moved on, their footsteps lighter, their movements slow and deliberate, the sounds drawing closer.

She was level with the door. She allowed herself a glance sideways.

The glass in the door was broken. Cracks spread throughout its pane like a spider's web. She could make out a face behind the glass, eyes staring back at her, cold and emotionless. And then it moved, a quick flick against the glass, another crack forming on the pane.

"Don't look!" Abe said, "We're nearly there."

Ellis closed her eyes, moved a few steps forward. She opened them again, stared dead in front where the doors stood waiting for her. It was her goal to reach them, to push them and hope to God they opened into somewhere safe.

More noise behind her.

Ellis turned back as a door from the other end of the corridor burst open, three figures wearing bloodied scrubs pouring out into the corridor. Ellis pointed her torch, searching for any sign that these men might be survivors like her. But, while she recognised all three as fellow ASOs, Ellis found only death in their eyes.

Abe looked at her. His gun hand was shaking profusely.

"Run," he said.

Ellis ran, bursting through the doors at the end of the corridor, the sound of gunshot ringing out behind her. She scrambled into a new corridor, dark as the last one.

The torch dropped from her hands, its beam snapping off as it skittered across the floor.

The dark swallowed her up.

Gunshots continued, muted behind the double doors, now closed. And there were other noises in this corridor. Shuffling footsteps. Spluttering, phlegm-filled coughs.

Ellis discarded the gym bag and fell to her knees.

Her hands blindly palmed the smooth, dust-filled floor, desperately searching for the torch. She found it, clicking it on and showering the corridor in light.

"Oh God," she whispered.

About ten bodies stood in front of her. They wore assorted lab clothing: scrubs, lab coats, shirts and ties. Ellis didn't recognise any of them. She couldn't see their faces, their heads hunched over their bodies, staring at their feet.

The torch was heavy in her hands, her fingers like butter. She couldn't move, frozen to the spot.

One of the bodies raised its head. Half of its face was missing, a single eye staring at her, lips torn from the mouth, teeth bloodied.

Ellis pulled herself to her feet. She reached for the handle of a nearby lab door, pulling, shaking.

Locked.

The dead thing came closer. The rest of the pack followed.

Ellis fell against the locked door. She opened her mouth and screamed. Squeezed her eyes shut, waiting for the first cold touch, the first incision, the first lock of jaws around her flesh.

But then the door opened. Hands from inside reached out to grab her.

FOURTEEN

Ellis screamed, struggling to get away as she was dragged inside the room. Hands reached for her face and she bit into them. The hands pulled away, their owner screaming out.

Ellis found the torch, pointed it in the direction of the scream. The beam fell upon her attacker, finding the frame of a man wearing a lab coat, his arms raised to shield his face from the intrusive light.

"Turn that damn thing off!" he said.

Ellis recognised the voice immediately.

"Blake?"

She dropped the torch, threw her arms around him. Darkness swallowed them up again, but she didn't care, searching all over his face for his lips and then kissing him deeply.

Blake Farrow relaxed into the kiss, wrapping Ellis in his arms and running his hands through her hair.

"Where have you been?" he said.

"The canteen. Abe found me and –" Ellis suddenly remembered. "Oh my God, Blake. He's still out there, in the other corridor. We've got to –"

"Wait a minute," Blake said. "Abe? You're with *Abe*?!"

"Yes, but he's still —"

Blake cut in, "Listen to me, Ellie, Abe's not to be trusted."

"What?" That wasn't true. Abe was about the most trustworthy person Ellis knew. He'd saved her, pulled her from the Animal House. He'd looked after her, kept her safe.

Ellis broke away from Blake, looked at him suspiciously. She found the torch again, shone it in his face.

Blake squinted against the light.

"What's going on here?" Ellis said.

"What do you mean?"

"You know what I mean. That Lennon guy sniffing around your office. The security shutdown —Johnson reckoned it was your work."

"Johnson! You trust *Johnson* over me?!"

"He's dead, Blake. Everyone in the lab is dead!" Blake went to interrupt, but Ellis raised her free hand, continued, "And Abe, another man you say can't be trusted, is out there somewhere, looking for me." Her eyes narrowed, "So you better tell me exactly what the hell you've been doing here to cause all of this."

Blake sighed.

A dim light bathed the room as he switched on a portable lamp.

Ellis switched the torch off, allowed her eyes to adjust to the softer light. It was a standard office she stood in, one that was shared by all the ASOs. There was a storeroom in the corner. A computer by the desk. Some files along the walls.

Blake sat down in a nearby chair, rubbed his bearded face. He looked tired. *Beyond* tired. Ellis noticed his lab coat was stained in blood, now dry and embedded in the white cotton.

She sat down opposite him. "Please, she said… what was in those samples you had us injecting the animals with? I need to know."

Blake smiled. "When you first started here," he said, "I couldn't believe it. A beautiful, young ASO. Fresh out of college, eager to change the world." He looked up at her. "Why the hell did they send you *here*?"

"Because I showed promise. That's what you said. Before adding that you couldn't see it yourself, but as you were stuck with me, I'd better make myself useful."

Blake allowed himself a faint laugh. "It was a joke."

"I know."

Blake looked towards the storeroom. "Flu virus," he said. "You probably knew that already. I'm sure Johnson told you we were working to find a cure or radical new treatment. Money to be made, yadda, yadda." He laughed, the laugh giving way to a cough. "But that wasn't the full picture. No, we were *building* a virus, Ellie, not curing it. A fast-acting, highly contagious and aggressive virus."

"What?" Ellis said. "But why?"

"I don't know," Blake replied. His voice held none of its former glory. It seemed weak, deflated. "I never saw any of the memos or files on who exactly was funding it," he continued, "but I know it was a government department of some description."

He looked away. His face was strained. To Ellis, Dr Blake Farrow had always been the epitome of manliness: forty-something, tall and thickset with a square-jaw and the shadow of a beard no matter how closely he shaved. Yet now he looked older to her. His beard was full and grey. His face pale and narrow.

"You hear of things," she said. "Read things online. About governments working on covert projects. Bio-weaponry, that kind of thing."

"I don't think it's that," Blake said. "We were on need-to-know, of course, but what was strange was even though this virus we were building was pretty nasty, it wasn't meant to kill. Not the way you'd expect for the likes of bio-warfare. The brief needed it to go through the system very swiftly and then die. An anti-virus was also ordered, although we were only in the early stages of development with that…"

Blake stopped talking suddenly. His eyes narrowed as he leaned in closer to Ellis.

She backed away.

"You're hurt," he said.

"It doesn't matter. I'm okay."

"No, your arms…" Blake gestured to the cuffs of her scrubs.

Ellis rolled up a sleeve, revealing the scars.

Blake pulled her arm close, studied it in the poor light.

A gunshot. Blake let go of her arm.

Ellis tensed up immediately. "Abe."

She went to move, but Blake grabbed her.

"Please," he said. "Abe can't be trusted."

But she broke away, moved to the door.

Abe was battling with the dead outside, bulldozing through them, heading towards the double doors leading to the next corridor.

Ellis wanted to open the door, call out. But she didn't. Instead, she let Abe go. Torn between loyalty to the man who had saved her and the man who had broken her heart. Ellis felt as guilty as Blake Farrow looked.

"Why don't you trust him?" she said.

But Blake raised a finger across his lips. "I think they're more or less deaf," he said, leading her away from the door. "In fact, some of the more heavily infected may even be blind, or partially blind.

He sat down again.

"They may look human," he continued, "but they're far from it, Ellis. They're primitive creatures. Drawn to heat, to bright light. Probably more in common with the virus itself than the human host." He frowned, waved his hand. "But all of this is mere speculation. I would need to do tests. *Proper* lab tests within a controlled…" His voice trailed off.

Ellis sat down again, looked Blake in the eye. "Abe told me you were dead," she said.

Blake laughed humourlessly.

"I don't know what to think anymore," she said, "Who to trust."

"Abe's been lying to you, Ellie."

"How do I know that? Sure, he was wrong about you, but he *saved* me, Blake. Put his own life at risk."

"You have to trust me. Abe was lying to you. He's not one of the good guys."

"Oh, and *you* are? Injecting people with that virus you made?"

"Oh, for Christ's sake, Ellie, it was a government contract!" Blake stood up. "You know how hard it is for private labs in this current climate? No HSO in their right mind would turn down a contract like that."

He stood up, walked to the other side of the room.

"You know the Milgram experiment, where they asked people to do stuff to supposed human test subjects under lab conditions? And those people agreed to all sorts of shit, just because a man with a white coat and clipboard told them it was okay. Well, *we were those guys*, Ellie. And the government memos that came through, the ones we were allowed to read? They were written on headed paper and I thought to myself, *Surely it must be kosher if it's on headed paper*." He shook his head, added, "I was in too deep by the time I realised just how wrong it all was."

"We can leave," Ellis said. "Tell the press. Get the word out."

Blake shook his head. "I'm not leaving," he said.

"What?"

"I don't *deserve* to live. Not after all I've done."

"Well, what about *me*?" Ellis yelled. She stood up, walked across the room to him. "Don't *I* deserve to live?!"

Blake held her gaze. His eyes filled with tears as he found more scars, this time on her face. He traced them with his finger. "When did you get these?" he asked.

"What?"

"The scars…when did you get them?"

"Few days, a week ago, who knows?"

Blake continued to study her.

Ellis felt very self aware. "Stop it," she said.

"I'm sorry, it's just that…"

"I should be infected? Walking around with messed-up eyes like all the others out there? You think I don't *know* that?"

He looked up at her, a smile threatening to break across his tired, bearded face. "You could be immune," he said. "I'd need to –" He looked to the door.

"What is it?"

"We need to take a blood sample, run some tests."

"Blake," she said, her voice more gentle. "There's *nothing* can be done here. Our only hope is to leave, to find someone we can trust, try and sort this whole mess out."

"Yes," he said, thinking. "You're absolutely right."

"But you need to come with me. I can't do this on my own."

Blake looked at the glass pane on the door. He recoiled as one of the dead sniffed, cleared its throat. "I-I can't…"

"You *have to*, Blake," Ellis pressed.

She kissed him, pulled him close. His body was frail against hers. Like the body of an old man.

"Please," she whispered into his ear, "I need you…"

He moved away from her, rummaged through a nearby set of drawers, pulled out a USB memory stick. "This is everything. The memos, the induction notes. Anything they've given me, it's all on here."

"Blake, I –"

"Take it," he said.

"You're coming with me."

"I'm not. I can't. I'm too weak."

"I can help you, I'll –"

"Ellie, I'm infected."

She stepped away from him.

"No, Blake."

"Yes. There's no hope for me. So go. Go now while you still can."

Her eyes were stinging. Had she any more tears left, they would have come. Instead Ellis stood dry and empty before him. "Blake, I…"

The words failed her, but he understood.

"It's okay," he said, smiling. "I know. But you have to go."

FIFTEEN

It made sense, what Blake was saying. With the flu virus raging through them, blocking their sinuses, the dead *should* have limited sensory perception.

But *blind*?

She recalled Jenkins, by the door to E21, seeming to stare through the glass into the white of her eyes…

A cold sweat ran down her spine.

There were a lot of them around now.

She knew they were drawn to light. Shining a torch full beam hadn't been the best idea in the world, when she thought about it. Yet Ellis would feel very vulnerable without *some* access to light. So she kept the torch with her, tucked away for now.

Ellis figured the safest way to get around in complete darkness was to half-walk-half-crawl. She used her hands to map her way, feeling along the floor, along the wall, listening for the heavy footsteps of the dead.

She'd managed half the corridor when her hands collided with something.

Ellis stopped, remained still for a second. Her breathing sounded so loud to her that she was sure she'd be heard, even if they were mostly deaf.

She ran her hands over the object, realising it was a dead body. Its flesh was cold and clammy to touch. She felt a gunshot wound on its head. It must have been one that Abe had killed on his way through. Ellis groped her way around it, moving past, all the while worrying it might reach out and grab her leg.

She pushed through a set of double doors into another corridor.

She felt her way along like before, avoiding the shuffling dead she encountered. She reached the end of this corridor, realising that the next would be the main throughway to A Block, back where she had started.

She pushed through another set of doors, immediately hearing the swell of shuffling and grunting noises ahead. It seemed the dead travelled in packs, like a herd of sheep. They were gathered along the end of the corridor, circling the security door Abe had most likely left through. It was the door Ellis needed too, in order to get back into A Block.

She made her approach carefully. Curled against a nearby wall and listened intently.

Ellis noticed a leg hanging out across the exit, wedging the security door ajar: it belonged to one of the dead. The gap created was just enough for her snake-like body to slide through.

She stayed low. Crawling more than walking. Slowly and quietly, Ellis edged her arms and torso through the exit, climbing over the felled body.

She went to pull her legs through, but the body suddenly stirred, grabbing her ankle. Ellis kicked out hard, freeing her leg and pounding the dead thing's head, sending it back into the other corridor.

She fell back against the door.

The pack of dead were drawn to the commotion. She could feel the weight of their charge upon her back, spurred on by the promise of her flesh. The gap was too narrow for them, but if Ellis moved, their combined might would push through the heavy security door, filling the corridor in seconds.

She heard a gunshot. It came from somewhere in the complex.

"Damn it," Ellis swore, finding her torch and flicking it to ON.

She'd made it back to A Block, along with more of the dead than Ellis could imagine. They had followed Abe through the complex and were now scrambling against each other, fighting to get through the double doors at the far end of the corridor where the security guard had left.

As Ellis' light spilled upon them, they turned around.

SIXTEEN

Ellis moved her torch away, desperately seeking out an alternative exit. She found office doors all along the corridor on each side.

She stood up, pulling away from the door at her back, allowing the dead from the previous corridor to bulldoze their way into this one.

Those from the other end of the corridor moved towards her.

She was trapped, sandwiched between two herds of the dead.

Frantically, Ellis tried each of the office doors, starting with the closest and working her way up.

The first was locked tight. Likewise with the second.

The third was open, and she went to enter, just as one of the dead reached for her, making contact, wrapping its clammy hands around her arm.

Ellis dragged the cursed thing into the room with her, threw it to the ground.

She slammed the door closed, then pushed a nearby trolley against it.

The body she'd dragged into the room was crawling back onto its feet.

Ellis searched the room with her torch, finding a letter opener on a nearby desk. She reached for it, and as the cadaver attacked, Ellis stabbed its throat. She held the blade fast, wedging it further into the rancid flesh. The body shook vigorously and then fell.

Ellis dimmed her torch.

Darkness. Always darkness. It was her friend.

Movement from the corner.

Ellis snapped her torch on again, searched the room.

She found a body stumbling towards her. She raised the blade again, still bloodied from her last attack, but the body raised its hand in defence, and then spoke to her.

She recognised the voice. It was Dave Lightfoot.

She caught him as he stumbled, helping him into a nearby chair. His hands covered a stomach wound.

"Jesus, who did this to you?"

"A-Abe…" he mouthed, blood spilling from his lips as he spoke.

He tried to talk some more, but Ellis shushed him, setting the torch and blade on the table, grabbing some bandaging from a nearby first aid cabinet and trying to stall the bleeding. But it was no good. The bullet was lodged inside. He was sinking fast.

"H-he's hunting us," Dave said. "He's killed everyone else."

Ellis was reminded of the storeroom in the canteen. The bodies stacked up inside. Abe told her they'd been infected, that they'd attacked him and he'd taken care of them…

Ellis raised a hand to her mouth, stalled a sob.

Was that what had really happened?

Another gunshot. Abe was close.

Ellis spotted a door adjoined to the next room. She remembered where she was. This was where the clerical staff worked. She could move through some of the rooms here without going back into the corridor.

She grabbed her torch from the table. Pocketed the envelope opener.

"Come on," she said to Dave, pulling him to his feet.

…

They moved through the clerical rooms, finding the door into Corridor A3. They left A Block, entering C Block. With the cats no doubt still trying to claw their way into the canteen, they were able to pass through C with little trouble, into D Block. There they found the doors leading to the fire exit stairwell.

They'd been ripped open.

Abe.

With Dave's energy depleting fast, his burden upon Ellis became heavier. But she managed to help him up the winding staircase, torch switched on and outstretched as they went.

They reached the double doors leading out of the complex. A sign warned staff to only open DOOR 2 when DOOR 1 was closed and all safety measures had been followed. This was important when entering and leaving a potentially contaminated lab. But both doors had been blasted wide open, the last person through not caring much about health and safety.

Ellis slid through the gap. Once in, she helped Dave.

They reached the foyer of the outer building. Ellis shone her torch along the foyer's generous reception. She could see shutters drawn across the windows. They were still locked in.

She swore under her breath, relaxing Dave into a waiting room chair by the reception desk. She was wracking her brain, trying to work out just how the hell to get out of the complex when she heard a loud crack.

Dave's head slapped against the wall, a short gasp leaving his mouth. His body tumbled forward onto the floor. A bloody smear was left on the wall, a separate pool of blood seeping across the tiles where his body now lay.

"No!" Ellis screamed.

She knew it was Abe.

"Where are you?!" she screamed. "Show yourself, you coward!"

Silence.

The darkness was paling. Daylight spilled through the tiny gaps in the shutter blinds.

"What are they paying you?" Ellis shouted. "It must be money. Because I don't think you're a bad man, Abe. I *can't* believe that…"

Abe stepped out of the shadows.

He looked ashamed, unable to keep his eyes on her.

"Where's Farrow?" he said.

"Dead."

"I don't believe you."

"He's in B Block. Take a look if you want, but he'll be dead by the time you get there. He's infected." She looked at Abe, noticed a gaping wound on his arm, sallow skin across his face. "You're infected too," she said.

He laughed, and for a second he became the old Abe; the affable Abe who would sit in the canteen and do his crossword; whose eyes would light up when Canteen Carol brought him his chips, or 'fries' as he'd call them, making Carol laugh every time. But this wasn't old Abe, and Carol was no doubt stacked with the others in the canteen store, a bullet in her brain.

"I have an ex-wife," he said. "Always going on about the shitty money I send her for the kids. How they'll never make it into college, end up deadbeat losers like their old man." He smiled, perhaps aware that Ellis had no time for his sob stories. "When the Jenkins thing happened, I shut the lab down, just as they'd instructed. I needed to contain the infection, take out everyone exposed, especially those working on Project QT. Farrow got away, but I knew he'd come out of hiding if I had you, Ellie."

"It was you who opened the door to Johnson's office," Ellis said. "You set me up."

Abe nodded. He showed her his security card. "It's not like yours, Ellie. It works. I used it to override the shutdown, open the doors I needed."

"The people in E Block," Ellis said. "You killed them in cold blood."

"I had to," Abe said. "They'd been exposed to the virus."

"We were *all* exposed!" Ellis protested.

Abe sighed. "You're right. They were never going to come for me," he said. "Even if I killed every damn person in that lab, even if I killed all those things…" He shook his head, looked at his gun. "They knew I was desperate. Desperate enough to do something like *this*. Desperate enough to believe their lies." He smiled. "I'm just the dopey security guard, after all…"

He looked to Ellis, aimed the gun at her.

Ellis closed her eyes, braced herself for the inevitable.

Nothing happened.

When she opened her eyes, she saw that Abe had lowered the gun.

He waved a hand.

"It doesn't matter anymore," he said. "None of it matters."

A breeze blew in, ticking the hair on the back of her neck. Ellis noticed one of the shutters partially open. There was a crowbar nearby. Abe had been working to create a gap. She could get through. Escape.

"Abe, please…" she said. "Let me go."

He looked at her, stepped forward, came right up to her face.

She reached a hand into her pocket. The envelope opener was still there. She curled her fingers around its handle.

Abe's face was strained, riddled with guilt. "I'm sorry, Ellis," he said. "I really am..."

"Please," Ellis begged. "You're scaring me..."

He touched her cheek with his hand. Smiled poignantly then raised the gun, this time forcing it into his own mouth.

Ellis backed away, shut her eyes.

The gunshot rang out, almost deafening her.

Abe's body fall to the ground.

"Fuck!" she screamed and it was probably the first time Ellis ever used the word. "FUUUCCCKK!"

His blood was all over her. She could taste it, still warm on her lips. She wiped it from her face, spat on the floor.

Ellis needed to get out of here. She couldn't spend another second in this godforsaken building.

She struggled through the gap in the shutters, clambering out into the open air.

The light blinded her, but she didn't care. She ran out into the grounds, eyes closed, the sun bathing her, the wind caressing her hair, the fresh air filling her lungs...

But something wasn't right.

Ellis stopped running, opened her eyes.

She looked into the face of a man wearing the same yellow suit and breathing apparatus that Abe wore. Others in similar garb stood behind him.

Ellis backed away.

They moved closer.

One of the men grabbed her, and in the struggle, she noticed the USB stick Blake had given her fall from the pocket of her scrubs. She watched as the device was trampled into the ground.

"No!" Ellis cried.

She reached into another pocket, finding the envelope opener. Jammed it into the neck of her attacker. It pierced the plastic of his suit, found his flesh. He stumbled backwards, one hand clamped upon the wound.

A broad shouldered man stepped forward. Ellis swung the blade again but he dodged it, brought the butt of his rifle down heavily across her face.

Ellis went down hard.

The broad shouldered man moved in closer, brought the rifle down again. Then again. He pounded Ellis' face until it was nothing but bloody mush. Grunting with each strike until he was sure there was no life remaining within her brutalised corpse.

He stepped back. Looked at his rifle, studying the blood and gore dripping from its end with disgust.

He turned to another man.

"Clean that shit up," he said, pointing to Ellis.

The broad shouldered man moved towards the laboratory entrance, flanked by more suits.

"The virus is out, gentlemen," he said. "So we move to Plan B." He pointed to the building. Let's get to work."

PART TWO

THE VIRUS SPREADS

ONE

"Mam, I got in."

The other end of the line was quiet. Ciaran looked at his mobile phone, in case he'd been cut off, but the screen was still bright.

"Mam? Did you hear me? I got in."

"I heard you", a voice said.

"Well then… what do you think? Isn't it great?"

Ciaran was still holding the papers from the open day in his hand. One sheet was signed and dated, and he'd put it into a clear plastic envelope to keep it good. He'd waited for this day since he was a child and didn't want anything to spoil it. He knew it wasn't every mother's dream to have her son enlist, especially in West Belfast, but couldn't she at least be proud of him?

"You'll be sent home in a box. Just like all the others." Her words hit him like a hammer.

"Mam, I've joined the TA! *Territorial* Army, not the *regular* Army. They won't send me anywhere."

He heard her tut. He knew that noise well; his mother made it when a lump got stuck in her throat. Before the tears came.

"Mam, don't you start –"

"You never listen to me!" she wailed, "Always think you know best."

"Mam…"

"DON'T YOU *MAM* ME!" Within seconds, she'd gone from longsuffering and weepy to something that reminded him of a boiling kettle. Ciaran often wondered how someone so small and delicate could make this many sounds, all so different. But that was the wonder of his mam.

"Mam, listen…" he said, "I'll not be home for dinner. I'm going to grab a pint to celebrate."

"Who with?"

"Jamsey. Maybe John."

"John who? You've never mentioned a John!"

Jesus. He was eighteen years old. When did this ever stop? "John Ford."

"Ford? I've –"

Ciaran held the phone away, shaking it in the air as if to kill it. He took a deep breath, returned it to his ear. "Look, Mam. Gotta go." He flicked the phone off before she had a chance to say anything else, pocketing it in his joggers.

He clenched both hands. She'd really pissed him off this time.

He stood near a lamppost. It was early evening and still bright, but the stupid thing was already lit up.

Ciaran slammed his fist into the rough metal. The pain was barely registering. He slammed again. A bloody mark showed up on the bleached grey hide of the lamppost. He went to swing again then stopped himself, turning his hand and looking at it. His skin was raw. It looked like mincemeat.

He turned to see if anyone else was around.

An old man pulled his dog across the road, the dog straining against its lead to glare at Ciaran. He'd scared them. He hadn't meant to, but Ciaran had scared them nonetheless.

He took a deep breath. There was no way he could get on like that in the army. He needed to cool himself down.

A drink would help.

He looked at his watch. Only seven o'clock. He'd get a taxi into town and grab a drink somewhere.

…

Half an hour later and Ciaran was sitting in the Garrick bar with a pint.

The TV in the corner broadcast some football match that he feigned interest in – United against someone. There was a good crowd in to watch the football, most of the seats filled.

Ciaran sat by the door, a constant to-and-fro as people poured in and out. Neither Jamsey nor John sat with him. He didn't expect to see them. John he'd made up, just as his mam guessed. Jamsey he hadn't seen for a couple of years, since a major falling out over something he couldn't remember (they had both been drinking). It was just going to be Ciaran tonight, and that was fine. He wasn't afraid of his own company.

His hand was sore from punching the lamppost. He took another swig from his half-empty pint glass to try to numb the pain.

His mind wandered, finding the rugged desert terrain of Afghanistan. Ciaran was dressed in pale, desert khakis. He carried a rifle, probably an SA80. The rattle of gunfire was all around him. The enemy was everywhere, and his unit was hemmed in. He lay flat in the sand, looking down the scope of his weapon. There was an enemy combatant in his sights – a sniper on a mound to his left. He squeezed the trigger, and the barrel of the rifle shook briefly before –

"Not watching the football?"

Ciaran looked up, pulled from his daydream. A girl stood by his table. She was a little older than him, probably early twenties. She held a glass in one hand, sucking her drink with a straw. She was on her own.

"Not big into football," he said.

"I thought every fella liked football."

She smiled, and he caught a glimpse of her teeth. Thick metal braces ran across the top row like train tracks. She saw him looking and closed her mouth. Ciaran looked away, embarrassed.

There was silence for a moment, both of them drawn to the football on the screen. The ball came flying towards the United goalmouth, only to be knocked wide by the keeper's fist. A low moan ran throughout the bar, followed by excited voices.

"I'm just waiting on a few mates," Ciaran said over the noise.

"Oh. Alright…" she said, looking disappointed. She stood glued to the spot, one thumb hanging on the belt loop of her jeans. She looked around, as if wondering what to do with herself.

"You can sit for a bit," Ciaran offered.

"You sure?"

"Yeah, why not."

She sat down in the seat opposite him. In the light coming through the window, she looked a little older than he initially thought. Maybe twenty-five. She wasn't unattractive, even with the braces. She looked over, and he knew she wanted him to buy her a drink.

"I'm… er… kinda not working right now," he said.

She smiled. "*Kinda not working*?" she said. "What does *kinda not working* mean?"

Ciaran looked down finding a beer mat on the table. He picked it up and twirled it around his fingers. "Been signing on. Got a new job today but don't start for a couple of weeks."

"Well, congratulations then. I'll get *you* a drink to celebrate." She pointed at his pint of Harp. "Another one of them?"

"Er, yeah," he said. "Thanks."

He watched her walk to the bar, looking her up and down. There were a couple of fellas standing nearby, pints in hand. One of them looked over and nodded at Ciaran as if to say, *Nice one, mate*. Ciaran looked away.

The phone in his pocket vibrated, causing him to jump. He retrieved it, looked at the screen. MAM CALLING. He swore then selected IGNORE CALL. He switched the phone off and slid it back into the pocket of his joggers.

The girl was back now. She sat another pint beside his half-empty glass and slid into her seat. A glass of what looked to be Coke was in her hand.

"That vodka?" he said.

She sniffed the glass. "No. Just Coke."

"Don't you drink?"

She looked up at the television as if the answer to his question might be there. Rooney was arguing with the referee. The bar erupted again, the group of fellas nearby pointing at the screen and shouting.

"I used to," she said, still watching the TV.

Ciaran nodded. New conversation needed. "What do you do?"

She turned back. "I'm a teacher," she said.

"Yeah? What do you teach?"

"Just everything. Primary school."

"What age?"

"P 7. Ten and eleven year olds."

Ciaran smiled. "They're wee shits at that age."

She laughed, took a sip of her drink, then asked, "What's your new job?"

Ciaran looked at the clear plastic envelop sitting on the table beside him. "Just joined the TA," he said.

His voice was muted. Apologetic.

"Wow," she said but she didn't look wowed.

"Yeah," he said. "It's just a job."

He lifted his pint and drank deeply. He went to set it back on the table, but she stopped his hand.

"Let's drink to your new job," she said, then put her lips around the straw. He watched the Coke move up towards her mouth. He lifted his own glass again, lightly knocking it against hers as she continued to drink. He drained his own glass dry.

Voices swelled suddenly around them. Someone had scored.

"What's your name?" Ciaran said, leaning closer to the girl.

"Julie," she shouted over the noise of the crowd. And then she smiled again.

TWO

The boot sale was less crowded than usual.

Martin's stall was gaining little attention; people weren't interested in the contents of his garage, the old records and books, the toolbox he'd never used. He'd dusted them all down, even polished a few things to give them a shine, but still no takers.

He reached a hand by his side finding his dog, Fred. He stroked the dog's fur as it slept peacefully. Fred was his right-hand man. The old dog lay beside Martin's deck chair, soaking up the heat, giving moral support.

Martin looked at the other stall-holders, the ones with trinkets and curiosity items. He wondered why folks bought such junk. Then again, these things were more social than anything else. All about the chit-chat.

He wasn't a boot sale regular; twice a year would usually clear him out.

People here wanted a bargain, something for nothing. Martin had learned to barter over the years, not allowing folks to grab his stuff for buttons. One time, when Martin was greener to it all, some old pro bought half the stuff on his table, only to add it to his own stall, selling at twice the price. These tools he brought today were brand new, hardly out of their packaging. Martin wasn't going to let them go for pennies. He'd rather give them to charity.

He spotted an Indian family. They were usually good for a sale, descending like hawks, mid-morning, filling plastic bags with clothes and toys for their children, anything they couldn't get cheaper elsewhere. Martin recognised them. He'd seen them haggling in the local shops, broken English sounding aggressive to whatever old dear was manning the till.

"How much for the tape?"

Martin looked around, finding an old man waving a roll of half-used masking tape. He wore a white string vest, formidable belly hanging over belted trousers, bare arms sun-scorched and covered with white hair.

"A pound," Martin told him.

The old man sniffed, turned his face up and set the roll back on the table. "Fifty pence," he said without looking at Martin.

"Pound," Martin said, reaching his hand over to ruffle the head of Fred.

The old man smiled, sticking his hand into his trousers pockets and jingling change. A rucksack hung from his shoulders, packed full. "Is the dog for sale?" he said smiling, then handed Martin a pound.

"You wouldn't want him," Martin said, already sick of the quip he'd heard about twenty times that day.

The old man dropped his rucksack, unzipped it and placed the masking tape inside. Martin noticed some other rolls in there along with a clear plastic tub filled with nails and screws.

He noticed Martin staring. "Stocking up," he said. "For the end of the world."

"That so," Martin said.

He knew the old boy as one of the regulars from the boot sale. A bit of a head-melter, always preaching to all and sundry about the latest conspiracy theory he'd picked up from some book he'd just read. No harm in him, mind. Usually filed along quietly, once you looked bored enough.

But today the old fellow was keen. He pulled a crumpled brown envelope from his rucksack. He looked over his shoulder, as if whatever new top secret he was about to divulge hadn't been shared to every other stall holder. He opened the envelope, carefully removed what looked to be a glossy leaflet. He placed it on top of Martin's pasting table, spreading it out flat, clearing stock to make room.

"These are going out next week," he said, voice almost a whisper. "I've a friend in the know." He smiled mischievously. "If you ask me," he continued, voice still low, face beaming as if this were all good news being shared, "I'd say it was all them wars landed us in this shit." His eyes rolled slightly backwards, gesturing towards the Indian family, the mother shifting through a cardboard box of old toys and showing them to a disinterested child in a buggy. "Probably one of them biological attacks you hear about…"

Martin said nothing, simply flicking through the brightly coloured leaflet detailing methods to prevent the spread of germs. There were pictures on every page with smiling, middle-class mothers helping to fit yellow surgical masks over the faces of their children. Other pictures showed a calm workman, also wearing a mask, stepping back to admire the handiwork of a window he'd fully covered with clear plastic using the same sort of masking tape Martin had just sold. All measures your family should take in the unlikely event of the flu virus becoming a 'Stage 2 Pandemic'.

Of course, none of it mattered. Just nonsense some joker on the internet had dreamed up from his bedroom. Fairly well done, mind.

Martin handed the brochure back, blowing some air out of his mouth.

"I'm telling you," the old man protested, reading Martin's mind, "This is the real Mc Coy!" He was getting more and more worked up. A volley of spittle left his mouth.

Martin felt Fred's hackles prick up under his hand and instinctually grabbed the dog's collar. "Not saying there's no truth in it," he said. "So calm yourself down, okay?"

The old man grabbed his brochure from the pasting table.

Fred was growling now, a low murmur vibrating from his throat like a distant roll of thunder.

The old man left them, no doubt to poison some other poor bastard with his paranoid bullshit.

"Easy," boy," Martin said, stroking the dog. "Everything's alright."

He looked back at the Indian woman, now bent over her child in its buggy. The child was crying, and the woman was trying to wipe its face with a tissue, despite its protests.

A sneeze exploded from the stallholder beside him.

…

It was late afternoon before the old man approached his farmhouse home, feet sore and mouth dry from walking and talking. He looked around, dropped his rucksack and retrieved a heavy bunch of keys. He turned each of the five keys in the five locks, looking around once more before letting himself in.

The sound of a parrot greeted his entry, the bird singing "Tom, Tom, Tom" and fluttering its wings with delight. Tom whistled back at the bird, tapping its cage.

He moved through the living room-cum-kitchen, setting his rucksack down by the desk in the corner, then flicked both internet and PC connection to ON. He listened as the old computer whirred, nodded in approval before moving through to the kitchen.

He filled the kettle, set it onto the gas cooker and turned the dial. He lit up a match, leaning it gently towards the escaping gas to ignite a small flame under the kettle, then pulled it sharply to his mouth and blew it out.

Tom moved back to the computer, moving the old stool out from under its desk before sitting down.

The monitor displayed its usual gibberish before throwing up his log-in page. Tom tapped in the sixteen-character password then struck the RETURN key.

He waited while his customised desktop loaded, tapping his fingers on the desk.

Once in, he connected to the internet and began his rounds, opening up the various message boards he frequented all on the topic of TRUTH. He searched each of the threads for new entries.

Tom was a regular on a lot of message boards. Sometimes he argued, striving to convince the idiot sheep of what was going on around them. Most users would laugh, make fun of him. That made Tom angry. He'd swear at them, tell them they were going to die, type feverishly in capitals. And then he'd get banned.

A pop-up box in the corner indicated an incoming request to chat. Tom moved the mouse cursor, accepting, the dialogue box flicking open onto the screen.

"Agent13", he muttered to himself reading the username in the chat box. "Wait til I show you what I've got…"

Tom had waited a long time for this. Finally, he'd something big to share. He reached for the rucksack on the floor, opened it and retrieved his prize. Carefully, he placed the brochure face down on the scanner next to the PC.

The computer beeped, the words 'Agent13 is typing' appearing on the chat screen.

"Just wait, will ye?!" Tom barked, frustrated.

The message NEW PLAYER appeared onscreen.

Tom stared at the words, rubbing the three-day-old stubble on his chin. He sighed. His curiosity got the better of him, despite himself. "Who?" he said out loud as he typed.

LOCAL, came the response.

Tom laughed. "Ever the cryptic bastard, aren't you?"

He typed again, this time in capitals: WHO?!

The message 'Agent13 is typing' appeared again, Tom laughing. "Just get on with it!"

CONNOR JACKSON

"Who?!" Tom said again as he typed.

THE CHAMBER came the reply and then MAHON ROAD.

"Only the old army camp there," Tom muttered back and then typed it in.

EXACTLY replied Agent13.

The kettle whistled in the corner. Tom walked back to the kitchen, retrieving his favourite mug from the draining board where he'd left it. He dunked a tea bag in, lifted a nearby bottle of milk, smelled it, turned his nose up yet still added a drop. He drowned the lot in hot water from the kettle. Lifted his mug and returned to the computer.

There was a link on the screen now, provided by Agent13. He knew the link as one of the regular truther user-groups he would download from.

Tom clicked on it.

The link brought him through to encrypted data. Tom swore. He opened the program Agent13 had supplied him with for decrypting code like this. He ran the data through it, waiting as the PC clucked and burped before throwing up a new page with the data decrypted.

Tom squinted, reading through the small type. It talked about something called The Chamber, a surveillance project running out of the Mahon Road Army camp. The project was particularly active during Northern Ireland's Troubles, interrogating suspects behind closed doors, employing CCTV to keep an eye on key suspects, using the information gained to blackmail, coerce and generally manipulate some of the key players on both sides of the conflict. The result was a swiftly drawn-up 'peace' deal.

Tom read on with interest, almost forgetting his own news.

Major Connor Jackson, whoever he was, was up to his eyes in all of this. He'd led the project in the 80s, soon bringing another player in, a young doctor called Miles Gallagher. Seems the pair were something of a Jekyll and Hyde, reports from Agent13's source confirming disharmony. Eventually, Jackson left, transferring his command to another officer.

LITTLE TASTE OF HOME appeared on the chat screen.

Tom smiled. Like him, Agent13 was based in Northern Ireland. They ran a truther group together. It was rare they'd uncover something local. Normally, they had to make do with whatever US truthers were pedalling: Bohemian Grove or the Bilderbergs or whatever. The Mahon Road was so close to him, Tom could almost throw a stone at it.

He had the urge to go out to the Mahon Road right now and take some pictures, feign a stake-out and talk it up for effect, uploading his story and pics to the group. But then he remembered the brochure. The tape in his bag, the plans he was making to stock up and lock up.

Tom returned to his scanner, scanning the brochure from cover to cover. It didn't take him long, weighing in at a scant 8 pages, all in easy-to-read bold print. He went into his e-mail account, uploading and e-mailing the whole document over to Agent13's e-mail address.

He returned to chat, a smile spreading across his face.

"Sent something to you, buddy" he typed, then leaned back in the chair, arms folded over his formidable belly. "Let's see what you make of *that*…"

THREE

"That'll be £19.99."

Colin folded the scarf and placed it into a bag. He twirled the package around, pointing its handles at the pretty girl at the other side of the till.

She pulled a twenty from her purse, set it on the counter.

Colin's eyes fell upon her t-shirt. There was writing across the chest which Colin squinted to make out. MISS BEHAVIOUR, it read.

"Ahem."

Colin looked up to find the girl staring at him, eyebrows raised. "Just reading your t-shirt," he said, lifting her twenty and ringing it through the till.

"I'll bet you are…"

Colin smiled, handing her the penny change and receipt. "No returns for sale items."

She pocketed her change, took her bag and walked off. She didn't look amused.

"Really not a boobs kind of guy," Colin muttered under his breath then turned to the next person in the queue.

A young, chavvy-looking bloke approached next, placing a pair of boxers on the counter.

"£6.99, mate," Colin said, his voice dropping a key or two.

The chav fumbled in his pockets for change.

Colin smiled as he waited, whistling along with some unknown tune playing on the store radio. He wasn't normally a whistler. It was something he would do subconsciously, an attempt at manning-up, when needing to fit in with whatever alpha-male was nearby.

Chavvy Bloke produced the cash, setting it on the counter. His face screwed up, muscles tensing as he went to sneeze, the spray blasting Colin. "Sorry about that, mate…" he said.

"Don't worry about it," Colin replied, through clenched teeth. He took the money, shaking it in his hand then ringing it through the till. He offered the penny change.

"Keep it," Chavvy said, rubbing his face with an old battered tissue. He flashed a grin then wandered off, bagged boxers in hand.

Colin turned to Sinead, who was standing at the till beside him, her pent-up giggle waiting.

"Fucking twat," Colin said, pulling off his snot-soaked t-shirt. "Should stay indoors if he has the flu. That's what the ads say!"

He left the till. Bare-chested, Colin strolled to a nearby railing and retrieved a vest-top. He could hear Sinead laughing behind him. "What?!" he said, looking back at her, face filled with mock anger.

Sinead was laughing so much now that she gave way to a coughing fit. She pointed at his bare chest. "It's your tan line," she managed, red-faced and exasperated.

Colin put his hand to his mouth, feigning diva-style shock. He marched to the full-length mirror at the other side of the shop, oblivious to the customer using it to try a coat on.

"Oh my GAWWWWD!" Colin burst, doubling over, screeches of laughter ringing out. "I'm such a milly!"

He replaced the vest top back on the railing, instead lifting a short-sleeved, high-collared shirt. He pulled the tag off and slipped it on.

"That looks nice on you," came another voice, accompanied by the familiar clap of high heels. An impeccably dressed young woman approached. "How will you be paying?" she quipped. "Cash or cheque?"

"What's up, Vic?" Colin said. He shot an acid look at Sinead, who rolled her eyes, then turned to the next customer.

"Call just came in from head office," Vicky said. "They want us to close."

"What?"

"It's this –" she looked to make sure no customers were within earshot, "this *fucking* flu," she said in a low voice. "Government's closing all businesses, except what they deem 'necessary'. They're going to announce it on the news later. Unless you're selling groceries or hardware, you're gone."

"We sell clothes," Colin said, "surely that's essential enough for them?"

"Colin," Vicky said, looking over her glasses as if he was irritating her with his stupidity. "This is the twenty-first century. Supermarkets sell all the clothing deemed essential. Our quaint little overpriced boutique just didn't make their list."

"Jesus…" Colin said, looking around the 'quaint little boutique'. "I need this job." He sighed heavily then added, "They're going to let us go, aren't they?"

"Full pay for four weeks, half-pay for the four after that," Vicky said. "And then… well, let's hope it's all cleared up by then and we're open again."

Colin laughed. It was a bitter, sardonic laugh. He retrieved a pair of jeans from a nearby shelf, threw them over his arms, straightened them out then replaced them.

"When do we close?" he asked her.

"Now," Vicky said. "We close up now."

FOUR

The tension was palatable, a nervousness that permeated the very earth. Dew was still heavy on the ground like sweat. The simmering heat was oppressive.

Colin stood on his porch.

Through designer sunglasses he watched as the people from number twenty packed their car full. It looked like they were planning a long break.

He looked to number twenty-four. A single ambulance stood parked by the front of the house, a police Land Rover parked right next to it. It was an old man who lived there. Care workers went in to get him up in the morning then put him to bed at night. Sometimes, they'd wheel him out onto the porch and he'd wave over if Colin was leaving the house.

Colin unlocked the door to his own house, removed the sunglasses and went inside.

To say it was his house was not *strictly* true even though it was *legally* true. Until recently, the house belonged solely to his ninety-two-year-old Aunt Bell. Colin had moved in with her after his marriage fell apart.

A lifelong singleton, as Colin would call her, making her laugh every time, Aunt Bell had no kids of her own. And so Colin became the child she never had, shaming his own parents, whose duelling-banjo religion forbade them from accepting a queer for a son.

But Aunt Bell treated Colin the same way she treated everyone else: just as she found him. And Colin returned the favour, giving her the care most ninety-two year olds needed to stay independent. He did everything for her, helped her wash and dress, closing the door on the bored, lack-lustre care workers who pulled old Mr Twenty-Four out of bed each morning.

None of it sat well with the rest of the family. Soon neither Christmas nor birthday cards came through the letterbox. But then, as if to stick her bony old fingers up at the family which had rejected them both, Bell wrote Colin's mother (her sister) out of her will, writing Colin in, and signing the deeds of her private semi-detached over to him.

"Aunt Bell," Colin called, hearing her television set blaring from the front room, *turned up to eleven*, as he would joke.

There was no reply.

He entered the room to find her sitting on the sofa, staring at the television.

Something was wrong.

She would usually hear the door bang, and he would come in to her muttering about whatever she was watching, half to him and half to the characters on the screen. But she was quiet now.

"Aunt Bell?" he said, again.

She turned to look at him, her big eyes wide and watery.

"They're closing the town," Bell said in a hoarse voice then looked back at the TV. The report that Vicky had mentioned earlier was playing, some reporter talking about Stormont's decision to 'temporarily close' Belfast's city centre.

"It's only for a bit," Colin said. "Just 'til this old flu goes away."

He pulled his jacket off, dropped it on the sofa.

Bell looked at him with daggers in her eyes. "Hang that coat up," she said, pointing to his discarded jacket on the sofa.

Colin shook his head, smiling. He lifted the jacket, left the living room, and hung it in the hall.

Something outside caught his attention. He opened the door, stepped back out onto the porch, looking across to number twenty four. A stretcher was being taken out by paramedics, the old man lying on it, wheezing and coughing violently.

Two cops followed.

The paramedics loaded the old fella into the back of their ambulance.

FIVE

The yanks were going mad about it.

People were calling into Alex Jones' radio show and talking about nothing else. There was chat about some laboratory in Belfast, with suggestions of foul play.

Nothing was confirmed.

Theories came thick and fast from the sites and podcasts Tom followed. They were citing everything from viral warfare to big corporations linked to Bilderberg, trying to make a quick buck out of developing a virus only they could cure.

It was both exciting and terrifying. Things were getting nasty out there, but a part of Tom revelled in it. He'd been the first to expose it all with the leaflet he'd been sent by his old mate Stan at the printers.

He'd heard nothing from Stan since…

It was as dark inside as it was outside.

So quiet he could hear the hum of the generator in his outhouse. He'd topped it up before sealing himself in. He'd used power sparingly. He really didn't want to go outside again.

Tom sat in his easy chair staring at the boards on his windows wondering if he'd done enough to keep the virus out.

He'd created three defences.

Polythene covers were pinned around the walls surrounding the doors and windows, then sealed using the masking tape he picked up from the boot sale. Tom had then nailed large wooden boards across most of the glass and external door, leaving his bedroom window as lookout. His last line of defence was cradled in his hands: a brown plastic bottle containing his meds. This was potent shit. He would wash them down with vodka. There was no way he was going to let some damn virus tear him apart...

He popped one of the pills now. Needed something to take the edge of.

He heard the familiar sound of his chat icon. Tom jumped up from the easy chair and hurried to his computer. He read the screen.

YOU OKAY?

"Agent13," Tom muttered, typing back his reply. "I'm okay, buddy, how are you?"

MORE INFO ON THAT CASE YOU'RE WORKING ON...

"Case? What case?"

A new link appeared, Tom following it to find a new file uploaded to their news group. He clicked on it, swearing as the all-too-familiar sight of encrypted data poured onto his screen.

"Damn it!" Tom exclaimed, feeding the file through his software. He hated the way Agent13 did this all the time. *Such a nuisance!*

The information was decrypted. Tom's eyes narrowed as he read. It was more on that Chamber thing, the old surveillance and interrogation racket. Government sponsored of course, but old news now with all this flu stuff. Still, it seemed important to Agent13.

The new file contained a list of people The Chamber worked on. Some of the names Tom recognised as key political figures. Others he didn't know.

Tom couldn't really concentrate on it.

DID CHRYSLER GET IN TOUCH YET?

Agent 13 was talking about Chris Lennon, another key member of their local group. Chris was working on something big. He'd allegedly been to this lab they were all talking about on the Alex Jones show but wouldn't share anything until he got all the facts straight.

"Still no word from him…" Tom said, once again typing.

HE'S GOT BIG INFO ON THE FLU. HOW IT STARTED.

"You see," Tom said, pointing at the screen, "Chris knows what's important."

WOULD HAVE LIKED HIS INPUT ON THE CHAMBER TOO.

"Would you, now?" Tom murmured. "My *input* not enough for you?"

SO WHAT DO YOU THINK?

"Jesus, we've no time for this Chamber stuff," Tom complained. He typed something to that effect back to 13.

IT'S RELEVANT, typed the other man.

"Hardly," Tom said as he typed: "Let's get back to the flu."

SURE, 13 replied. IT'S GETTING WORSE. THEY'VE STARTED QUARANTINES.

"Quarantines?" Tom said. "What do you mean, *quarantines*?"

SIX

TA Centre, Co. Armagh
15th June

Ciaran was still half asleep as he carried his breakfast across the canteen.

He set his tray down at the table beside another lad his age, called Grady. An older man sat opposite. He was one of the newbies, wearing an old tracksuit instead of the khakis that Ciaran and Grady wore. His hair was dark, his beard full and sporting flecks of grey. There was an Eastern European look about him.

"How's it going?" Ciaran said to him, extending his hand.

The other man looked up from his food. He seemed a little startled but shook with Ciaran enthusiastically.

"I'm Ciaran."

The newbie looked vacant, confused.

"It's my name," Ciaran said.

Grady was laughing.

The other man smiled, pointed to himself, said, "Ron. Name."

Grady was in stitches. His body was shaking as he hid behind his arm, laughing from across the table. Ciaran shot him a dirty look.

"No uniform?" Ciaran asked.

Again the confused look.

"Uniform," Ciaran said, pulling at his own green khaki shirt.

"Ah," the newbie said, smiling. He shrugged dramatically, hands raised, palms pointing upwards. He said something that Ciaran didn't understand.

"Probably here cleaning toilets," Grady said. "Until they signed him up…"

"Shut up," Ciaran whispered.

"Don't worry. He can't understand a word of English. That right, mate? Yeah?" Grady mocked looking to Ron.

Ron nodded, still smiling. "Yeah," he repeated parrot-style.

"See?" Grady said, grinning.

"Leave him alone," Ciaran said half-heartedly. But he knew Grady was right. An asshole, maybe, but pretty much on the money. It looked like they were signing up anyone who could walk in a straight line these days.

The news was playing on the television. Ciaran was drawn to it. The words FLU: LATEST were written across the screen. There was a riot outside City Hospital. Place was going mad.

"This flu thing's out of control," Grady said, pointing his fork at the TV. "There's talk of them doing quarantines."

"Quarantines?"

"Yeah, like going into towns where infection rates are high and locking the place down. That sort of thing."

Ciaran laughed. "You watch too much sci-fi, mate…"

"Maybe." Grady said. "But that's how they're dealing with this thing now. There's talk of them bringing the Irish Army across the border to help out. More brits are being sent over too."

"All hearsay."

"You think?" Grady looked to Ron, who was looking back, concern etched across his face. "You wanna see some of the stuff they're putting online. Man, that stuff's crazy. What they're doing at the docks and airports, keeping people in and all…"

"It's just a precaution. To keep the virus from spreading. The army's just keeping the peace, that's all."

"Mate," Grady said, lowering his voice, "People are tearing the fuckin' hospital apart." He shovelled another mouthful of food, chewed speedily. "Some worrying shit going down."

Yet Grady didn't seem too concerned to Ciaran. Excited, maybe. But not concerned. He was the kind of asshole Ciaran was hoping to get away from. He'd known guys like Grady in school, guys who thought they knew everything when they really knew jack-shit. Mouthy bastards who talked a hell of a lot more than they listened, who took nothing seriously, who slagged everyone and everything off around them, just for the hell of it, just to hear the sound of their own voices. Fucking prick.

Ciaran looked back at the TV. They were playing footage from some office building.

Several cops dressed in yellow suits were dragging a middle-aged man out of the building. But the man didn't look right. It wasn't just the flu: he'd a crazed look about his face. His eyes were vacant, like he was on something. As the camera zoned in, he lunged at the nearest cop, sinking his teeth into his arm. The other cops were trying to pull him off, beating him with their batons like he was some mad dog.

Ciaran noticed one of the kitchen staff watching the scene unfold. He was resting against his mop, a pool of spilled juice gathered at his feet unattended to. The man's face said it all, pale and drawn like he too wasn't feeling the George Best. Sweat soaked his back, seeping through his clothes.

"Someone turn that off," barked the Sarge.

The kitchen hand snapped out of his trance then called to one of his colleagues to switch over.

Ciaran watched as an older woman with a remote flicked through the channels, most carrying the same story. She settled on MTV, which, as always, was playing some dicky reality show.

The Sarge approached Ciaran's table, carrying a neat pile of clothes. He lifted what appeared to be a white boiler suit from the pile, set it on the table next to Ron. "Uniform," he said to the Polish man. "Ran out of regular GI threads," he mocked, "so this will have to do you, soldier."

Ron looked at the clothes, smiled and gave the thumbs up to Sarge.

Sarge looked to Grady and Ciaran, shook his head, then moved on.

SEVEN

The Sarge was a hardass. A weathered face and beer belly suggested more than a few miles on the clock. Ciaran reckoned the old bastard would have beaten the training into them, if he could get away with it.

"Most of you should know by now what to expect from me," he said now, strolling up their line. "I expect the best. And I don't mean *your* best, I mean *the* best. You'll be in active service within the week, and, while that means your training will be fast-tracked, I don't want you to think you can half-arse your way through it."

The Sarge stopped and looked a particularly spotty young lad up and down, shook his head, then moved on.

Ciaran stole a glance at Grady beside him. "Fuckin' tit," the other lad whispered. Stifled laughter filled their end of the line.

The Sarge looked sternly in his direction, but Ciaran kept his eyes looking forward, his face straight. The Sarge stepped in front of Ciaran.

"Something funny, boy?" he said.

"No, sir."

"Well, why are you laughing?"

"I'm not laughing, sir."

The Sarge held his gaze on Ciaran, sizing him up.

He moved on, staring suspiciously at each man he passed.

He reached Grady, stopped. "Something funny, Grady?" he said.

"No, sir."

"Well, wipe that smirk off your ugly face then, boy. Cos I'll tell you this – none of you cunts have anything to be laughing about."

He turned to address them all, then continued. "It may have bypassed you clowns, but it's getting pretty ugly out there, and you're going to be dealing with it sooner rather than later. It's my job to make sure that when you're faced with a tough call to make you've all got the strength of character and bloody fucking training to make it. Cos a laughing solider is a nervous soldier, and the army is no place for nerves. You hear me?"

"Yes, sir!" Ciaran called in unison with the others.

"Good," the Sarge replied, sizing the men up as he paced the line again.

"Now, I've got something very special in store for you ladies today," he boomed, marching down the line again. "This exercise is known as Fighting In Built Up Areas. FIBUA for short. We've kitted the range out with makeshift buildings and obstacles. It's not exactly Baghdad; a little imagination and improvisation might still be required on your part…" The Sarge stopped at Polish Ron, the new recruit standing proudly, eyes straight ahead, wearing the white boiler suit he had been given as a uniform. "But you bozos know all about improvisation," he added then laughed.

"In your hands is an SA80 assault rifle," he continued. "Standard weapon of the British Army. Let me remind you that this is your gun. She belongs to no one else, so I want you to look after her."

The Sarge stopped in front of a young lad with blonde highlights and earrings. Ciaran didn't recognise him. He wore a white boiler suit like Polish Ron's. His eyes were watering. A gun rested awkwardly in his hands, like it might explode any minute. The Sarge looked at the lad with disdain, shook his head then progressed on down the line.

"I ain't gonna give you any bullshit about this rifle being your best friend, your lover or any other war movie bullshit," he continued. "But you need to become familiar with her. You will need to strip, clean and reassemble her and do it quickly.

"Most of you already know some of the basics. You've taken her for a walk, marching around this godforsaken camp like a pack of queers. Some of you have even been firing live ammo on the range. But today, ladies, is a very special day. Today, you'll get the chance to actually use your mother-fucking gun." The Sarge's eyes widened, a smile breaking across his lips. "Does that excite you?"

A low murmur along the line.

"I can't hear you!" roared the Sarge. "Are you ladies excited?!"

"Yes, sir!" the recruits returned.

"Good!" The Sarge barked back.

He reached the end of the line, turned and proceeded to walk back down it.

"Now, on the muzzle of your SA80 you'll notice an attachment. This is to stop you idiots from killing each other. You'll be firing blanks for this exercise, not live ammo." His voice lowered as he added, "Thank God." Another low murmur throughout the line, this time amusement. "You'll be dealing with all kinds of shit when you're out on those streets," the Sarge boomed, "and I don't want any of you jokers panicking, shooting the place up. A good soldier shows restraint. There'll be no friendly fire on my watch. You got me?"

Another parrot-style reply from the line.

"A built up environment is the hardest to work in. You'll have limited vision. An attack can come from anywhere. This exercise will have plenty of surprises: targets that you will not fire upon as well as targets that you will fire upon."

The Sarge stopped, smiled and looked up the line. "Now, who wants to go first?"

He was met with deathly silence.

The Sarge sized up to Ciaran. "What about you, soldier?" he said, gazing into the young recruit's eyes. "Are you ready to walk the walk?"

Ciaran thought about the Sarge's question for a moment.

His mind travelled back to the TV in the canteen. The riot at the hospital. The infected man being dragged out of the office block. He thought of the kitchen hand standing with his mop, sweat soaking his back as he watched it all play out in on the screen.

Ciaran remembered how excited he was on open day, how proud he'd been when telling that girl, Julie, he'd met in the pub, about enlisting. But now he wished he'd listened to his mam. Because the Sarge wasn't exactly selling the job of soldier to him.

It was hot. Ciaran tugged at the collar of his khaki shirt.

There were flies everywhere, and he swatted one across the nearby wall of the first makeshift house.

He swore under his breath, wishing he were somewhere, anywhere else but here.

The FIBUA, as the Sarge called it, was poorly organised, half-arsed and, frankly, pointless. It reeked of box-ticking. The Sarge had made a list, marking each recruit off on his clipboard as they performed each manoeuvre. Room clearing was the next thing on the list.

And Ciaran was up.

They were to move in groups of three, keeping their eyes on the streets (read: space between each wooden shack) before storming the plywood houses one at a time, clearing each, room by room. Throughout the houses, the Sarge had pinned paper targets, some representing hostiles, others meant to be civilians. The recruits were to clear each allocated room, showing quick response to hostile targets, while leaving the civilians unharmed.

Ciaran was in a group with Ron and Grady.

He was tired and jaded and couldn't be arsed with any of it. His clearance of the first house was slow and pretty sloppy. He missed several key cut-outs.

The Sarge told him he'd be a dead man, were this the real thing. That levelled Ciaran more than he thought it would. The deeper he got into this stuff, the more he realised he wasn't the badass soldier he thought he was. It was really getting him down.

Grady, on the other hand, was buzzing. He'd proven to be a good aim on the range and in this exercise looked just as sharp. Too much so, mind, the zealous little cunt emptying his mag into two cardboard children in the second house. The Sarge barked at him for that, but Grady didn't seem to take anything to heart the way Ciaran did. As long as his trigger finger was clicking, the little twat seemed happy.

It was Ron's turn to take the lead next.

Although visibly nervous, the Polish man surprised Ciaran, taking care as he cleared each room efficiently, his nerves seeming to sharpen his senses as opposed to dull them. Even the Sarge seemed impressed, his silence throughout Ron's run saying it all as he shadowed the recruit through the wooden set. Looked like the Pole had some military experience after all.

They came to the last house, Ron still taking the lead.

Ciaran and Grady held back with the Sarge as Ron took the biggest room at the end of the corridor. Ciaran watched the Polish man glide through the doorway, his rifle aloft and ready for action. Even with the white boiler suit, Ron looked more like a soldier than Ciaran ever would, and that pissed him off.

He was jealous. The jealousy turned to resentment, Ciaran wondering just why the Polish man was even allowed in the TA in the first place. Surely only *British* citizens should be allowed to join the *British* Army! But Ciaran was reminded of his own passport. How it was *Irish*, not British.

His mam's face crossed his mind. Her disapproving look.

Army's no place for a Falls Road boy.

There was a sudden scream. It sounded like Ron.

Ciaran ran to the bigger room, looked in.

"Ron?" he said. "You okay, mate?"

It was dark, the sunlight dimming, affording Ciaran little light despite the plywood building's open top.

In the corner, he noticed Ron struggling with someone – or something.

Ciaran raised his rifle even though it was loaded with blanks.

Ron stumbled towards him, the Polish man clutching his own throat, blood soaking the brilliant white fabric of his boiler suit.

Ciaran froze, dropped his gun. "What the –" he mouthed.

Ron reached for him, one arm outstretched, panic in his eyes.

Ciaran backed away, looking for help. Grady was in the corridor, the Sarge beside him.

Another man staggered into view. It was the man Ron had been struggling with. He looked young: tall and thin, wearing a chef's uniform. Ciaran realised it was the kitchen hand from the canteen yesterday, the one standing by his mop as the news played on TV.

Only, something was very wrong with him.

He looked a mess. His face was blue, his whole body bent over itself as he crept forward. One of his feet dragged like it was broken.

Ciaran backed down the corridor, the kitchen hand following.

"J-Jesus, Sarge…" Ciaran said, looking to his CO, "What the fuck's wrong with him!?"

The kitchen hand's mouth opened, a viscous cough erupting. As he stepped into the better light, Ciaran could see blood gathering on his chin. He realised with horror that it wasn't the lad's own blood but Ron's.

"Stand aside, Private," the Sarge said.

Ciaran pulled back, watching as the Sarge raised his handgun, aiming it point-blank at the lad's head.

He fired.

The shot rang out louder than Ciaran expected. The noise was everywhere, echoing around the plywood walls of the house.

It was the first time he'd watched a man die. Sure, he'd watched stuff online – suicides and beheadings, anything he could find, genuine or otherwise. Ciaran thought it would prepare him for the real thing. He thought he'd be ready to see this.

But he wasn't.

And he certainly wasn't ready for what came next.

Ron was on the floor, choking on his own blood, his lips forming a gargled plea.

"Sh-shouldn't we call for help, sir?" Ciaran offered, but the Sarge ignored him, instead standing over the wounded European man and unloading two rounds into his head.

"Fuck!" Ciaran gasped, jumping with each shot. "Jesus Christ!"

His voice broke, giving way to sobbing. Tears flowed down his face, and he rubbed them away with his hand. He looked to Grady, finding the other lad's face dry like stone, eyes glued to the two bodies on the ground, chest rising and falling in short bursts as if excited.

EIGHT

Nobody wanted to talk about the FIBUA. It wasn't that it hadn't affected them - most of the other recruits looked as shocked and scared as Ciaran – it just seemed best not to talk about it. Not directly, anyway.

Lunchtime, and pretty much everyone had started drinking already. The officers seemed to turn a blind eye to it, perhaps realising the recruits needed an outlet after the day's horrifying events.

But Ciaran was sober.

He left the others as they filed into the canteen.

He pulled the mobile phone from his pocket. Slid it open, accessed his contacts list and chose MAM.

The phone rang twice before a familiar voice answered.

"Hallo?"

Ciaran went to say something but his voice was shaking.

"Ciaran? Is that you son? What's wrong? Where are you?"

"Nothing's wrong, Mam," he said, sniffing back the tears. "Just wanted to hear your voice."

"Ciaran," she said. "I've been trying to get you for ages, son, but you never answer. Listen, we're leaving the city. Your Uncle John's got a caravan in Newcastle. We're going to stay with him for a bit, wait this whole *flu* thing out." She said the word 'flu' the same way she said words like 'Brit' or 'Police' or 'Paisley'. "You know where he is, don't you, son? Bunny's Caravan Site. You'll come join us as soon as you get out of there, hear?"

"Sure, Mam," he said. "Soon as I can."

"How's training going?" she said, and he could still hear the disapproval in her voice. "You know they're going into houses now, locking people up? Your Granny's friend was locked up the other day. Don't you be locking people up, son, you hear me?"

"I hear you, Mam."

"Don't know what you're doing there anyway," she sighed. "Come on home now, and sure you can go up to Newcastle with me and your Uncle John. He's plenty of room. It's a big caravan he has."

"I'll try and get away, Mam." But he knew he wouldn't. They weren't letting anyone leave, unless the doctor signed them off. And Ciaran wasn't keen on admitting anything that even *smelled* like illness after what had happened to Ron.

"Well, that's where we're heading," his mam said. "Get a taxi, sure. They're still running where you are, isn't that right?"

"I'll do that," Ciaran lied.

He could hear some raised voices at the other end of the line.

"Listen, son, that's your Uncle John now. I've got to go. But you take care of yourself."

"I will, Mam."

"And Ciaran," she said. "You know I love you, son."

"I know, Mam," he said, face twisted as he fought to hold back the tears. "Me too."

He ended the call, bent over and threw up on the ground.

A couple of recruits passed him on their way out of the canteen.

"Fuck's sake," he heard one say. "He's infected! Like the ones on the news!"

"I'M NOT FUCKING INFECTED!" Ciaran yelled at them, grabbing one of the lads and pushing him up against the wall.

"Alright, alright," the recruit said. "Calm down, mate."

Ciaran released the man, pushed him away and then stormed off in the other direction.

"Fucking psycho," he heard the lad shout as he retreated. "You'll never make a soldier getting on like that!"

NINE

The television sat in the corner of the room, ornaments built around its base. It was jet black, the smooth finish glistening as the brightness of day leaked through closed blinds, bleeding into the screen.

Shaun stood by the living room doorway, his arms crossed. He was reading the words along the bottom of the picture, following the ongoing debate between a rather zealous TV host and his bureaucrat victim of the day.

A hand patted Shaun's arm. Lize was baying for his attention.

"Are you just going to stand there, watching that?" she said, her lips strained. She was holding a dishcloth, evidence that she *wouldn't* be standing there with him.

Shaun waved her away, looking back to the screen.

The debate was heating up. It was about the flu, of course. What the government were doing about it.

A middle-aged man from the studio audience was shouting, hands pointed aggressively as he hammered his point home. Once done, he sat back into his seat, arms folded.

Everyone clapped for him.

A news update appeared at the top of the screen: STORMONT DENIES POLICE BRUTALITY.

The blue lights of an ambulance flashed past the front window, pulling Shaun away from the TV.

He looked for Lize, finding her bent over the sink in the kitchen. He called her, but she didn't answer. He called louder, not sure what background noise he was battling against. Still she didn't look around, dipping her head towards the sink. Her hands busied with the dishes, yet produced nothing.

Shaun closed in from behind, wrapping her in his arms. He could feel her body shaking, little reverberations moving through her. He turned her face gently to his. She was crying. She pressed her soggy hands against his chest and leaned in on him.

"What's wrong?" he said.

Her mascara was running. She checked her eyes. "This whole thing…" she said, "Shaun, it's getting worse, not better."

It was more difficult to read her lips when she was like this. They turned up at each corner just like when she was smiling, telling him a joke or playfully flirting. Shaun wanted to sign to her, but she was standing too close to him.

"It'll be okay," he said weakly.

She looked up, as if to say, *Do you really believe that?*

She stepped back, creating space. Her eyes found his. Shaun knew that look: she wanted to tell him something important, something he may not want to hear.

"I think we should leave," she said, "Take Jamie and head down to Daddy's place."

Shaun frowned.

"Please, Shaun. It's only getting worse in the city, but the country could be safe. And Daddy is really good with this sort of thing. You know he is…"

What sort of thing? Shaun thought. *There has never been this sort of thing!* He wanted to yell at her. Any mention of her father usually led to them rowing, but Shaun knew how comical his voice sounded when he shouted.

He still remembered the kids from school laughing when he got worked up, riled by their constant abuse and hurtful remarks. He remembered how they would gather around him, like a pack of hyenas, laughing, giggling, waiting to pounce.

Their favourite game was to point at parts of their bodies and get Shaun to say the word. ASS and TITS and COCK. He would say each word, and they would laugh and he would get satisfaction from their laughs, a feeling of inclusion. He remembered feeling angry with his mother for chasing them away and dragging him by the arm back home, like he'd done something wrong.

"I couldn't stay with your father," he said, signing as he talked. "Not for a day. Not even for an hour."

Lize shook her head. "Shaun," she said, and from the shape of her lips he knew she was almost whispering. "Do it for Jamie."

He looked to the sink, dishes still floating around in there, unwashed. The suds frothed up like bubble bath. Sparkling, calm, serene.

He felt her hands on his face.

"Shaun. I'm frightened," she said, and he could tell from her eyes that she meant it, that none of it was fabricated to get her own way, to win this latest fight within the constant battle they seemed to be waging with each other these days.

He pulled away from her, returned to the living room where the debate still raged on TV. A young woman was getting quite agitated, screaming as two security guards dragged her out. LAB CLOSURE SAID TO BE

CONNECTED TO FLU OUTBREAK, read another news update.

Lize pursued him, wrapping herself in his embrace once more. She wasn't for giving up. She really wanted them to leave.

Shaun sighed, planting a kiss on his wife's forehead.

"Okay," he said. "I'll get Jamie ready. You phone your dad and tell him we're coming."

…

Shaun paused by the door of Jamie's bedroom. Their nine year old was very grown up for his age, insisting that his parents knocked before entering his room.

Shaun rapped his knuckles on the wood.

Being deaf, he'd no way of knowing whether Jamie had replied.

A few moments passed.

Shaun knocked again.

Still no answer.

Rather than burst in, Shaun left Jamie's door, wandering into the spare room.

He found a large suitcase in the cupboard and dusted it down. The case hadn't been used in ages.

Before Jamie had been born, he and Lize used to holiday frequently. City breaks were their favourite. A long weekend in Rome or Berlin or Amsterdam really did the trick. A meal out in some fancy restaurant with a nice bottle of wine thrown in. They did none of that anymore.

He noticed a smaller case, this one handheld. Lize had used it on her latest business trip. Shaun reached for it, thinking Jamie could use it to carry his Nintendo and books (the boy was chain-reading teen horror titles these days; they couldn't keep up with him).

As Shaun pulled the smaller case from the wardrobe, something fell out and tumbled to the floor. He bent to his knees and picked it up. It was a white envelope. Lize's name was written on the front. Shaun checked the seal. It was open.

Shaun looked around seeing that Jamie's door was still closed. He peered across the doorway, finding the stairs empty.

He reached inside the envelope and pulled a card out. On the front of the card was a picture of the Eiffel Tower. Shaun hadn't been to Paris, and he thought the same could be said for Lize, until he opened the card and found a photo inside. It was taken in front of the tower. Lize was in it, standing beside an older man. His arms were wrapped around her. The picture looked recent.

Shaun felt his stomach churn.

He went to read the card but a tap on his arm disturbed him. Jamie looked up at him, his eyes drawn to the card in Shaun's hands.

"What's that?" Jamie said.

Shaun shoved the card and photo into his back pocket. "Nothing," he said.

Jamie shrugged. "Did you need me?"

"Yes," Shaun said, his mind still a million miles away. He reached for the smaller handheld case and handed it to Jamie. "You need to pack for a trip away."

"Cool," Jamie said excitedly. "Where are we going?"

"Grandpa Martin's."

"Oh," Jamie said. His face dropped. "Really?"

"We have to," Shaun said. "The countryside's a better place to be right now. So don't make things any difficult than they already are."

"Okay, Dad," Jamie said, still frowning. He picked up the case and slumped back into his room.

Shaun watched him go, then reached for the card in his back pocket, opened it and read:

Dearest Lize,

Fondest memories of a wonderful weekend in 'Gay Paris'...

Love always,

Alan

Shaun's eyes welled up with tears.

Jamie came out of the room. He was saying something, but Shaun couldn't focus on it.

Shaun pushed past the boy, headed for the bathroom. Closed the door behind him and locked it.

He looked in the mirror, tried to steady himself. He blew his nose, dropped the tissue into the toilet and flushed it. *Come on*, he told himself. *Keep it together.* He looked into the mirror again, practised a smile, holding it as he reached to open the door.

He found Jamie standing on the other side of the door, like he'd been knocking.

Lize was on the stairs behind him, a worried look across her face. "What's wrong?" she said.

"Nothing," Shaun said, his smile still holding.

"Is Jamie packed?" she asked.

Shaun looked to Jamie.

"Not yet," the boy answered for him.

"Did you talk to Martin?" Shaun asked Lize, careful to hide his angst.

"Not yet," she said. "Phone's playing up. Mobile's no better. Seems to be a common problem. It's all over the news."

"Try mine," Shaun said, reaching into his back pocket. As he pulled it out, the card and photo tumbled across the floor.

All eyes stared at them.

Shaun placed his hand on Jamie's shoulder, leading the boy back into his room. "Come on, son. Let's get you ready," he said.

He glared at Lize as he passed.

He could see the guilt in her eyes, and it broke his heart.

TEN

"Aunt Bell?"

Colin placed a hand on his aunt's shoulder.

She was getting worse. Lying in bed with her hair net on and no make-up, she looked every second of her age and more. Her small body looked frail. Her skin was so hard and dry that Colin worried it might crack open.

This fucking flu…

"Peggy…?" she muttered, half awake.

"It's me, Aunt Bell," Colin said quietly, wiping the dried blood from her nose.

"Ah," she said. "Did you bring the soup?"

"Soup?" he said, discarding one wet wipe and picking out another.

"Yes," she said, her eyes opening. "I'll have the mushroom. Always liked mushroom soup."

A moment of lucidity seemed to flow through her as she looked at him. One bony hand moved up to touch his face. "Colin," she said. "I'm so cold." Her face screwed up like newspaper. Her pain was tangible.

Colin left her, moving downstairs to the phone once again. He tried the emergency helpline from the television, getting the same pre-recorded message he always got. He left his name and address on their answer machine, listening again to the first aid instructions, almost able to recite them in time with the nice English lady's voice at the other end of the line.

Colin entered the kitchen.

He stood for a second looking around, like he'd forgotten what he was there for.

He remembered: "Soup," he said, raising his finger in the air.

He searched each cupboard, finding teabags and sugar, tinned beans, Jammy Dodgers. But no soup.

Aunt Bell hadn't eaten *anything* today. Colin tried to give her all the things he'd seen her eat over the years: salted porridge, well done toast with thin slices of cheese and lashings of butter, spaghetti hoops, Jammy fucking Dodgers, but she turned her nose up at them all. And now she was asking for mushroom soup, which Colin had never once seen her eat.

"Soup," he said again, wondering if he could check to see if any of the neighbours would spare some. But most of them were gone, packing up their cars and hitting the road. Those left were bedding in, probably too scared to open their doors. Probably stocking up every last scrap of food for themselves.

Colin would have to go out.

He went back upstairs to Aunt Bell's bedroom.

She was sleeping, the fever still damp across her brow, the hair net soaked. She was so hot that Colin could feel the heat in his own throat. The infection was radiating from her. He wanted to kiss her but stopped himself, instead kissing his fingertips and pressing them gently against her chapped lips.

He left the house.

Outside, it was quiet. Tense.

The doors and windows of most of the houses were boarded up. Colin also wanted to flee. But with Aunt

Bell so unwell, he knew it was a bad idea. She needed to rest. She needed sleep and comfort. And now she needed soup.

His car, nicknamed Vince, stood solemnly in the driveway as if waiting for him, begging him to hit the open road. Colin opened the door and climbed inside. He sat for a moment, checked himself in the mirror, noticing he hadn't combed his hair today. Must have forgotten.

"Come on..." he whispered to himself. "Get moving."

But the car remained still. Colin realised he was scared.

He picked his phone out of his pocket, called up his contacts list and hovered over the name VICKY, then, thinking again, threw the phone to the passenger seat. This was no time for weakness. He needed to be strong. He needed to be in control. He needed to be manly.

He stuck the keys in the ignition, firing up Vince and pulling out of the driveway.

ELEVEN

Vince was a green Volkswagen Beetle. Having bought it second hand, Colin had owned the little car for almost ten years, Vince being the single constant in his life. And the Beetle was loyal to a fault. Even when Vince broke down, his sputters and squeals were tepid, as if embarrassed about falling ill. Thankfully, he was revving like a beast today.

Colin drove down the Antrim Road, towards town. The streets were so deserted that it seemed like the world had already ended and Colin somehow missed it.

He stopped just short of Belfast's city centre, spotting a small Spar corner shop still doing business.

Colin pulled up on the pavement just outside the shop, wanting to keep Vince well within his sight. He ignored the double yellow lines roughly painted next to the pavement. A parking ticket was the least of his worries.

Colin locked Vince before walking towards the shop.

A wide-eyed young woman exited, knocking against him. Something fell out of her pocket and Colin stopped to pick it up, calling her back. It was a packet of hay fever tablets.

She turned as he called. Her red hair was almost golden in the sun.

Colin reached the tablets to her.

She grabbed the packet from him, without saying a word, before moving on.

Colin shook his head.

He opened the door and entered the shop.

Inside was a queue of people, moving all the way around the walls, stocking their wire baskets with pretty much anything they could grab.

A wiry Goth lad stood busily restocking the emptying shelves, but everyone just pushed past him, lifting goods directly from his trolley.

An older man, still wearing his Spar t-shirt, stood hunched over the only functioning till, scanning bar codes and piling the goods into bags.

A tall security guard with a perfectly pressed uniform and slickly parted hair stood by the door, holding a gun. He looked scared, displaced.

Colin joined the queue, meekly smiling at an unhappy couple at the tail end.

He pulled his phone out of his pocket, noticing the message NETWORK UNAVAILABLE written across the screen. He put it away again.

...

He was in the queue for at least an hour, and, in that time, the wiry Goth managed to empty five trolley loads from the storeroom. Colin was counting, all the while stacking his own basket to overflow, making sure to include a six-pack of mushroom soup.

Two people were ejected from the shop.

The first one, an older man, lost his head whenever the till operator refused to take card or cheque. The customer (if you could call anyone that in this glorified bread line) tried to make a break for the door, basket in hand, shrieking like a child as the tall security guard quietly blocked his exit, calmly prised the man's hands from the red plastic handles of the shopping basket, then pushed him out the door.

Not a single person offered to help or pay for the poor bastard's purchases. Colin watched on with shock, but, like everyone else, did nothing.

Another customer, this one looking like a student, tried to make a grab-and-run for a packet of cigarettes. He too was evicted from the premises in the same manner, the security guard grabbing him literally by his collar and sending him on his way with a push from his size tens.

It was Colin's turn to line up and pay the man. He made sure to have the cash ready in his hand, smiling at the morbid till operator.

Face to face, he realised the man was younger than he at first thought. His hair, thinning and combed to the side, fell against a red glowing forehead. His eyes held nothing even resembling emotion. He was lost in the till, scanning items with robot precision.

It reminded Colin of a local history book that Aunt Bell had once shown him. There was a picture with lines of women standing rigidly at the factory, operating sewing machines. "See that one on the left," Bell said, beaming proudly, "that was me." And even when Colin looked closely, he still couldn't tell her apart from the forty others in the picture with identical uniforms and hairstyles; their clock-in cards just visible by the door in the far left of the picture.

Colin was pulled out of his thoughts when the door crashed open.

"Okay, everyone stay cool!" yelled a thin man with tattoos and a shaved head.

He stepped through the door, brandishing a revolver.

He grabbed the security guard, the big man reaching for his own weapon.

"Don't even think about it", Tattoo spat, forcing the guard to put his gun down and lie on the floor.

Tattoo moved towards Colin, pushed him aside. His eyes were swollen and blackened, like the very thought of sleep was long forgotten. He seemed wired, waving the revolver at pretty much everyone who was looking at him until he reached the till.

The till operator panicked, slamming the drawer open, offering handfuls of money, eyes fixed squarely on the revolver.

But Tattoo laughed. "No cash. That shit's useless," he said.

He looked to Colin, then down at the basket in his hands. "Give me that," he said. "All your food. Give it to me now!"

But Colin stalled, thinking of Aunt Bell, thinking of the soup.

Tattoo grabbed the basket roughly, pointing the gun straight in Colin's face. "Don't be a dumbfuck," he said.

But Colin *was* a dumbfuck. He held on tight, staring into the other man's eyes, begging, pleading, challenging.

Tattoo increased his grip on the basket handle. "Sorry, boss," he said. "Not your day…"

He head butted Colin then pulled the basket away.

Colin fell to the floor. Reached for his nose, staring at the others who stood like useless statues around him.

Tattoo waved his revolver in one final warning and then turned to leave.

"Please," Colin said, still on the floor.

Tattoo stopped.

"Just the soup. The mushroom soup. It's for my aunt. She's dying…"

The tattooed man laughed. It was a hollow laugh with a distinct absence of humour. It rang throughout the shop like breaking glass. He shook his head, muttered to himself then fumbled in the basket. He broke one of the tins of soup from the six pack and lobbed it.

Colin caught it.

He looked up in gratitude, but the tattooed man was gone.

TWELVE

Vince was growling.

Colin swore under his breath and drummed nervously on his steering wheel.

An accident on the Antrim Road stalled the light traffic. Two cars blocked the road, one having collided with the other.

A woman sat in the passenger seat of the offending car. She was screaming. From his vantage point, Colin noticed the head of the driver dipped forward to pierce the shattered windscreen.

The second car, the one they had driven into, was strangely empty.

Colin pulled up behind the two cars.

None of the other traffic stopped, instead mounting the pavement to pass.

This bothered Colin.

The incident in the Spar was still fresh in his mind; how food was seized from his very hands, yet no one offered him anything from their own baskets. He'd left the shop empty-handed, save for the single tin of mushroom soup – a mercy-throw from the man who'd robbed him.

Ironically, the tattooed man's fucked-up benevolence proved the most selfless act Colin had seen all day. And now, as he watched each car pass, ignoring a woman in pain as she screamed out for help, Colin could feel nothing but anger.

His hand hesitated on the car door handle. He reached into his coat pocket and took out his phone. He found the same message from before: NETWORK UNAVAILABLE. Colin swore then tried his luck anyway, tapping in 999.

It rang dead, as he expected.

"Fuck," Colin said.

The sound of the woman's screams continued to haunt him.

He reached for the car door handle once more.

He wasn't good with this sort of thing. The sight of blood terrified him. He couldn't even get through an episode of *Holby City* without breaking a sweat.

Sighing, Colin stepped out of his car.

He left Vince revving, the familiar and healthy murmur somehow heartening.

From his new vantage point, Colin could see the woman's car sat one third on the edge of the road, one third against a lamppost and one third up the rear of the still, dead car in front.

The screams kept coming. Colin felt his stomach knot as he began to imagine just what horrors lay ahead.

He made his approach, still looking around for someone more suited to this type of thing. Someone older, wiser or less tanned.

He pulled his Gucci sunglasses from his hair, feeling very aware of himself. This wasn't the time for accessorising. This was serious shit, *real life* shit.

Colin reached the passenger side of the car, noticing how many tiny shards of glass lay on the ground. Most of them were stained. A reddish-pink that reminded Colin of strawberry syrup.

But there was something else down there. Something that looked like overstretched elastic…

Colin swallowed hard, not wanting to face the woman; her screams now spent, giving way to laboured, wheezy breathing. He was right beside the car window now. He was hoping to glance quickly then look away. But she was waiting for him, reaching from the car to grab his arm.

She went to say something, but the words were drowning in the frothy, mucus-filled blood gurgling from her mouth. It suddenly dawned on Colin what the elastic was on the ground: it was her entire top lip. Her two remaining teeth protruded from under her nose like tusks. They looked longer than he expected, more horrific than he could have imagined.

Two heavily bloodshot eyes, one semi-mangled by the piece of glass embedded in the socket, stared at him. A constant stream of red tears streamed from the bad eye, the good eye blinking constantly as if trying to dispel something unreachable.

Her hand searched Colin's arm, finding his hand. She sputtered something, yet again it was indecipherable.

Colin screamed. He couldn't help it.

He wanted to go. Tried to pull his hand away, but she held firm, her vice-like grip cutting into his wrist like little razors.

Colin tried to avoid her gaze, looking instead to the clearly dead man in the driver's seat. Part of his head was embedded within the remainder of the windscreen. The rest spilled out onto the bonnet.

Colin started to heave, managing to dip his head to throw up on the ground instead of over the woman's face. He jerked his hand away from her grip, stooping by the car to finish retching.

When he stood up again, wiping his mouth before turning back to face her, it was too late. Her good eye stared dead ahead, as if there was someone important coming towards her. Her head rested against the car's doorframe.

She was gone.

Colin ran a hand through his hair, squinting against the sun. He looked out onto the road, where a steady stream of traffic continued to pass by, each car filled with people only too eager to stare at him. He wanted to shout at them, scream at them like the dying woman. Why had they left him to deal with this on his own?!

He began to imagine the lives of the couple lying dead in the car, of how their family, maybe even young kids, could be waiting for them somewhere. He thought of reaching in, searching for a wallet or purse, checking for a number to ring, then remembered, with some relief, how his phone wouldn't work.

Turning, knowing nothing else to do, Colin simply walked away.

The gruff chorus of traffic continued to fill his ears.

As he drew closer to his own car, he could hear Vince's engine still running smoothly.

THIRTEEN

The ambulance was the first thing Colin saw as he pulled onto his street. The second thing to strike him was how everyone standing around the ambulance wore protective yellow suits.

"Oh God, no," he breathed.

Colin pulled up on the pavement, opening the car door. He left it hanging as he ran towards the house.

A tall, suited figure stepped forward to block him. He wore breathing apparatus, an oxygen tank strapped to his back.

"Can't go in there," his muffled voice came.

"My aunt…" Colin yelled, trying to push past.

The suit struck him square on the chest.

Colin fell back onto the garden path. He pulled himself up.

The suit now held a police baton. "I said you can't go in there," the voice came again.

Colin stared into the suited man's face, trying to find some glimpse of humanity. He found nothing, save his own reflection in the mask's visor.

A sound from inside the house distracted him. A mechanical sound. Like the sound of a drill.

Colin stared back at the visor in front of him.

"Please! Tell me what's going on!" he said.

Another sound, this one more fluid or gassy, the two sounds working their way, in disharmony, around the house.

Colin pushed forward, but again the yellow suit pushed him back, this time swinging the baton to connect with Colin's head. The blow seemed to vibrate right through his skull, and he fell straight to the ground.

For a moment Colin lay still, dazed, the sounds swelling around him. When he looked up, he found not one but two masked heads staring back.

One of them bent down.

"Now look," this one said, and immediately Colin could tell it was a different voice than before, "Your aunt is infected. She's not even conscious. I know this is difficult, but we've had to quarantine her. The house is a no-go area."

Colin tried to process the information but failed. The drilling noise continued making it even more difficult to focus. His head was starting to throb. It felt warm and soft at one side. Colin reached into his hair, finding dampness. When he brought his hand back, it was bloodied.

The second suit called over yet another suit. This new suit attended to Colin's head, dressing the wound.

The friendlier suit continued to talk to him, battling to be heard over the noise.

"Have you somewhere you can go?" he asked. "Friends, family…"

Colin looked back towards the house, his home for the last year. Aunt Bell was in there, and she wasn't coming out. Ever. The full reality of that dawned on him.

"Look, for what it's worth," the kinder suit said, placing his arm onto Colin's shoulder, "I'm sorry…"

The sounds died down, more suits leaving the house, industrial gear in their hands.

Colin noticed metal sheets where his Aunt's hideously mauve curtains used to hang.

The gentle suit stood facing Colin, as if trying to hide what was going on in the house. With the sun behind him, Colin could see the man's eyes through the visor. His face looked tired, sad. His apologies were heartfelt, and in the moment that meant something to Colin.

"What's your name?" he heard himself say, because somehow that was important, somehow it was vital to know the name of the man who called time on his Aunt's life and locked up his home.

"George," the suit replied. "Sergeant George Kelly. I'm a police officer."

FOURTEEN

Colin sat in his car, staring out the window.

He was parked at the side of the Antrim Road, not knowing what the hell to do with himself.

He tried his phone again. It refused to work, so he slammed it into the seat beside him.

He began to cry.

His tears flowed unchecked, as if in allowing them, in welcoming them, Colin was honouring his Aunt Bell. She was a traditional, hard-working woman. A proper church burial would have meant the world to her. For those bastards to cage her up like that, without so much as a prayer…

Colin's eye caught sight of the tin of soup, rolling on the floor under Vince's passenger seat.

He thought of everything that had happened to him today: the Spar, the tattooed man with the revolver, the woman screaming then dying in the car as he watched, the yellow suits, Aunt Bell. The world was falling apart, yet no one wanted to admit it, no one wanted to shout out unless they were forced to, unless they were trapped and beat, dying or in desperate need of help. Society and every stitch that wove its fabric together were unravelling like a cheap sweater. And Colin could only watch, stand by helplessly, too sensitive to ignore it like all the others, yet too much of a fucking homo to do anything about it.

He thought of Vicky.

Until that point, Colin hadn't known where he should go. He would have been happy just to start the engine, pull onto the road. Turn corners and find new roads. To motor on (as Aunt Bell used to say when each new day greeted her, along with her relentless pains: *We'll just have to motor on, won't we?*) until Vince ran out of juice. But now, he had a destination.

"Vicky!" he said, as if the word was magical. "Vicky, Vicky, Vicky."

FIFTEEN

Vicky sat in her small bedsit on the Stranmillis Road, staring at the television. She was still in her bathrobe. She couldn't remember getting up or if she'd taken a shower. The news report was a repeat, one she'd probably watched at least twice that day already.

Since closing up shop, she'd shut herself indoors. As much as she didn't want to admit it, Vicky had no one to go to. And that was a shame; the end of the world should be something a girl shares with someone special.

Her bedsit was a mess. Glasses and cups – some with half-drunk coffee, others with her tipple of choice, Merlot – lingered on the window sill.

Outside was quiet. She heard random screaming coming from another flat across the way, but little else.

Her phone was dead, yet the television still soldiered on.

Another safety announcement was running, several actors in a lift dealing with the outrageous attack of another's sneeze. A pious voice narrated, instructing the masses to blow their noses and then dispose of the tissue in an 'appropriately marked bin'. These 'appropriately marked bins' were all around the city, the voice said.

Her flat's buzzer sounded.

Someone at the door.

It wasn't the first time the buzzer had sounded. Vicky had learned to ignore these calls regardless of when they came, whether in the middle of the night or middle of the day. But this time the caller persisted, and something about the rhythm of the buzzer struck a chord with her. The timing seemed oddly familiar…

"Colin," she muttered to herself. It was his ring.

She moved towards the buzzer. She pressed the answer button. "Hello?"

"Vicky!" came the voice, and it was Colin. "It's me, let me up."

She pressed the buzzer unlock immediately. She unlatched the door to her flat and entered the hallway.

She descended the hallway stairs meeting Colin as he entered the flat.

He was crying. There was a bandage on his head.

"What is it?" she said. "Are you hurt?"

Colin wiped his eyes on the sleeve of his jacket.

"I'm alright," he said. "Would murder a cup of tea, though…"

…

They sat on the edge of her Murphy bed, its wire frame and battered mattress pulled down from the back wall of the bedsit, near the built-in plywood cupboards. The sheets hadn't been changed in weeks.

Colin's eyes were surveying the flat as he sipped on his tea. Vicky realised it was the first time he'd visited. In fact, it was the first time *anyone* had visited.

"Been a mad week," she said. "Haven't been much in the mood for domestic Goddess duties, as you can see."

Colin smiled, then placed his lips against the hot cup, flicking his fingers back and letting the tea move towards his mouth until he was sipping again.

Vicky hated to watch him drink. So robotic, so precise. So fucking camp.

She looked away.

"They –" he started, but his voice broke, his free hand clenching into a fist and pressing against his grimacing mouth. He steadied himself then looked back at her. "Aunt Bell," he said. "She had the flu. They came and locked her in the house."

Vicky searched his eyes for any hint of a lie or a sign that this was one of the elaborate jokes at her expense he was known for in work.

"They did *what*?!"

"They quarantined her," he said, holding her gaze and talking in a low voice as if the room was bugged. "Came dressed in yellow protective suits and *fucking quarantined her*."

It took Vicky a while to digest this, to understand what the word 'quarantine' could mean outside of some stupid sci-fi film. She'd known Aunt Bell. She'd chatted to Aunt Bell on the phone. Aunt Bell gave her tea, made small talk about the weather, the soaps, her bloody knee operation. Vicky had sent Aunt Bell a birthday card last year, *and* a Christmas card. Aunt Bell was real to her.

"Jesus Christ…"

Vicky stood up.

She felt trapped. She needed air.

She walked to the window and peered out.

The view was pitiful: a yard with overflowing bins. Cigarette butts littering the ground, leading to a pale, concrete wall with barbed wire running along its top.

"I haven't been out since they closed the shop," she said in a flat voice. "I was scared."

She turned to face him.

"I'm sorry," Colin said. "I should have called. But everything was just so…" His voice trailed off.

"It's alright," she said. And she meant it. There was no sarcasm in her voice.

Colin looked up. There was a determined look in his face. "Let's get out of here," he said. "The city, I mean. Let's hit the road, head down the M1 as far as it'll take us."

Vicky looked at him with disbelief in her eyes.

"I mean it," he stressed. "Vince is outside, full of juice. Running better than ever. We'll leave this godforsaken city and wait until the whole thing blows over. I've friends in the country, just outside Portadown. We'll check in with them. They'll be only too glad of the company."

"And how's that going to help?" The question seemed contrary, but it wasn't. Sure, she wanted nothing more than to be out of this flat, but she also needed to feel safe. Vicky wanted to believe that Colin and his half-baked plan with his half-baked car (Christ, that thing was almost antique!) was the escape hatch she had been waiting for. But, when it all boiled down, Colin just wasn't a man who inspired confidence in her. God knows, it wouldn't be the first time he'd let her down.

And then there was the gay thing. Colin wasn't a *real man*, a man who would fight for her, shout and wave his fists at other men when her honour was threatened. Political correctness meant nothing to Vicky now; the truth of the matter, plain and simple, was that she didn't feel safe with Colin.

But Colin remained persistent. "Vicky," he said, "When this thing hits, and I mean *really* hits" he stretched his hands wide apart, several bangles on his wrists jingling, "you don't want to be in the city. In fact, the further you are from the city, the better."

Vicky looked out the window. She could see rooftops stretching for miles. Very little greenery. The sun had dipped behind a cloud, dimming the light. A fly buzzed around the glass, trying to get out, struggling to find an opening.

"Listen to me," Colin said. He was on his feet now. He grabbed her shoulders, looked her in the eye. "The air's fresher in the country. Cleaner, less infected. Seriously, it's the right thing to do. And if they do get their shit together and start treating this fucking virus properly, with drugs and stuff, well then... maybe we can come back."

"Okay," Vicky said.

But she didn't move. She just stood there, like she was frozen to the spot.

"I-I just need to grab some things," she said, finally.

SIXTEEN

It was only when Vicky disappeared to the bathroom that Colin got a proper look around her flat. It was a hovel. Several prints hung on bleached walls. A dirty brown carpet spread across the floor, coarse and hard, like sun-baked sand. Dark rot pierced the white paint of her window frames.

This was the very last place you'd expect a girl like Vicky to live, a girl whose idea of dressing down was Armani socks under Calvin Klein jeans, a girl who had once described public transport as 'undignified'.

Colin was reminded of those celebrity shows where '80s has-beens would be sent to live in the jungle or on a farm. And here was middle-class, designer-boutique-manager Vicky roughing it every night in a bedsit.

But that wasn't the only thing that struck Colin.

Vicky's OCD with tidiness was legendary in the shop. Yet the flat was a mess. Black bin bags, stuffed with clothes, gathered in a corner near the sofa, awaiting the wash or skip. A dozen or so trashy magazines littered the sofa, as if she were sleeping under them.

Colin could maybe understand if Vicky had just moved in, but she'd been here about a year.

He walked through to the kitchen, finding a sink full of dishes. An empty carton of Cup-A-Soup lay dead on the worktop.

He opened the fridge. Grimaced at the smell of stale milk and God knows what breed of fruit festering – *no, colonising* – in the pull-out tray.

He closed the fridge quickly, reached to open the cupboard above. There was tea and coffee in abundance. The odd tin of fruit. More Cup-A-Soup. Nothing else.

What the hell does she eat?

"What are you looking for?"

Colin startled.

Vicky stood in the kitchen. Her hair was brushed. She was wearing jeans and a sweater.

"Er, nothing," he said, heat rising to his face. "Just thinking about making some tea before we get moving. Fancy a cup?"

She looked suspiciously at him.

"Not really," she said, still sizing him up over her glasses. "Let's just go."

Colin looked at the small bag in her hand.

"Is that all you're taking?"

Vicky didn't reply, as if bored of his questions already. She made for the door.

"Okay," Colin muttered to himself, taking the hint, "Let's go, then."

He followed her out into the corridor of her apartment block.

She closed the door behind them, without locking it, and descended the stairs.

"Hey," Colin shouted after her, "Aren't you going to lock up?"

But Vicky just turned to look at him, her eyes once more peering over the glasses. It reminded him of libraries, of banks and official scary places, of every teacher he hadn't liked very much.

"Are you coming or not?" she said, her voice irritable.

SEVENTEEN

Before long, Vicky was sitting in Vince's passenger seat.

The car always smelled the same, regardless of how many air-fresheners Colin hung from its mirror. A smell of age, experience. A smell that said, *I've a few miles on the clock, you know. Been around a corner or two.* It was comforting, and Vicky found herself relaxing back into the seat, despite herself.

Colin started up the engine, Vince roaring to life with an angry quality that surprised her.

"Jesus," Vicky said. "The old boy's got wind in his sails."

Colin smiled proudly. "Told you."

He pulled onto the Stranmills Road, heading up towards Malone. From there it would be a quick journey to the turn-off for the M1 motorway. But Colin didn't go that way. Instead, he took the first left at the Stranmillis roundabout and headed towards the Ormeau Road.

"Where are you going?" Vicky asked.

"To get Sinead," he said like she should have known.

"*What?*" Vicky glared at him. "Colin, you didn't mention anything about Sinead coming!"

"Look," he said, raising one finger from the wheel and pointing at her, eyes still on the road, "Sinead's one of us. She's on her own. There's no way I'm leaving her, and that's that."

"Oh, for God's sake!"

Vicky should have known he would do this. Colin and Sinead were thick as thieves. Two peas in a fucking pod. Christ, Vicky even considered they might be sleeping together at one stage, right before Colin came out, surprising her and just about no one else.

Sinead lived in a shared house off the Ormeau Road, a spot known as the Holylands. The place was notorious, each street lined with tall robust houses, packed to the rafters with undergraduates, drug dealers and migrant workers. Rumour was that the area was a dumping ground for those intimidated out of other areas for bad behaviour. Either way, the Holylands was becoming less holy by the day, with increasing reports of burglaries, joyriding, rape and muggings. And that had been before the flu hit.

They moved up University Road before pulling onto Damascus Street. As Colin parked Vince by the pavement, Vicky noticed a crowd gathered just outside one of the houses.

"Jesus," Colin said, pulling the handbrake then unclipping his seatbelt.

"What is it?"

"That's Sinead's house."

...

Colin got out of the car, Vicky following closely behind. He prodded one of the bystanders, a lanky guy with floppy hair and a long, narrow face.

"What's going on?" Colin asked.

"Dunno," lanky guy mumbled.

His friend, of similar build and dress, spoke up: "It's the flu. They're sending an ambulance out. Think it's that house there." A long finger peeked out of the cuff of his cardigan, pointing towards Sinead's house.

Colin grabbed Vicky, said: "We've got to get her out of there."

Vicky laughed. "What? Are you crazy?"

Colin left her, moved quickly through the crowd.

Vicky followed, reaching for his arm. "Colin, what if it's Sinead that's sick?"

"We're taking her with us," he said.

"Like hell we are!" she protested.

But Colin was in the doorway now.

"Listen to me!" Vicky called, "COLIN!"

Still he ignored her. "Sinead!" he shouted.

A few people were on the stairs. He recognised them as her flatmates.

"Where's Sinead?" he said to one, a small mousy looking girl with round glasses.

"Upstairs," came the reply. "In her room."

Colin turned to Vicky, pulled her aside. They stepped into the nearby kitchen, finding privacy.

"There's going to be a crowd of men showing up, wearing yellow plastic suits," he said to her, "Just keep them from following me, got it?"

Vicky grabbed him. "Colin, think about this. If she's sick –"

"Just do it!" he said, pulling away.

Vicky watched Colin go, storming up the stairs towards Sinead's bedroom. A dark and wrong part of her wondered if he'd be so quick to act if it was *her* up there.

She turned to look out the open door, hearing the sound of sirens.

EIGHTEEN

The landing was what you'd expect in a gaff like this. Mildew climbed the walls. Dusty old carpet covered the floor. It was your typical house share in Belfast. Cheap but not very cheerful.

Colin tried each door, knocking with his fist, calling out Sinead's name.

He heard the sound of strained coughing coming from the next floor.

He took the stairs, found a single door at the end of a short corridor. He knew this was Sinead's room. Everything about it screamed her name.

A poster, featuring a white kitten with the word 'Miaow!' inscribed below, was tacked to the door. A small whiteboard and pen hung above the poster with the words 'Stacey called at 8.30' inscribed in pink, the date from two weeks ago. Even Sinead's smell was here, a sickly sweet perfume that always reminded Colin of the confectionary counter at the Movie House.

Another cough, this one more aggressive.

Colin knocked the door.

"Sinead?" he called quietly.

He could hear sirens outside.

"Sinead, it's Colin," he said, opening the door gingerly.

"Colin?" Her voice came, raspy and forced.

He pushed the door wider, finding a small box room decorated much the same way as her door. More posters of cats. Pink wallpaper. A dream catcher hung from her open window, flirting with the breeze.

Sinead was lying on the bed, a fever breaking on her forehead. Her duvet was slung to the side. Her pyjamas were soaking wet.

"Jesus, babe," Colin said to her, his voice low and comforting. "You're all sweaty."

She rolled her eyes like she always did when he said something silly, but he could tell her heart wasn't in it. She was scared, and he knew it.

Colin entered her room, sat on the edge of the bed.

"Colin, I feel awful," she said.

"I know, babe," he said, pulling her close, rocking her gently in his embrace.

Her body was red hot, her sweat like acid on his skin. Colin felt his eyes water as he rocked her, his face straining hard not to cry. He needed to be strong.

The sirens were louder now, as if they were right at the house.

NINETEEN

The crowd around the house seemed to thicken as the flashing blue lights made their final approach. A police Land Rover pulled up and parked.

Two officers climbed out, dressed in yellow plastic suits, just as Colin had described. They attached bulky breathing apparatus to their backs.

Ripples of panic ran through the crowd. Some people fled immediately. Others stood their ground, angrily hurling abuse.

But the cops ignored everyone, moved towards the house.

"Fuck this," whispered Vicky.

She stepped in front of the two cops as they continued their approach. Smiled flirtatiously.

The bigger cop grabbed her roughly, pushed her against the doorframe.

"Hey! Get your hands off me!" she protested.

"Do you live here?" he said, his voice gruff and threatening.

The other cop placed a hand on his colleague's shoulder, pulling him back.

"I'm sorry, miss," he said to Vicky, "but we need to know your relation to the patient." His voice was softer, younger than the other cop, but the suit and mask still held a certain menace.

"I'm her employer," Vicky said.

"Well, do you know where the patient is now?"

"You're too late. An ambulance called just before you guys came." She wondered why the hell she was doing this. "You just missed it."

"Bullshit!" barked the bigger cop.

"Leave it, Norm," the younger voice reprimanded and then to her said in a stern but calm voice, "Miss, you know that lying to the police is a crime?"

"Leave me alone!" Vicky looked to the crowd, feigning panic. "Help!" she cried. "They're trying to take me!"

The crowd, already riled, became even more worked up. More people bolted. Those remaining surged forward aggressively.

Another Land Rover pulled up, more cops descending like hawks, batons swinging. They rounded up the troublemakers, beat them viciously.

Vicky panicked. She couldn't breathe.

There was chaos now. People were running, screaming, bleeding around her. Vicky fought her way through the crowd and ran, stopping only when she was a safe distance from the house. She was hot, sweating.

A few people stood at the doorways of their homes, staring at her, suspiciously, as if she herself might be sick or infected.

"What are you all looking at?!" Vicky yelled.

They sloped back inside, closing their doors.

Vicky thought for a moment then reached into the back pocket of her jeans, retrieving her mobile phone. She flicked through the contacts list, chose COLIN then pressed the phone against her ear. She didn't expect it to work. The network had been patchy for days.

"Come on, come on," she whispered.

It was ringing.

"COME ON!" Vicky cried.

"Vicky", Colin answered. "Where are you?"

"Outside, down the street a little." She peered back towards the house. "Place has gone mad, Colin. There's cops everywhere. Get out of there now."

She could hear the sound of commotion from his end, a door banging closed and the descent of steps.

"Colin? Talk to me, damn it!"

She thought the connection had died but then Colin spoke. "It's okay," he said. "I'm on the fire escape. Grab Vince and meet us round back. And hurry!"

"Oh, for God's sake!" Vicky muttered, snapping her phone shut.

She made her way back along the street towards the house again. She walked slowly, trying to keep a low profile.

The crowd was still lively. A line of cops held them back, some now armed with guns. Yet another van showed up, more suited cops climbing out to join the others.

Vicky slipped past them, dipping her head.

She found Vince.

Vicky opened the Volkswagen Beetle's door, jumping into the driver's seat.

The keys were in the glove compartment as always. Vicky shook her head, marvelling at how easy it would be to steal from someone like Colin.

She started Vince, once again surprised by the car's enthusiastic sounds.

Vicky pulled away. She drove down the road a little, took a narrow side road. She hung a left, finding the rear entry to Sinead's house.

Colin was shuffling down the back alleyway, Sinead in his arms.

He opened the back door of the car, sliding Sinead in, before jumping in beside her.

"Go!" he yelled.

A booming noise, not unlike a firework going off, rocked the air.

Vicky looked in the side mirror, catching sight of the two cops from earlier, moving towards them, the big one brandishing a firearm.

Are they shooting at us?

Vicky felt her heart rise up into her mouth. She wasn't breathing. It was like someone had hit the pause button, time slowing down like a scene from some action movie.

Colin was lying on top of Sinead, as if to shield her. His eyes bulged out of their sockets. He was screaming now, "FOR GOD'S SAKE, MOVE!"

Another booming sound. The glass in the back windscreen shattered.

Vicky pressed her foot on the pedal, skidding back up the entryway and swinging out onto the road. She fought with the steering wheel. Sank her foot on the accelerator again.

She pulled out of University Street, onto the Ormeau Road.

Her hands seemed glued to the steering wheel, her foot to the accelerator. Her eyes were wide and staring dead in front. The eerily light traffic seemed to just part before her like the waves of the Red Sea.

When she thought she'd put enough miles between herself and the chaos from Sinead's house, Vicky slowed down.

She looked into the back seat, finding Colin still cradling Sinead. He was covered in glass from the blown-out windscreen. Shards filled his hair like tiny pieces of diamante.

Vicky pulled over, stopping the car.

"This is t-too much," she said to Colin, her voice shaking. "You drive."

TWENTY

Although Shaun couldn't *hear* any of the sirens throughout the city, or the random shouts and wails, he could *smell* them. Tension filled the air like poisonous gas. A cold sweat broke across Shaun's back as he packed his family's meagre valuables and belongings into the back of their car.

The city seemed empty.

Shaun looked around the housing estate he had lived in for the last ten years, finding few signs of life. Empty driveways. Wire grills placed across doors and windows. His neighbours had slipped away like thieves in the night, no advance warning given, no gathering together, the way a community should. The people he'd waved across the road to for ten years were gone, and Shaun realised that he couldn't even remember their names, never mind guess where they'd taken off to. All he knew for sure was that while the government announcements on TV said one thing – to stay at home, to await further instruction – most people were doing the complete opposite.

A hand pressed, gently, on his shoulder.

Shaun turned, finding Lize. She was smiling, even though there was nothing to smile about.

"It'll be alright," she said. "Daddy will know what to do. He still has contacts in the Armed Forces."

Yeah, that'd be right, Shaun mused. *Good ol' Daddy to the rescue.*

He'd be more understanding if this were the first time, but the reality was that good ol' Martin was who Lize would go to for *everything*. He'd watched her talk on the phone to Daddy about anything from which school to enrol Jamie at, to what to do when the car kept stalling or where the best place was to buy new tyres. Martin – Daddy dearest – seemed to be the font of all knowledge in their family, and, frankly, it sickened Shaun.

It would be annoying even if Martin were one of the good guys, a doting father simply looking after his little girl. After all, shouldn't she be going to her husband for all these things? But Martin was far from good. A grumpy bastard on a better day, his normal form was despicable.

Martin was in the Armed Forces but didn't like to talk about it. Posted abroad, with her father doing God knows what, God knows where, Poor Lize had been dragged through every base across Europe, never settling.

No wonder she'd cheated on him…

"Lize, you know how I feel about him," Shaun said. "I'm doing this for you and Jamie. But I need to be sure that when it comes down to it that you'll take my side, that –"

"*Sides*?" she broke in, "What *sides* are there?"

"Lize, you know what he's like, how he tries to rile me!" He could see her struggling to read his lips, all too aware of how slurred his speech would become when he got excited.

"That's nonsense, you're imagining…"

Her voice was lost to him as she turned away, but Shaun grabbed her hands, held them. His eyes met hers, and he realised just how frightened she was, how frightened *he* was.

He wondered if Martin was frightened, if Martin was a man who *ever* got frightened, or if he, in some sick way, thrived on situations like this, situations where he could take hold of the reins and fix everything for his little girl, further alienating Shaun in the process.

"I'm serious, Lize. I need you to promise me you'll be on my side. Please."

But she couldn't promise anything. He knew that from experience.

She pulled away from him.

Shaun turned to find Jamie coming down the path, carrying his Spiderman lunchbox. Shaun watched as Lize lifted Jamie in her arms and planted a kiss on his cheek.

As Jamie climbed into the car, Shaun wondered what the boy thought of him. Did he see him as a boy should see his father: a provider and protector? Or did he see him the same way Martin saw him: some stupid dummy.

A liability.

Weak.

TWENTY-ONE

Colin closed his eyes and swore silently to himself.

"Oh, this is brilliant," Vicky said, as they sat in a heavy line of traffic. "Brilliant!"

One hand clutched her purse, the other playing with a battery-operated hand fan, blowing air into her face.

"The motorway will be quicker," she mimicked in a camp accent, turning her head from side-to-side. "Back roads are soooo slow." Then she turned, all trace of humour gone from her face, and peered at him over her glasses. "Brilliant," she said again.

Colin ignored her. Blew out a little air. Tried to hide his frustration.

He looked at the car in front. In the back were some kids and a large dog, awkwardly moving along the back seat. The kids were playing with the dog. The dog seemed tired, warm, its long tongue hanging out one side of its mouth as it humoured the kids. A bumper sticker ran along the bottom left of the back windscreen. 'Don't follow me,' it said. 'I'm lost too.'

Colin looked at the nearest road sign for perhaps the fiftieth time. He wasn't any closer to it.

One of the destinations on the sign was Portadown.

That's where they were heading.

He turned in his seat, looked to Sinead. She seemed so helpless in her pink jim-jams. Colin had swept the glass shards from her skin and hair as best he could. He'd placed some cardboard against the blown-out windscreen to keep the draft out. He'd secured her with the back seatbelts. But the poor girl still looked awful. She sounded worse, her constant spluttering and wheezing coarse and jagged like thorns.

"You okay, pet?" Colin said, knowing full well she wasn't.

"Does she *look* okay?" Vicky asked, seizing the point indulgently.

She wound down the window, hanging her head out to look up the queue of traffic. She swore, then muttered, "Come on."

"What's the hold-up?" Colin asked her, conceding. Huffing with Vicky was pointless. He should have known that by now.

"Ten thousand cars fleeing a disease-ridden city," she said. "On the fucking motorway." She looked back at him in that teacher way again. "That's the hold-up," she said.

"You're impossible."

Colin undid his seatbelt, reached for Vince's door handle.

Vicky shouted, "Wait, where are you–?!"

Colin pushed the door open and stepped out of the car.

A warm, heavy breeze attacked him; the air was dense, the heat gathering every speck of dust, every belch of exhaust fumes, every fucking germ and mixing it all together.

Colin fumbled in his pocket for a handkerchief to press against his face.

He looked along the crowd of cars, most of them packed to the brim with bags, clothes, furniture, bikes, dogs, cats, children and just about every combination of the aforementioned you could think of.

He could hear the dull rumble of coughing along the line, the infection spreading like wild fire.

He spotted what the hold-up was: at the front of the line stood what he assumed to be a patrol of soldiers, all brandishing rifles.

"Jesus," he whispered to himself.

He climbed back into the car.

Vicky was at him again like a Rottweiler, nagging before he'd even closed the door.

"Listen," he said, raising his finger to her, "I need you to stop talking and help me."

She looked at him suspiciously.

"There's a line of soldiers up there," Colin said. "I think they might be after us."

"Great," Vicky said, dryly. "And you know *why* they're after us?" Her lips were twisted. "I'll tell you why: because you wanted to play the fucking hero and risk BOTH our lives for an infected girl – a girl you may or may not be sleeping with."

"What?!" Colin spat. Her words cut him deep. Tears suddenly filled his eyes, but he didn't want Vicky to notice. He wouldn't give her the pleasure. "She's your friend too," he said. "Have you forgotten that?"

"NO!" She slapped her hand against the dashboard. She put her face into her hands, and he thought *she* was going to cry for a moment. Instead, she took a breath. "No, I haven't forgotten, it's just –" She sighed deeply before continuing in a quieter voice, "We need to hide her. God knows, they probably know the registration of the car already. And even if they don't," she continued, "well, Vince isn't too hard to pick out of a crowd, is he?"

"We're fucked. That's what you're saying, isn't it?"

"Colin, I'm just being –"

"You're being the same, miserable bitch you've always been!"

They were interrupted by the sound of commotion building further down the line of traffic.

A blast of gunfire. Both Colin and Vicky jumped in unison.

They stared at each other.

"What was t-that?" she said.

"What do you *think* it was?"

Colin looked into the back seat. Sinead was shaking, curled up in a ball, arms wrapped around her petite body. Her face was red, her lips stretched across her teeth. She was in pain.

"We can't stay here," he said.

But Vicky wasn't listening. Her hands were clasped over her ears. Her eyes were closed tight, her lips working as she muttered, "Oh God oh God oh God…"

Colin swore, straining to look up the line of traffic.

He breathed in, then out again.

He undid the handbrake, reached for the gearstick and revved the engine.

"What the fuck are you doing?!" Vicky said.

"Just hang on," he said.

TWENTY-TWO

"What is it? What's going on?"

Shaun waved his hand across her face as if that action alone might magically silence Lize.

"Shaun, what is it?!" Lize said more slowly, as if to flaunt both her ability and absolute right to speak.

But Shaun kept his eyes dead ahead.

Lize spotted a number of armed soldiers. They were moving along the line of traffic.

Lize clicked her seatbelt open then reached for the car's door handle.

"What are you doing?" Shaun asked.

"I'm going to ask them what the hold-up is."

Shaun sighed heavily. She knew he felt powerless in situations like this.

"Mummy?" she heard from the back seat.

Lize looked into the rear of their people carrier.

Jamie peered back at her, his face a deathly shade of white. He was scared, and Lize shouting at his dad wasn't going to help matters.

"I'm just going to ask the soldiers what's going on, darling," she said in the voice that adults reserved for patronising children.

There was a sigh from the back. It sounded just like his dad's sigh: all grown-up, less of a huff and more of a moan. It seemed to put years on the boy.

"Listen," Shaun said. His voice was measured, less fraught. "Let *me* go."

After ten years of marriage, she knew him only too well; he wouldn't want the other men in their cars, with their wives and girlfriends beside them, to see him sending his woman out to talk to the scary men with guns.

"Okay," she said.

But it wasn't to save his pride. It was her fear talking. The nerves performing summersaults in her belly, the bouncing heart *he* could probably feel from the seat beside her, telling her to step back and let the invalid handle things.

It was always his joke to her whenever she was control-freaking him, making him feel as if he were paralysed from the neck down as opposed to being deaf: *Let the disabled guy do it*, Shaun would say, and Lize would laugh.

But Lize wasn't laughing now.

She leaned back into her seat.

She watched him open the door, heard Shaun make the same sighing noise his son had made only seconds ago.

It was then that Lize had a moment. More of a panic, really.

Maybe it was the sighing, the way her son would breathe out in a similar way to his father, but there was a certain poignancy about this scene. Lize sensed very strongly that something was going to change from now: their dynamic, their life together as they knew it shifting down a gear. It was an all-consuming fear, and she felt the urge to cry. Instead, she swallowed hard and reached to touch her husband's arm.

Shaun leaned his head back inside the car. "What?"

"Be careful," she said, clearly annotating each syllable.

His eyes fixed upon her as he read her lips, drawing the sincerity from her words like water from a well.

He nodded.

…

Lize watched through the windscreen as Shaun moved up the line of traffic.

From the car in front, she could hear coughing, a dull echo hammering out like a drum, deep and throat-ripping. From somewhere else came sneezing.

Lize looked into the back seat.

"Put your mask on," she told Jamie. "Now!"

Once the boy pulled the surgical mask down over his mouth and nose, Lize reached for her handbag, retrieving her own. She didn't place much faith in them. They'd been distributed by the government when the initial panic had reached 'Fever Level' (as the experts were now calling it), along with a plastic water bottle, described as VIRUS PROOF, and an overly cumbersome fold-out leaflet with the words KEEP CALM written across the front in gaudy colours.

"What's keeping him so long?" Lize muttered to herself.

She craned her neck to see past the cars in front.

Shaun was drawing near to the soldiers at the front of the line.

One of them stepped away from the main pack, his rifle half-mast to signal Shaun to stop where he was.

Lize watched Shaun raise his hands into the air, like a foiled bandit from some old Western. She could see him speaking, his lips moving as he no doubt tried to form his words in a way that would be easily understood. He was nervous, and he didn't always make sense when he was nervous.

"Mummy, what's happening?" came Jamie's voice from the back, slightly muffled under his surgical mask.

"Shhh!" she chastised.

She looked back through the windscreen.

Lize noticed the soldier turn his head, midway through whatever useless, indecipherable tirade Shaun was dealing out.

She was beginning to wish she'd gone instead of him. She wasn't too old to flirt. Open a few buttons on her top, flash a bit of tit. God knows, it had worked on Alan.

No, don't go there.

Something was happening.

The soldier talking with Shaun returned to the main pack, his rifle still drawn. The others surrounded another car, about four or five up from their own. They all aimed their guns forwards and Lize heard an exchange of raised voices.

"Oh shit," she muttered. "This doesn't look good."

Lize undid her seatbelt before winding the window down and leaning out. The gunfire made her jump.

Shaun was looking back at her and couldn't see it.

"Shaun!" She waved her hands at him, calling him back.

"Mummy?"

She ducked her head back into the car.

"Keep your head down!" she said firmly to Jamie. "Just like they tell you on the plane. Duck it between your legs."

When she turned back, she found Shaun running back to the car.

He pulled the door open, jumping in.

"What's –" she began, but he broke in.

"They're shooting people," he said, imitating the action with his hands. Then he fiddled with the keys to get the ignition started.

"*What?*" Lize said, but he had turned away.

Shaun fired the car up.

"Wait," Lize said. "Even if you do get out of the line, how are you going to get past them?"

Shaun banged his hand on the steering wheel, swearing.

Lize glimpsed into the back finding Jamie, head still tucked obediently between his legs, just like she'd told him.

The sound of commotion made her look outside again, the occupants of several other cars in the queue simply leaving their cars and making a run for it.

An old woman, clearly infected by the virus, stumbled around by the side of the road.

A short burst of gunfire split through the old woman's head, splashing bits of her brain, hair and blood against their car.

Almost as a reflex, Shaun switched the wipers on, spreading the concoction like spilled soup across the entire windscreen. He flicked another switch, jetting some fluid into the mix, turning the mixture pink, the wipers continuing their work to create larger patches of clear glass.

It was through one of these patches that Lize watched the soldiers continue their cull, firing into another car, the windows shattering against the hail of bullets.

A vintage Volkswagen Beetle turned onto the hard shoulder, revving like a cat ready to pounce, aimed squarely at the ready-made roadblock ahead. As Lize watched, it fired on ahead, skidding against the loose gravel.

A volley of shots rang out, the car still firing ahead towards the blockade.

Lize looked over at Shaun.

His hand was on the gearstick.

TWENTY-THREE

It was his first day on the streets. Ciaran had been in active duty for all of two hours, and he'd already killed.

He stood back from the car, the SA80 warm in his hands.

There was a girl inside.

She was infected, and he'd been told to fire at her.

With the windows blown apart, Ciaran could see her more clearly. Blood spread across her body, but he still recognised her. It was the girl from the Garrick. Julie. The primary school teacher.

She'd bought him a drink, made him feel good about getting the new job (this job!) when even his own mother couldn't be proud.

And in return, Ciaran had ripped her apart with the squeeze of his finger.

"Oh fuck," he said.

Ciaran stepped back, dropped his rifle to the ground.

There was a man clambering out of the front of the car, an older man, clearly in shock. Blood flowed from his forehead, most likely from flying glass, a bitter aftershock following the hail of gunfire.

Ciaran looked to Grady, standing beside him. The other lad's rifle was still aimed at the car, awaiting the order to disengage.

"What have we done?" Ciaran said to him.

The Sarge squared up to Ciaran, standing mere inches from his face. "You did what had to be done, Private! Now pick up that rifle!"

"No, I…"

"PICK UP THE FUCKING RIFLE!"

Screaming from a nearby camper van.

"Sir, more infected!" shouted Grady.

A man exited the van and leapt upon the young soldier, trying to wrangle his gun from him. A younger woman descended from the back of the camper van, helping an older woman wrapped in blankets to climb out after her.

The Sarge moved in to help Grady wrestle the gun free from his attacker. He pulled the man away from Grady, kicking him to the ground. Once Grady was clear, the Sarge aimed and fired two rounds into the bettered man's chest.

"If they're hostile or infected, put them down!" shouted the Sarge to the other soldiers. As if to demonstrate, he aimed at the retreating women and fired another volley of shots, felling them both.

The younger woman was still alive, lying on the ground, screaming and trying to clamber away. As Ciaran watched on, horrified, Grady fired two shots into her back.

Chaos erupted, people leaving their cars in droves now.

The Sarge stepped forward, eyes wide, and took aim at those fleeing. "INFECTED!" he bellowed, before firing indiscriminately.

Ciaran closed his eyes, prayed silently for the hell that he was witnessing to be over.

He could hear the sounds of cars revving up, some trying to drive their way out of the death trap.

His eyes snapped open.

Someone was on the ground next to him, trying to pick up his rifle, but Ciaran grabbed it, fought to wrestle it back.

His attacker lashed out, punching him repeatedly in the head.

Ciaran let go of the rifle, stumbling backwards onto the hard shoulder.

Impact.

Noise everywhere.

Ciaran found himself halfway through the windscreen of a car. He couldn't see too well but made out the face of a young woman, hands raised as fragments of the windscreen showered her.

And then he lost consciousness.

…

The crash of glass gave way to Vicky's scream, both arms crossing her face as the car hit something or someone.

Colin shielded his eyes and sank his foot on the accelerator, hoping a dead straight line would take them down the hard shoulder and past the carnage.

When he opened them again, he found a man's head jammed in the devastated windscreen.

Vicky was pulling her seat back, her feet kicking against the dashboard, trying to scuttle further away from the horrible sight.

Blood gathered in the cracks of the glass. Colin couldn't tell if it belonged to him, Vicky or the man embedded into the windscreen.

Everything was happening too fast.

He stole a quick glance in the rear view mirror.

They'd cleared the carnage, but Colin didn't dare slow down.

He could see Sinead, still lying in the back, barely conscious yet safely strapped in by both rear seatbelts.

"Get him off me get him off me get him off me!" screeched Vicky, still scuttling against the bloodied head and shoulders on her side of the dashboard. Colin could see the rest of the man's body hanging across the bonnet.

He looked down the M1, finding an open road, few cars in sight.

He pressed his foot on the pedal, squeezing every last drop of Dutch courage out of Vincent's fuel tank. The little car whined like a wounded animal. It wasn't a sound Colin remembered hearing from Vince before. Then again, he didn't think Vincent would ever have reached these kinds of speeds.

The soldier remained stuck in the windscreen. His head rested on the dashboard, occasionally bouncing as they progressed further down the motorway.

Within time, Vicky calmed, her seat still pulled as far back as she could manage, but no longer trying to burrow her way through it. She was shaking, both hands pulled up to her face.

"Is he…?"

"Dead?" Colin looked over to the man's head. Blood seeped into the soldier's hair, creating a mess of red and black that looked like slick oil. Colin felt his guts churn. "Don't look at him."

"I can't help but look at him," Vicky barked. "He's right in front of me!"

"Well, just close your eyes, then!"

"You close your eyes!"

Colin stared at her quizzically. He could tell from her face that she knew her last quip didn't make any sense. For some reason, a smile spread over his face.

Vicky looked at him incredulously.

He started to laugh, not knowing how he could, or why he needed to.

"Oh, I'm sooo going to hell for this," he managed.

PART THREE:

THE COUNTRY

ONE

M1 Motorway, Southbound

Shaun followed the little Volkswagen, eventually overtaking when they got to the open road, his own people carrier easily outdoing the brave little banger when it came to speed and power. As they passed, all three of the people carrier's occupants stared in disbelief at the soldier hanging out the windscreen of the Beetle. They marvelled at the driver laughing.

Several other cars had made it out of the city, now following them south.

On the other side of the road, more cars could be seen heading north, towards Belfast.

That worried Shaun.

Were the people of Northern Ireland chasing their own tails, fleeing the frying pan only to get burned by the fire? Shaun began to wonder if the rural areas were going to be any different to what he'd just left behind. Was this, indeed, the beginning of the end?

Twenty minutes passed. The excitement of before was still fresh in Shaun's mind.

He felt Lize's hand on his shoulder and jumped. "We need to stop," she signed to him. "Jamie needs to pee."

Shaun looked into the back, finding the screwed up face of his son looking back, eyes pleading with him. He looked to the road, finding nowhere appropriate to stop, save the hard shoulder. He looked to Lize who raised her eyebrows in a 'hurry up' kind of gesture.

Minutes later, Shaun took the turn-off for Lurgan, one of Northern Ireland's larger towns.

He drove a couple of miles, entering a built-up area, surprisingly deserted. There was no one around. Cars remained parked in driveways. Blinds were closed, some windows boarded up with metal sheets.

They drove past a sprinkling of glass on the pavement, the result of a blown out streetlight. A nearby shop window was broken, random items spilling out from its doorway. The door itself hung on one hinge, gently swaying.

A flash of siren caught Shaun's eyes in the rear view mirror. He feared it might be the police or the army or someone else with a gun and a uniform. But it was an ambulance. It bolted past them, tearing up the empty roads as if there was somewhere worth taking the wounded and the sick.

Lize tapped him on the shoulder, pointing into the back.

Shaun turned, and Jamie signed to him, *Daddy. Need to go!*

They continued to move along the street, driving slowly so they could spot somewhere that looked like it might have a toilet.

A service station dead ahead.

Its lights were still bright, although it was unlikely to be open. There were no cars around it. The pumps looked unmanned, but a sign reading 'customer toilets' sealed the deal.

Shaun pulled in, parking in one of the spaces provided.

Jamie grabbed Shaun's shoulder from behind. He asked permission to leave the car, but Shaun raised his hand.

He looked to Lize then carefully opened the car door.

It was much warmer outside than in, thanks to the miracle of air con. Shaun shielded his eyes from the bright sun, and looked over to the Spar mini-market joined onto the service station.

Still no sign of life.

He looked left and right before jogging across the forecourt towards the customer toilets. He checked the gents, finding no one inside. He came out and waved across to the car.

Within seconds, Jamie was running across the forecourt and into the toilets. Shaun watched as the boy relieved himself in the urinal, one hand against the wall to its side, his face turned sideways. Once finished, the boy stood for a moment, seemingly enjoying the feeling of an empty bladder.

"Come on!" Shaun called.

Jamie zipped up and headed straight back over to the car.

Shaun went to follow, but a quick movement from a townhouse opposite caught his eye.

He looked across to the people carrier. Jamie was climbing back in.

The movement in the house caught his eye again. It was the first real sign of life he'd seen, save for the ambulance. He found himself gravitating towards it.

The townhouse was a typical small terrace. The décor was dated. Pebbledash finish. Old wooden door with a single pane of glass at the top. Shaun reckoned it was an older person or couple who lived here, just by the look of the place.

He wiped the glass of the door with his sleeve, peered in to investigate.

The hallway was empty.

Patterned carpet led up the stairway, with mahogany banisters looking freshly polished. An old telephone rested on a coffee table just by the door to the living room.

Shaun was about to turn away when he noticed movement again. The living room door was pulled open, but, from where he stood, Shaun couldn't see exactly what was happening. He looked through the side window. But the blinds were partially closed, and he couldn't see much from there either.

Shaun stood back, thinking it probably best to just go, join his wife and son and hit the road. But he couldn't seem to leave well enough alone.

He strained his eyes, twisting his head to stare through the door's glass pane once more. He hadn't noticed before, but there was a stain on the pale carpet leading through the now half-ajar living room door. It looked like blood.

The body of a man fell heavily across the doorway to the living room.

Shaun stepped back, yelled: "Jesus!"

He knew he should leave but instead found himself going back to the glass.

The man was still there. He was older than Shaun, probably late forties. His hair was dark and thinning at the temples. Blood soaked his white shirt. His eyes opened, his hand rising then falling back to the carpet.

The head of someone else... *something else*... appeared from the living room doorway, towering over the body. It didn't look human. It looked down at the body on the floor. Its lips parted, a thin line of drool seeping out; hanging like silvery string before pooling on the felled man's face. Then it stopped, like it knew it was being watched.

Its head turned slowly, viscous white eyes looking at Shaun.

Something grabbed his shoulder, and Shaun screamed out.

Turning, he found Lize.

"What are you doing?" she said.

She looked through the glass, her face twisting, losing colour as she no doubt found what he was watching.

"Don't look," Shaun said, grabbing her. "Come on! We have to go!"

"Wh-what is that!?" she stuttered.

But Shaun pulled her away, both of them running back towards the car.

TWO

Waringstown, Co. Down

He usually tuned in for the weather forecast. It was a habit more than anything else, one that gave his day routine. But today was the first day that it didn't broadcast and, for a man like Martin, that was a worry.

Sure, he'd seen the news reports: riots in the city, hospitals on the brink of closure, sanctions on trade and travel. But all of these things seemed distant to Martin, as if part of some end-of-the-world movie. None of it was real in *his* world.

But no weather forecast…

He looked out the window, trying to formulate his own forecast. The sky was a rich blue colour. A few clouds moved in from the west; Martin wondered if there'd be rain later on. He hoped so. His vegetable patch out back was dry as a bone and, with things going the way they were, he might be needing a bit more growth out there.

Martin switched the television off, sick of the same old footage; the same debates and interviews; the same announcements from the same politicians saying little about anything. The TV channels were repeating everything on a constant loop; helpline numbers and out-of-date 'community announcements' rolling along the bottom of the screen. Curfew times for each county. Wasn't there anything else to report? Was anyone actually out there recording anything *new*, reporting on what was going on *now*? Or were the journalists just as scared as everyone else?

Martin wasn't scared. Martin was prepared. He'd stocked up early, filling his locked garage and shed with as much food and bottled water as he could get his hands on. The house was secure. The doors and windows were locked.

He wouldn't be walking into Waringstown village, where everyone was talking crazy talk, like old Tom at the boot sale, spreading rumours about locals who hadn't been seen in a while. *Caught the flu*, they whispered. But they may as well have been saying, *Caught the plague*.

Martin wondered if the internet would have anything different. He thought so, but with no connection in his house, no computer even, there was no way of finding out. Martin was a proud technophobe. He liked the radio or the television or the newspaper; tried and tested ways of getting information across in a way which didn't require some whizz-kid on stand-by, lest your system crash, or whatever.

He heard a familiar noise.

He looked down, finding Fred staring up at him, head poised to one side, concern in his eyes. Martin ruffled the dog's fur. Even old Fred could feel the tension in the air. Maybe the dog could sense that something was about to happen, that visitors were coming. Like most dogs, Fred wanted his whole pack together. And Martin felt the same right now: he'd talked to them on the phone only an hour ago, but he couldn't fully relax until Lize and little Jamie were in the house and he could lock the doors up tight.

But that dumbo, Shaun…

It wasn't that Martin hated the man. He just hated him being with Lize. She was his little girl, after all. He'd brought her up single-handedly after her mother had died in childbirth, and while Martin would have to admit that he hated her in those first weeks, blaming her for taking the only woman he'd ever loved, he soon grew to love little Lize for the very same reason: she was all he had left of his wife, Liza.

As the years went by, all he could see was Liza in her. In fact, he meant to name Lize after his wife, but a careless scribble on some form or other and she was registered as Lize. And so it stuck. In a way, it suited her very well. To Martin and everyone who knew her, Lize was one in a million.

Where was she?

Martin lifted his phone and punched in some numbers. The dead tone screamed in his ear like a siren. He slammed the receiver down, swore loudly.

Damn phone company!

Fred sloped off to the back of the room, hiding under the dining room table.

Martin was all worked up now. He hated himself for that. He should be calm, relaxed.

He cracked his knuckles, paced the living room. Blew some air out of his mouth then breathed it all back in again.

He switched the television on again. Still the same old footage and numbers and announcements on repeat, over and over and fucking over again. Martin wanted to put his foot through the bloody thing.

Suddenly, Fred's ears pricked up, and he ran to the door barking.

A car had stopped outside the house.

Martin followed the dog to the door, unlatching the safety and turning the key in the lock.

THREE

Ballynarry,Co.Armagh.

They'd pulled off the motorway at Portadown.

Colin said they should avoid the town centre, head straight for the country roads, and Vicky wasn't going to argue. She'd seen enough of urban life back in Belfast. She was ready for a bit of country air.

Soon the world turned green around her. Cattle and sheep stood huddled together by hedges. Even the birds seemed quiet, their normally cheerful chorus muted against the overwhelming sound of silence.

They passed a few houses, mostly barricaded from within, crudely erected signs saying things like 'Trespassers will be shot' or 'Beware of the dog.' Country folk weren't fond of townsfolk, period. But this was a whole new ball game.

"Are we nearly there yet?" Vicky said for the fourth time within twenty minutes.

"What are you, four years old?" Colin said. He sighed. "Okay, yes. We're nearly there. It's just up here to the right."

Sure enough, they followed a small lane off the main road. Furrowed mud had dried in the shape of large tractor wheels, leading as far as the eye could see. Fields flanked each side of the lane.

They passed by an old-style barnyard, small cottage by its side. Again, if anyone were in, they weren't for advertising the fact.

Eventually, they neared another house, a newly built bungalow with a wide lawn and freshly stoned driveway. Hedges shaped like animals guarded a beautiful flowerbed and artificial waterfall.

But still no sign of life.

"Are you sure they're expecting us?" Vicky asked.

Colin didn't reply.

"Maybe they saw the car coming," Vicky pointed at the solider lodged into the windscreen. "I know *I* would hide from *that*."

Colin parked the car on the driveway, opposite the garage.

"Oh, thank God," Vicky said, swiftly exiting and putting some distance between herself and that bloody soldier she'd been staring at for the last hour. She stood by the waterfall, carefully brushing the glass from her clothes using the rolled up cuffs of her sweatshirt.

"You stay here," Colin said to her. "And watch the car."

"Yeah," she said, looking once more at the soldier in the windscreen. "Like it's going anywhere."

…

The house belonged to Chris Lennon and Ben Reilly. They were friends of Colin's. That much was true. But Colin hadn't talked to them in weeks. He'd lied – told Vicky the couple was expecting him just to get her out of the city.

The last time Colin had visited Chris and Ben, they had just moved in, and had been were boxes all over the place. There were no floors laid, and everything was cold to touch. The couple held a painting party, paying guests with beer and wine. Colin got very drunk. He stayed over on their couch, remembering the white dust from the concrete floors being everywhere. It was like talc. Got into his hair, between his fingernails. It was infectious.

Now, of course, over a year later, the house was a veritable palace. Chris and Ben were country boys at heart, so this was their dream home, both of them selling their apartments from Belfast to move here.

Ben was self-employed and conducted most of his business online.

Chris was in sales; he worked for some pharmaceutical firm and found that the more travelling his job involved, the less it mattered where he was based. He just needed to be near the motorway, and, regardless of how remote it seemed out here among the cows and turf, he was only half an hour from the nearest slip road.

Colin knocked the door lightly. There was no answer, so he gently pressed the doorbell, listening as a familiar gong sounded from inside the house.

He looked over to the garage window, noticing both cars inside. They were obviously scared of looters, even out here. A house like theirs was already going to draw attention, so no need to give the wrong sort any other excuse to stop by.

Colin wondered what kind of reception *he* was going to get. Perhaps the couple had spotted Vince coming down the drive, just as Vicky said, and decided to lock down until the sorry looking car moved on. You could hardly blame them.

Colin stepped back from the doorway.

He looked at the side window, finding the blinds open. He stepped closer, cupping his hands around his eyes then pressing against the window, but he couldn't see anyone..

He wandered round the house. Reached the back door, looked through its glass into the small utility room. Nothing.

He was just about to give up, return to the car and the inevitable earache from Vicky when something startled him. It came from inside the house.

Colin reached for the door handle, slowly twisted it. It wasn't locked. He looked around then pushed the door open.

He stepped onto the ivory-coloured tiles of the utility room floor. A washing machine and tumble drier stood side-by-side. A digital radio was plugged into a nearby wall, an almost inaudible hiss escaping from its silver speakers.

Colin approached the door straight ahead, knocking gently.

"Hello?" he called out. "It's Colin. Ben? Chris? You guys home?"

There was no reply, so he pushed the door open.

It led into the kitchen cum dining area.

His eyes traced the room.

Everything looked so clean. There was not as much as a used cup in the sink.

A red plastic clock with no numbers kept time. A single plastic coffee table sat in the corner. A naked Barbie doll sat on top, its head turned slightly to one side, its arms raised and pointing forwards. It was staring at Colin as he moved through.

"Guys?"

Still no one.

Colin began to wonder if they were gone.

Maybe Chris had scored a ticket on some private plane, and the couple had left this godforsaken island altogether, heading for sunnier climes. That was the kind of people Chris dealt with, after all. People with money. People with class. People with the kind of capital that could afford fancy cars and villas on the continent.

Colin could imagine Chris and Ben relaxing in Spain, cocktails in hand.

But why leave the door open? The cars in the garage? The radio on?

Colin moved through to the hall, finding a rich red carpet.

A strange smell greeted his nostrils. It was like treacle mixed with bleach. It was unpleasant, even though he couldn't put his finger on why.

He wondered if the smell was coming from his own body, all that excitement from earlier making his sweat all the more pungent. He checked under his arms, finding a slight hum, effectively masked by a familiar brand of deodorant – expensive shit he'd picked up from *House of Fraser*.

The living room was the next door along, and Colin peeked his head though, still calling as he went.

He made his way along to the next door, finding the study. It was empty. Just a desk with a computer. Bookcase in the corner.

The next room was the bathroom. A huge corner bath sat next to a separate walk-in shower. Toothpaste and two brushes rested in a stainless steel cup by the sink.

But still no sign of life.

The smell from before was in the bathroom, and Colin wondered if it was a burst pipe or some blockage in the system. The more pungent it got, the less pleasant it became. Colin unrolled some toilet roll and blew his nose, dropping the spent tissue in the toilet and flushing it.

The next room was a bedroom – one of three, it seemed. Colin pushed this door like all the others, calling as he went.

He stepped inside.

The air was thick in here, the acrid smell catching in his throat like out-of-date milk. He immediately felt himself gag and bent over to wretch onto the floor. When he backed up, he saw the source of the smell, the bodies of his friends side by side in bed together.

A cold, icy sweat broke across Colin's back.

Ben was hardly recognisable. He'd always been slim, but he'd lost even more weight, his bones now stretching through parched skin, scarlet-stained teeth protruding through pale, narrow lips.

His eyes were barely human, no longer fixed on any particular view but instead blending into his skull like dusty old glass. They reminded Colin of the eyes of dead fish when they were washed up and left to fester on the beach.

The poor bastard had clearly reached the latter stages of flu, his nose and ears clogged with hardened blood.

Chris, however, looked healthy. As healthy as a dead man *could* look. There were no signs of infection, his body unmarred by the symptoms that Ben displayed. Instead, his face portrayed sadness, emptiness. And while Colin suspected that he had taken his own life, it seemed easier and more romantic to assume he had died of a broken heart.

FOUR

"Where is he?"

Vicky was never the patient type, and on a day like today, her nerves were shot.

She stood, arms folded, a safe distance from the car. She was staring over her glasses at the sight of the soldier buried in the windscreen. In the back was Sinead. Poor little infected Sinead. Riddled with the very pandemic that was killing half of Ireland.

Vicky held a handkerchief against her mouth. She didn't trust the freshness of the country air to dispel an airborne virus, a virus Colin thought it wise for them to carry around in the back seat of the car.

God, he was a prick sometimes.

She approached the back window and peered inside.

Sinead was half awake. Blood gathered around her teeth like messy lipstick. She started coughing. A pink gob slapped against the window. It held, sticky like jam, before sliding down and discolouring the clear, sun-sparkled glass.

Vicky inched away, finding her back against the fountain in the garden.

She looked towards the bonnet of the car, the body still buried in the glass, both arms hanging from its side as if the silly twat had taken a running fucking dive for the windscreen.

She remembered, as a child, being alone in the car with her dad. She couldn't remember where they were going, just that it was only the two of them in the vehicle and it was dark. A bird slammed into the windscreen. Vicky could hear the crack of its breaking bones, even now. She remembered her dad turning to her, swearing loudly, and then laughing. It was her first memory of death.

She had buried that memory. But a regressive therapy session unearthed the bird, cleaned its tiny corpse, rotting in the back of her mind for nearly thirty years, and presented it to her like a proud cat.

"Why do you think your dad had laughed?" the counsellor asked her.

Vicky didn't know. She thought it might have something to do with him being a drunken prick who beat her and her mother on a daily basis, but she couldn't be sure.

What's keeping Colin?

She stared towards house. No sign of him.

She lay down on the grass lawn, looked up into the sky. The sun was still blinding. There were very few clouds.

Vicky was just beginning to relax a little and enjoy the sunshine when the body on top of the car began to move.

...

As Colin looked at the two bodies on the bed, he recalled the young woman he'd found at the car crash earlier. How he'd watched her fade from life like steam from a teacup. But this was different. These were people he'd known in life, spent time with.

He thought about Aunt Bell, and a heavy weight seemed to fill the empty pit of his stomach. He wondered how she would spend her last moments. He wondered if she were still waiting for her soup, if they'd given her anything to drink or some fresh blankets. Had they explained what was happening, why they were in the house, barricading her inside? Did she try to resist or just quietly roll over and let the virus take her?

Colin moved closer to the bed. It smelled of sick and sweat.

He moved one shaking hand over Ben's eyes and closed them. The poor bastard had obviously struggled towards the end, trying desperately to cough up some lump in his throat or fight for his last breath.

Colin wondered who had gone first. Had Chris decided he wouldn't be able to watch his lover die and selfishly ended his own life before the flu took Ben?

Colin knew he'd have to drag their bodies out into the garden, along with their bedding, and burn them. He knew that the whole house was likely to be contagious. But what did it matter? The flu was everywhere now, rampant throughout Ireland, thick in the very air he breathed into his lungs.

There was no escaping it. It was all around him.

He could be next.

Colin opened the wardrobe, finding a blanket. He spread it across the two friends on the bed.

"Sorry," he whispered.

Then he heard Vicky scream.

FIVE

When he reached the car, he found Vicky on the lawn, scrambling backwards, eyes wide, and her glasses on the ground.

On the car bonnet, he found the soldier's body shaking, arms flapping. He was struggling like a frightened fish, head still wedged in the windscreen, blood spreading through the shattered glass.

"J-Jesus." Colin said. He didn't want to look but couldn't tear his eyes away.

He ran to Vicky, scooping her up in his arms.

She released an ear-splitting shriek that he would hear ringing in his ears for hours afterwards. Her glasses flew from her head, her eyes narrowed, wrinkling at the corners as tears rinsed out. Colin tried to pull her close, but she struggled against him, her fingernails digging into his back, fists flying. She was inconsolable, so he released her, left her on the grass, writhing and keening like a woman possessed.

Colin moved towards the car. He got right up close to the trapped soldier.

"Hello?" he called.

There was no reply. Colin hadn't expected one. Maybe he just needed to hear a voice, *any* voice, even his own.

He opened the car door, finding the soldier's face, bruised and sliced. One eye staring back at him. With his head raised and his face visible, Colin could see how young he was.

Just a child.

"Stop struggling," Colin said. "You're making things worse!" Blood was pooling on the dashboard. "Stop moving, for Christ's sake," Colin said again.

Colin rolled his hands into the cuffs of his cardigan sleeves. He tapped at the windscreen until it split into pieces, falling back onto the bonnet.

The lad pulled his head free, his body slipping down the bonnet and falling to the side of the car.

Colin exited the car, finding the soldier on the ground, choking.

"Think! Think! Think!" Colin muttered to himself, wracking his brain, trying to remember his first aid training.

He threw himself to the ground by the lad's side.

With one hand, he forced the soldier's mouth open, reached into his throat to find he'd swallowed his own swollen tongue. Colin searched inside, feeling the lad gag, warm, bloody juices belching through the gaps between Colin's hand and the soldier's throat. He found the tongue then pulled it free, relaxing it back into the soldier's mouth.

Carefully, lest he break any more bones, Colin bent the wounded lad over his knee, patting his back like a sick child as he expelled the rest of the shit in his throat onto the stoned driveway.

"It's okay," Colin said as he continued to pat the lad's back. "You're going to be okay."

SIX

18th June

They'd put both Sinead and the soldier in the spare bedroom. They lay in two twin beds, side by side.

Sinead was barely conscious. Her airways were clogging up with blood-filled mucus and needed to be cleared on the hour, every hour.

The soldier was seemingly not infected but still swaying in and out of consciousness. He was badly injured. It wasn't just the cuts on his face and neck. His legs, neck and some of his upper body had suffered in the collision, meaning bones were most likely broken, perhaps beyond repair. Without proper medical help, he might die or, at the very least, his bones would heal wrong. It was hard to imagine the pain the young soldier was going through, but there was nothing could be done for him.

There was little could be done for either of them. Some water when they were able. Some soup through a straw. Yet either one of them could pass away in their sleep at any time. And with the way things were looking, that mightn't be such a bad way to go.

As Vicky stood at the doorway, looking in on her former colleague, she remembered the girl Sinead used to be and would never be again. Bright, carefree. A people-person, born to do the job she did. Good with customers, laughing at their jokes, building rapport.

Everyone loved Sinead.

They *hated* Vicky.

In the old world, Vicky had been retreating into herself. Hiding in the office, going over sales figures, retail reports, dealing with invoices and purchase orders. She would only come out onto the shop floor to meet difficult customers, the arsey ones who didn't respond well to Sinead's soft approach. That was something Vicky *did* excel at: she could put the fear of God into anyone with little more than a look.

Vicky closed the spare room door, made for the bathroom.

She clicked the light on and locked the bathroom door behind her.

She washed her hands, scrubbing them feverishly with soap. Threw some water on her face, looked in the mirror. Her eyes were like tea bags. She felt old and withered. It was obvious she hadn't been sleeping well.

Her make-up bag sat between the taps on the sink, unzipped. But Vicky couldn't bring herself to retrieve anything from it.

She wondered when it was she had stopped caring about how she looked.

The general rule was that staff should wear products from the shop. Head Office would send them ideas on what new products retail assistants should be promoting. Staff would get huge discounts on these items.

Sinead and some of the others would put their own twists on Head Office's ideas, but Vicky would wear them *exactly* as they were presented, the same accessories, same shoes and make-up.

But now, there was no model for Vicky to copy. No pictures or memos from head office. She was expected to put on make-up because she wanted to.

Vicky looked away from the mirror.

Her eyes fell upon the large corner bath.

Like everything in this fucking house, it was spotless.

A few potions set along its sides. Expensive bath salts and cremes. Essential oils and a burner.

A razor.

Vicky's eyes lingered on the razor.

SEVEN

The study was the only place where Colin had found any trace of clutter in the house, but even then it wasn't anything to shout about. A few photocopies stacked by the computer. A coffee mug, stained at the bottom, resting on the desk near the printer. All things he would expect to see in the average house, but here they stuck out like sore thumbs.

He liked the study. Had spent most of his time over the last couple of days there. Sitting in the easy chair, thinking. Watching the news reports and updated YouTube footage on the internet. It had become his cave, somewhere to retreat to.

Something caught his eye now as he sat himself into the swivel chair by the computer desk: a single piece of notebook paper was taped to the wall. Colin hadn't noticed it before.

He reached his hand, pulled the paper from the wall and peered more closely at it.

There was something scribbled in biro pen:

12/08

Looked like a date. Someone's birthday, perhaps? Colin knew the date of Chris' birthday but not Ben's. He'd been to Chris' 30th last year. Something of a knees-up it was, too, with beaucoup de booze consumed.

He smiled at the memories

Colin visualised the pair now in their deathbed together. Sleeping peacefully. He knew he should have taken their bodies outside, but just couldn't bring himself to move them.

He threw the piece of paper across the desk, switched the computer on.

Google's search engine loaded up. Colin did a search on 'the flu'. As expected, the news pages were completely swamped with headlines about the pandemic.

Colin left the news pages, finding YouTube. There were literally thousands of videos uploaded on the flu, most of them censored as soon as they were uploaded – seemed that YouTube weren't keen on videos showing people dying.

Colin found one from Belfast that interested him and clicked in. The video began to play. An insane man was being dragged from an office building by the cops. They wore the same yellow suits as the ones who had come for Aunt Bell and Sinead. But the man was beyond angry, his jaws snapping at the cops' arms as they tried to feed him into the back of a Paddywagon.

A noise from behind startled Colin.

He turned to find Vicky leaning against the doorframe.

"Hey," she said.

"Hey," he said, feeling flustered, like she'd just caught him looking at porn. "How're you feeling?"

"Knackered. Haven't been able to sleep." She yawned, looking out the window. Evening was drawing in again. "Apart from that, I'm –"

Her eyes drifted over to the monitor.

Colin tried to minimise the YouTube video, but she stopped him.

"No, let me see," she said.

Colin stepped back, resigned to her viewing the video. He didn't watch the footage as it ran again, instead watching her eyes.

She stepped back and pointed at the screen. "What's wrong with that man?"

"I don't know," Colin said, his voice low and measured.

"He doesn't look right. What's *wrong* with him?"

"I said I don't know!"

Colin grabbed the mouse and closed down the page.

There was a sound from the hallway, an almost animal-like rasping.

Vicky looked towards the door.

"What the hell was that?" she said.

Colin pushed past Vicky, following the sound to the spare bedroom. Inside he found Sinead, her breathing so laboured that he expected her to give up at any second.

He pulled several baby wipes from the tub by Sinead's bed, cleaning her mouth and nose of the mucus, noticing how her breathing became steadier. He tried to get her to drink some water, managed to get some down before she rejected it, coughing and spluttering the water along with blood and thick globs of bile.

"I want her out of here," he heard Vicky say from the hallway. "She'll infect us all if she stays."

"Well, why don't *you* throw her out, then?! Right after you move Chris and Ben?" He turned to face her, rage and fear and grief exploding from within. "This isn't the shop, Vicky! You're not the boss lady now!"

Vicky turned and marched down the hallway. Colin heard the living room door slam.

"Fuck!" he said.

He ran both of his hands through his hair.

He could feel the dampness on his fingers. Sinead's blood and germs.

"Fuck," he said again.

EIGHT

Waringstown, Co. Down

Tom ran fresh tape across the wall above the bedroom window, resealing the clear plastic sheet that had come away.

He was running operations from his bedroom now. Everything had been moved upstairs. The important stuff, anyway: his computer, his old record player, the birdcage.

The bedroom boasted the only glass not boarded up. It was his window to the world. He stole a glance through the plastic sheet, finding the same yellow, sun-parched fields as always.

Nothing had changed.

Tom's eyes searched each corner of the window for further signs of give. He cut another piece of tape from the roll with his teeth, running it along a corner that clearly didn't need it. Then another.

He stepped back, appraising his handiwork. It looked secure.

Tom wiped his brow with an old handkerchief. This was thirsty work. A cup of tea would be good.

He headed downstairs, cutting through the living room, making for the kitchen. He almost tripped over a spent gas cylinder on his way. He'd still a few left. Should keep him in tea and baked beans for at least another while.

He fired up the gas, lighting the hob. He made his tea, poured it into his favourite mug. As he poured the tea, Tom noticed his hands were shaking. He'd run out of pills, scoffed the lot. He saw a bottle of vodka sitting on the worktop. It was his last one, and most of it was gone too. Tom added a drop or two to his tea. Maybe that would steady his hands a bit.

He carried the mug out of the kitchen, through the living room, heading for the stairs.

The smell of leftover food mixed with the ever-rank fumes coming from the toilet. It was getting too much to bear, and Tom made a mental note to tidy up later on, to seal all the rubbish in black bin bags and spray some more air freshener around the place, regardless of how much that shit hurt his throat.

Christ, he wished he could open a window, but he knew it would be suicide to do so.

This fucking flu.

According to the internet, it was everywhere now. All across Ireland. Cases reported in England, Scotland, Wales...

Yet still Tom saw no physical signs of the flu where he lived.

He reckoned rural communities would fare better as a rule. People were better at sharing, at trading without money and stocking goods. They kept quiet, too. Hid their sick and stayed out of sight.

Tom moved over to the computer, setting his mug of tea on the desk. He grabbed the mouse, doing a round robin of his daily haunts. It was *all flu all the time*. No one was talking about anything else.

The goons were getting more vicious. There were reports of death camps being set up. Of mass executions. Shootings on motorways.

One video caught his attention, and he hovered his cursor over the play button. The internet was slowing of late, but bit-by-bit the video began to play, delivering slices of another riot, this one from an apartment block in Finaghy.

The footage seemed to be taken by a mobile phone.

Two government types, maybe cops, were moving through a crowd of people, entering the apartment block. They wore oxygen masks and yellow plastic suits. "Good colour," Tom smirked.

The crowd was getting wilder as the suits moved up the stairwell. The person carrying the phone was swearing at the goons, yelling.

Tom smiled gleefully at the tirade of abuse she was levelling at them.

They reached their destination, an apartment surrounded by a crowd of other government types.

Tom watched a quarantine take place. He'd seen a few, already, but this one was particularly gruesome. A perfectly well woman was trying to escape her house as the goons in yellow proceeded to seal her in.

"Bastards!" Tom shouted at the screen, shaking his fist.

The footage flipped to something coming from the back of the crowd and Tom thought he could make out a number of heavily infected people in the crowd. But they seemed riled, angry. They were struggling with other people in the crowd, people who weren't goons.

Tom paused the video at that point, rewound. He squinted his eyes as the scene replayed, trying to work out what was going on. He saw the infected people again, seemingly agitated. He watched as other people – *everyday, ordinary people* – beat down the infected, some using sticks.

Why were they doing that?

He let the footage play on.

All hell broke loose.

People from the back of the crowd started to scream and push forward. Someone was shooting a gun. The crowd hemmed in on the cops, and they bolted for another flat, closing the door behind them.

The mobile phone shifted back to the crowd at the back. There was still some sort of disturbance going on, the other government types trying to fight their way out of the block while others pushed past them, heading for the flat the first two suits had disappeared into.

The phone zoomed in on the infected people. Tom leaned closer, trying to get a better look at him. There was definitely something not right here. They weren't sick in the everyday sense of the word. They seemed feral, violent, as if the flu had twisted their minds.

The phone changed angle again, moving with the main push of the crowd towards the flat door. People were beating against it, the pressure soon pushing it through.

The crowd piled into the flat, finding the first two goons standing with an older lady and yet another heavily infected man. The phone seemed to pass hands at this point..

Tom twisted his eyes, trying to make out what happened next.

Filming resumed, the camera shaky with pressure from the surging crowd.

In the corner of the screen, Tom noticed the smaller goon draw his firearm and shoot in the direction of the crowd.

The footage ended.

Tom stepped back.

"Whoa…" he breathed.

He looked around the room, suddenly paranoid.

He clicked out of that footage, finding other popular videos in the same vein. He clicked into another, watching a similar riot, this one from North Belfast.

A crowd of hooded youngsters were facing off against suited police. Again, the camera shifted to find some heavily infected people moving amongst the crowds. But they didn't look like people anymore.

They looked like monsters.

NINE

The sun pierced the thin fabric of curtains, waking Shaun early. Beside him, Lize continued to sleep. Next to her was Jamie, wrapped up in the duvet like a pig in a poke.

Shaun reached out his hand and stroked Lize's hair. They said that when you lost one sense, the others grew more sensitive, and Shaun believed that every time he touched his wife.

He kissed her head softly. Ruffled Jamie's hair then lay staring at them for a moment.

His family.

Dark thoughts intruded his mind. Shaun tried to push them away but failed. His wife had had an affair, and they still hadn't talked about it. Both Shaun and Lize had just continued as normal, ignoring the huge white elephant in the room. For now it was more important to remain strong for Jamie, to provide a united front.

Shaun quietly climbed out of bed. He left the room, closing the door behind him as gently as possible.

He descended the stairs, entered the living room to find Martin hammering nails into a series of wooden sheets.

Fred circled the room, whimpering with each slam of the hammer against nail.

For a while, Martin didn't see Shaun, his pursed lips suggesting he was whistling. When he did notice Shaun, he simply glanced at him and then checked to see if Lize or Jamie were there. Satisfied they weren't, that it was just Shaun, Martin returned to the job at hand without uttering a single word.

Shaun's heart sank.

At times like this he felt invisible. And God knows he felt that way a lot.

Once people realised Shaun was deaf, they would often forget he was even there. For some, it was simply ignorance: they treated Shaun the same way they treated someone in a wheelchair or someone with Down's syndrome. With Shaun, the impairment wasn't so obvious, so a person might talk to him, and he would read their lips and reply. But once they heard his voice, his twisting of certain words and letters, his speech a few decibels louder perhaps, Shaun would see the face in front of him change.

Sometimes, if Lize were with him, they would smile at Shaun benevolently before turning instead to address his wife.

Once, when Jamie had been no more than four years old, standing holding his daddy's hand, he was asked, in front of Shaun, if someone *normal* was around to look after him – a *real* adult. And while this wasn't something Martin had ever vocalised, it sure as hell was what he thought.

Fred came over to Shaun, tail wagging, still nervous.

There was a space in the hammering.

Shaun took it: "What are you doing?"

It was to be their first *real* conversation in five years – an indication of how well the last one had gone.

Martin stopped whistling, turned around. "Boarding up the windows," he said, and by the shape of his lips, it looked like he was shouting.

"Yes, I can see that," Shaun pressed. "But why?"

Martin turned again, this time setting the hammer down on the windowsill. He pointed at the television.

Martin went over to the television and switched it on. He lifted the controller, waiting patiently until the satellite kicked in. News 24 flicked up, midway through playing footage that would become legendary throughout the world.

It looked like a recording from a security camera. The time and date was written on the video's footer. The name of some laboratory from Belfast was rolling along the bottom of the screen.

A doctor wearing medical scrubs stood by a bed where another man's body lay. It looked like he was in the middle of an autopsy. Beside him stood a trolley holding what looked to be the dead man's heart and lungs stored in containers.

Suddenly, the body rose up, like a vampire from some old movie, stepped off the bed and grabbed the doctor.

The doctor pushed the body away, retreated off camera.

"What the hell –" Shaun mouthed.

The footage continued for a while, the dead man wandering around the room, pausing to look closely at the camera filming it. Shaun leaned closer to the television. He could see the dead man's face clearly and recognised it but, at first, couldn't tell where from.

The footage played on fast forward for a while before returning to normal time.

The doctor from before returned on screen, working at his trolley, seemingly trying to prepare an injection.

He was attacked by the dead man again.

A young girl, maybe a nurse or lab assistant, intervened, attacking the dead man with a blade of some sort. As Shaun watched, she ripped at the dead man's neck until his head was all but torn away.

There was blood everywhere.

Shaun turned away in disgust.

He looked to Martin, the older man's face smug, "I told you so" written across it.

Satisfied, Martin lifted the hammer from the windowsill, retrieved another nail from the small tin box nearby then moved to position it on another spot.

"Wait," Shaun shouted, his mind struggling to process all that was going on, his words slurred and barely legible. "You can't just lock us in!"

He sensed a hand on his shoulder, turned and found Lize, her dressing gown wrapped around her body, one hand grasping the fabric at her neck.

"What's going on?" she said.

Shaun threw his hands up in the air, "Your father's locking us in."

Martin stopped hammering, turned to Lize. "What did he say?"

"I said –"

"Oh, both of you, please!" Lize protested.

She sat down on the sofa, both arms folding across her chest. Her eyes were drawn to the television, the same footage from before rerunning, heading towards its dramatic conclusion.

"Watch that," Martin ordered Lize, pointing his hammer at the TV. "And *then* you'll see why I'm doing this."

"But how can we be sure it's even genuine?" Shaun protested.

"It's the BBC," Martin said, still looking at Lize. "It's good enough for me."

"It's an isolated incident in Belfast, for Christ's sake!" Shaun argued. "Some… medical anomaly. It's got nothing to do with what's going on here." Shaun moved closer to Martin, now standing in front of the television. "You can't go locking us in whenever –"

"Oh sweet Jesus," Lize said, her face paling, one hand moving to her mouth as she continued to watch the footage.

"Everything's under control," Martin said to her. "Nothing for you to worry about, sweetheart."

"He's overreacting," the younger man countered.

But then Lize did something that cut Shaun to the very bone: she lifted one hand and raised it in his direction like a cop stopping traffic.

"This is insane!" Shaun yelled, the anger distorting his voice, a line of spittle escaping his mouth. "*He's* insane!"

Both Lize and Martin glared at him, their faces then softening as they looked away from Shaun, to the door.

Shaun turned with them to find Jamie standing in the doorway, his Spiderman pyjama top on inside-out.

"Daddy?" Jamie said, and Shaun went to him, lifted him and carried him through the doorway, back upstairs, away from the excitement, the tension, the confined space that Martin was creating in the living room.

Away from the zombies on television…

…

Lize was terrified.

She couldn't even *look* at the television.

That man. Surely it can't be –

She swallowed hard, looked to her father.

She knew how headstrong he could be when he got an idea into his head. She thought it came from his army background, the black-and-white mentality they drilled

216

into him. Either way, Martin had always been a zealous man. Especially when it came to security.

Lize remembered coming home from school one day, back when they were living in Germany. One of the other kids had pushed her in the playground, causing her to fall, cutting her knees and ripping her jumper. She recalled trying to mend the jumper herself with a needle and thread she found in the garage, but her daddy found her searching through the many toolboxes and tin tubs that had populated his garage back then, just as they did now.

At the time they were living at a military base, with all the other army families, and when Martin found out it was a local kid who had pushed her over, he marched her to the boy's house, demanded the parents bring the kid to the door and then instructed her to push the little toe rag to the ground.

Justice was served that day. Her father believed in an eye for an eye, tit for tat. Do onto others before they do it onto you.

Martin pushed past his daughter, snapping her back to the present. He had boarded up the whole downstairs of the house and was proceeding upstairs.

Lize felt confused. She thought about the television, about what she had seen. God knew, she didn't need *that* anywhere near this house. But there was truth in what Shaun was saying. Locking themselves in meant no escape.

"Daddy, please stop. Think about this!" Lize reasoned with him. "You're upsetting Jamie!"

Martin stopped for a moment, laughed. "*Upsetting* Jamie? I'm giving the boy a chance to live! I'm giving us *all* a chance to live."

"You're going too far," she reasoned. But her voice was weak. She didn't even know if she believed her own argument.

She watched Shaun come out of their bedroom, closing the door behind him. Martin ignored him as always, pushing past the younger man and heading for the master bedroom, hammer in hand.

Shaun looked at Lize, shook his head.

Lize remembered their meal together, the first night they arrived. Shaun at one end of the table. Martin at the other. Lize and Jamie in between.

Martin was lecturing on how to conserve fuel used by the generator he'd rigged in the garage. "We only turn the cooker on once a day," he told Lize. "Make sure and tell him too," he added, looking over at Shaun.

Tell the dummy.

But Shaun didn't need to be told. He'd read Martin's lips. Lize had felt the anger resonating from him like a heater that night. Good God, the beam coming off his face could have powered the bloody generator for a week.

Lize followed Martin through to the master bedroom.

He had stacked some wood there, intent on covering the glass with it.

Lize grabbed his arm.

Martin turned, his face filled with rage. He raised the hammer, and she fell back onto the bed, her arms raised in defence.

Martin immediately crumbled, dropping the hammer and going to her.

"I'm sorry, darling," he said.

But she retreated from him.

And then it happened.

The first blow surprised Martin as much as it surprised Lize. The second blow he managed to block, pushing his attacker away for enough time to allow him to reach for the hammer.

But Shaun recovered quickly, bringing his foot down hard on Martin's hand.

Martin pulled his hand away, but Shaun followed through with a kick to the head. His shoe connected with Martin's jaw, a single tooth flying from the older man's mouth, a splash of blood spoiling the nearby wallpaper.

"Stop it! Both of you!" Lize screamed.

Jamie was at the doorway, looking in, clutching the doorframe with both hands, tears streaming down his cheeks.

"For God's sake, stop it!"

But Shaun was like a man possessed. His eyes were full and red, his fists beating repeatedly on Martin's face as the ex-soldier fought to defend himself.

Then Jamie was in the room.

Lize held her arms out to receive him, but the boy ran past her, grabbing the discarded hammer. He lifted it in both hands then brought it down hard on his Grandpa's leg.

"Oh God, Jamie, no!" Lize yelled, going to him and scooping him up, but the boy was persistent, pulling away, the anger in his face mirroring that of his father.

Shaun stepped away from Martin, the boy's attack enough to pull him out of whatever spell he'd been under.

He went to Lize and Jamie, throwing his arms around them both.

Lize received him but, while they embraced, she watched Martin roll away, reaching into a nearby drawer.

The older man rose up brandishing a hunting knife. He pointed it at Shaun.

Lize stepped in front of Shaun. "Daddy, no!" she said, her hands raised, palms forward.

Martin's hands were shaking, his breathing heavy, almost like he was growling.

Shaun immediately pushed Jamie away. "Get out of here, son," he ordered, but Jamie stayed close, hammer raised in his hand threateningly.

"Fucking dummy!" Martin spat. "You won't get the better of me, you fucking invalid!"

"Come on, then!" Shaun goaded.

"I'll fucking slice you!"

"No you won't, shit chicken!"

Lize would usually laugh when Shaun muddled his words, often when he was drunk or excited. But there was nothing to laugh at now in this room where a knife was waving in the air and her father's blood ran down the wall like wet paint.

She moved closer to Martin.

"Daddy, please… it's okay."

Martin's face softened, tears gathering in the corner of his eyes. "I…nearly hit you!" he said to Lize in a voice that she'd never heard him use before. "With a fucking hammer!"

"But you didn't," she said, "I'm okay, look at me…"

He looked at her, stared right into her eyes.

She reached for the knife slowly. He released it, and Lize laid it on the bed.

She took her father's hands and placed them on her cheeks.

"See?" she said. "I'm okay. You didn't hurt me."

He pulled her tight. She could feel his heat. His body started to shake as he burrowed into her embrace.

When Lize looked up, she found Shaun and Jamie glaring back at her. There was still anger in their eyes.

And something else.

Jealousy.

TEN

Ballynarry, Co. Armagh

Colin woke with a start, finding himself in the study's easy chair.

He'd been dreaming.

In the dream, he was driving the car with Sinead in the back seat. Vicky sat beside him, wearing a wedding dress covered in blood. The young soldier stood on the road, his gun aimed at them through the window of the car. Yet, no matter how fast Colin was driving, he was never able to hit him.

And then Sinead rose up from the back seat, snakes instead of hair on her head, each one alive and vicious, snapping the air, like alligators, then lunging for him.

It was then that Colin had woken.

He got up from the chair, his body stiff. He thought of checking on Sinead and the young soldier but didn't. He was too freaked after the dream.

He went to the bathroom, took a piss.

It was still early, but he decided to stay up. Maybe run a shower.

He peeled his t-shirt and shorts off. Paused by the mirror, examined himself for the first time in days.

His body-grooming had fallen by the wayside of late. His chest hair was filling out. Where his skin once looked golden, it was now pale and blotchy. A nervous rash covered the right side of his neck and he went to scratch it.

He'd lost weight, too, the normally problematic Buddha belly (as Sinead used to call it) almost gone. .

He turned the shower dial, quietly thanking Chris and Ben and their countryside ways; the house's generator ensured that home comforts such as water and electricity continued to work while the urban world crumbled. Colin made a mental note to check the generator for fuel as he stepped under the gloriously warm water.

At first, he didn't move. He stood under the shower, closing his eyes and enjoying how the noise, the moisture, the feeling of being cleansed brought him to another place, a place where the virus didn't belong, where it couldn't survive.

He reached for the shower gel, hanging from a nearby rail, the noise of it squirting into his palm loud and obnoxious. He lathered the gel into his skin, working it across every inch of his body. He could feel the germs all over like fleas, and he wanted rid of them. Medusa Sinead from his dream kept appearing in his head, and he fought to make her disappear, closing his eyes tight as he scrubbed, trying to think of anything else to overwrite her enduring, nightmarish image.

The sound of something breaking pulled him back to reality.

The noise rang out again, coming from the next room over.

The master bedroom.

Colin turned the shower off, listening again. There was a thumping noise, like someone was banging the door.

Colin stepped out of the shower, wrapped himself in the bathrobe hanging on the wall.

He opened the bathroom door and looked out into the hall.

Across the way, he found the couple's bedroom. The door was still closed.

Another thump. Or maybe it was a knock.

There was movement in the hall. He turned quickly, but it was Vicky, an oversized t-shirt draped around her wiry body.

"What is it?" she said but he shushed her, stepping closer to the bedroom door.

All kinds of things started going through his head. Was one of the couple still alive? Had someone broken into the house through the bedroom window? He would have heard a crash, surely.

Colin reached for the door, opening it slowly. It seemed to jam halfway.

He tried to swallow, but his throat was too dry and his tongue felt like an old facecloth.

A low moaning sound came from the room.

Colin pushed the door through.

It opened, light from the bathroom illuminating what appeared to be a pantomime ghost standing next to the bed.

"Who's there?" Colin cried. "Go on, show yourself!"

But there was no response, the figure simply stumbling forward.

Colin could see behind it now, noticing that where Ben had been lying in bed, there was no body. Chris remained on the other side of the bed.

Sweat was streaming into Colin's eyes, blurring the sight before him.

A heavy scent of decay attacked his nostrils.

He pinched his nose with one hand.

Reached for the sheet with the other.

It came easily, revealing Ben.

"Jesus, B-Ben?!" Colin said.

But there was still no response, the face before him showing no more signs of life than it had when it was on the bed. Vacant eyes stared somewhere *around* Colin but not *at* him. A mouth hung open, blood dried on its lips. And then that low moan came again, as if Ben was trying to tell him something.

Colin knew that Ben wasn't alive. He knew it because of what he'd watched on the YouTube videos, how the infected looked less and less human by the day. But those were videos and a small part of him could deny them as true or relevant, hide the truth until it was right in front of his eyes, no less real than the flu itself.

Colin did the only thing that he could think of, pushing Ben back with a hard shove, then closing the door again.

He heard the body tumbling to the floor.

He listened as Ben clambered to his feet again, made his way back to the door and began the pointless drill of thumping his head against the wood.

He looked to Vicky. He was still in shock and couldn't think of anything to say to her.

Vicky retreated down the corridor, knocking over a vase as she went.

Colin followed her.

She came out from the living room, wearing a coat over her t-shirt, jingling the car keys in her hand.

"What are you doing?" Colin asked, although he knew exactly what she was doing: she was leaving.

She didn't look at him. She seemed angry. Colin knew her too well. She'd found some way to blame *him* for this, just like she blamed him for *everything* he had absolutely no control over. The shop closing. The video on YouTube. Ben walking around when they both knew he was dead. All of it was Colin's fault.

"Vicky, stop!" he said, reaching for her.

He knew she wouldn't fare well outside, regardless of what was going on. In the real world, Vicky suffered. Colin knew now why her flat looked so run down: she went home every night late and crawled into bed alone and broken.

And that, of course, was *also* his fault.

"Vicky," he said, grabbing her, "Think about this! Where are you going to go?"

As she pulled against him, her coat came away, and Colin could see fresh scarring on her arms. It looked like she'd been cutting herself.

"DON'T TOUCH ME!" she screamed. She shook his hand away and stood, poised, fists rolled up tight. The anger was vibrating through her, breath coming hard and fast as if she were about to explode. "DON'T EVEN LOOK AT ME!"

"Vicky–"

"YOU!" she cried, pointing a finger. And then, more quietly, "You…" Water filled her eyes, her mouth turned up as if something were trying to crawl out and couldn't stretch her lips wide enough. A soft low wail left her, not unlike the noise Dead Ben made. "You stood there in your suit. Me beside you…"

"Vicky, please…"

But she persisted, talking over him, "And you said those words in front of all those people. And I loved that day, I *really* loved that day. And I loved *you*."

"This isn't the right time –"

"When *is* the right time? You come into the shop every day and everyone is laughing with you, having fun, sharing jokes, and then I come over and everyone's quiet…" She wiped her face. "When did you tell them all that our marriage… our life together was A FUCKING JOKE?!"

"Vicky, it wasn't like that."

"It was EXACTLY like that!" she barked. "And YOU… Everyone told you how brave you were, how difficult it must have been." She beat her fist against her chest, and he could actually hear the vibrations. "WHAT ABOUT ME?!"

He grabbed her and pulled her close, and while at first she resisted, pounding with her balled fists, she soon crumbled against him, releasing more tears and noise than her frail body seemed capable of. And Colin took it all from her. He took it because he knew that when it boiled down to it, a part of her was right; he *did* lead her up that garden path. He married her, spent the best days of her life on a whim, on an experiment to see if he could make a go of the mainstream life, the life his parents, his friends wanted.

As her sobs subsided, Colin could hear the gentle thuds against the door of the master bedroom.

…

Later, Colin was lying on the sofa bed in the living room, Vicky asleep beside him. Colin nursed her until she went over, exhaustion claiming her. He waited until he could be sure she was out, and then he carefully unfurled the duvet and stood up quietly.

He lifted his pillow, carrying it with him as he opened the door and left the living room.

In the hallway, he could hear the soft thumps against the master bedroom door as Ben continued his tireless campaign.

Colin ignored the noise, entering the spare bedroom, finding the two twin beds. The sun was strong now, attacking the blinds. He could see Sinead's face clearly. Still breathing heavily, her mouth and nose smeared once again with more of that thick, bloody mucus.

Colin stood over her bed. He was shaking.

"Sorry," he said, and with hands that felt like jelly, he pressed the pillow in his hands against Sinead's face.

He held it firm, feeling only the slightest bit of resistance as her hollowed-out body tried to keep going, her lungs fighting to get air that was no longer available. Within moments, she relaxed, but still Colin held the pillow, pressing harder, feeling something break under the force of his hands.

He heard some noise leave his mouth, perhaps the beginning of a keen, but he held it in, closing his eyes and pressing harder.

ELEVEN

He stood over the three bodies in the garden, stacked like old mannequins one on top of the other. In his hand he held a petrol can. He doused the bodies with the pungent liquid then dropped the can to the ground. He struck a match, dropped it onto the bodies then stepped back as they were swallowed up by flame.

Colin was numb.

His mind travelled back to earlier.

After dealing with Sinead, Colin had found a baseball bat in the spare room.

He'd gone to the master bedroom, finding Ben on his feet; the dead man's head sloped to one side, tongue protruding, eyes looking up and to the left. It was like his whole body was hanging from some invisible rope.

Colin brought the bat down heavy against his old friend's head. The noise was duller than he expected it to be, and so he hammered again, digging into the soft part of the dead man's brain, his body shaking, a short gasp leaving his lips before he was still.

He recalled bringing the bat down on Chris too, and then his memory blurred into random images of lifting each body in his arms, of carrying them outside to the grass.

The fire roared painfully.

Colin watched Sinead's sweet face through the flames until he couldn't bear it any more.

He left the garden, heading back into the house.

He found Vicky curled up on the sofa, staring into space. He sat down beside her, rubbed her feet aimlessly.

She allowed him but didn't seem to gain any comfort from his massage.

They heard a scream.

Vicky looked to Colin, her eyes like two bright lights.

Colin grabbed the baseball bat, followed the noise.

He entered the spare room.

He found the soldier on the remaining twin bed.

The lad's eyes were open. He stared at Colin. A low rasping sound escaped his lips.

Colin raised the baseball bat, but the soldier cried out again, and this time Colin could make him out.

"Please," he was saying.

TWELVE

24ᵗʰ June

Ciaran was full of pain. It flowed like waves through his mangled body. His breathing was strained, each gasp fighting against broken ribs. Both arms were throbbing, crudely wrapped in a makeshift sling.

He'd been conscious for days now. He wished he hadn't been. He wished he could sleep, but he couldn't. He wished there were drugs he could take, gear he could smoke, but there was neither.

There was a television set at the other side of the room. As Ciaran writhed on the bed, the damn thing played a constant loop of violence and panic.

Colin entered the room. He carried a bottle with him.

He reached into his pocket, dropped a mobile phone onto Ciaran's bed.

"That's yours," he said. "Found it on you when I pulled you from the car. I'd be surprised if it works, mind. My network's packed in. You see, this," and here he pointed at the TV screen, "seems to have spread across the whole of the UK. What you're watching is quite new. Seems Scottish, from the accents, but we rarely hear a commentary anymore."

Ciaran stared at the phone. A little antenna icon appeared in the top left corner.

"The internet's better," the other survivor continued. "A few servers are still connecting. We've AOL here. Some of the other search engines have powered down. Unpaid bills, you think?" Colin laughed, took a glug from his bottle.

"Pick it up for us," Ciaran said to the other man, gesturing to the phone, his one good eye pleading. "Pick it up and search for my mam on the contacts list."

"Your… *man*?" Colin seemed to look at him funny.

"MAM! M.A.M."

"Ah." Colin laughed quietly, reached for the phone. His hands were moving slowly with all the booze he'd consumed. His brow furrowed as he struggled to work out how to use the thing. "Jesus," he said, noticing the antenna icon. "Looks like you've got a signal."

"Middle icon," Ciaran urged. "Address list."

The other man waited for a moment, his eyes meeting Ciaran's. "Look, are you sure you want me to do this?"

Ciaran couldn't understand what he meant, what he possibly *could* mean. Of course he was sure! He needed to talk to his mam, see if she was okay, tell her he was going to come for her, that he was still out there, that he still loved her. His face must have said it all, because the other man nodded, smiled faintly then pressed the CALL button. He looked again at Ciaran.

"Ready?"

"Yes!"

The phone was held to Ciaran's ear.

On the television, he watched a young woman trying to pull away from an older man wearing a suit and tie. The older man's mouth was wrapped around her arm. A stream of blood seeped from the man's mouth.

The number was ringing.

THIRTEEN

The phone lay on the bed.

Ciaran's face was turned away from it, looking out the window at the empty fields that seemed to go on forever, stretching out like a fluorescent desert, many miles from the concrete West Belfast he called home.

He imagined his mam's phone lying in some puddle or ditch up in Newcastle, or anywhere else that lost things seemed to accumulate. Behind the sofa. In a taxi. Anywhere at all apart from in her hand, or at the bottom of the brown leather handbag that never left her side, the bag that contained her life, her medication, her fags, her address book.

Her phone.

If he allowed himself to believe that she still carried the damn thing, then Ciaran would know that his mother was dead.

Tears broke from Ciaran's one good eye. It cried all the harder. His nose streamed with clear snot that he constantly fought to sniff away.

Colin sat beside him. The other man reached over, gently tipping Ciaran's head and wiping his nose and eye every few moments, before leaning back and without as much as a word, allowing Ciaran to continue weeping, exorcising his grief the way it had to be done.

After some time, the tears just seemed to dry up. There was a salty taste in his mouth. It still hurt to breathe, perhaps even more so now.

Ciaran looked over to find the other man. He was still drinking.

Ciaran looked out the window again. Then to the television, still playing the same footage on repeat. "It hasn't reached us then, has it?"

"Not as such…" Colin set the bottle down and Ciaran noticed that his hand was shaking. He tried to steady it. Cleared his throat then continued: "We're fairly isolated out here. Very few neighbours about."

Ciaran nodded, looked back at the phone.

"Still can't believe it's working," Colin said. "You should maybe turn it off, save the battery."

"Yeah." But Ciaran didn't care about the phone anymore. If he had the use of his arms he would probably have opened the window and thrown it as far as he could. "Maybe best to stick it in some drawer. Just in case." He didn't mean any of what he was saying. These words were just something to fill the air, the phone just a focus point, irrelevant amongst the scenes of riots and barbarity on the television screen.

"What's wrong with them?" Ciaran asked.

He watched another scene unfold: an older man sinking his teeth into a nurse at the hospital. The man's face was empty as he attacked, his eyes heavy and tired looking, as if he was bored.

"They're dead," Colin said. He lifted the bottle again, drank from it.

"What do you mean, *dead*?" Ciaran asked.

"I mean, like, not living. Horror movie stuff where people climb out of their own graves."

"Like ghosts?"

"Have you ever watched a zombie film?"

"Of course. I used to love them," Ciaran said.

"Well, that's what seems to be going on here."

Ciaran laughed, but Colin looked at him sternly.

He stopped laughing.

"The guys who own this house," Colin said, "we found them dead when we got here, lying side-by-side. But one of them didn't stay dead. He got up and started moving around. He attacked me, and I had to –" Colin sighed, shook his head bitterly. "Outside is clear, though. Not a sinner for miles. So maybe we can wait it out here. Maybe the army or the government will get their shit together, beat it, and we'll be able to go back to the city."

Ciaran looked back to the screen. It was different footage now. A mob of people were closing around some cops in someone's living room. One of them took his gun out and was threatening to fire.

"Maybe," Ciaran said, but he didn't believe it.

FOURTEEN

Waringstown, Co. Down
28th June

"Shit!" Tom barked.

His chat icon appeared. Agent13 was incoming.

The alert sound had woken Tom suddenly, and he'd knocked over the mug of tea resting on his desk. Forgetting the spilt tea, Tom moved his shaking hand back to the mouse and opened the dialogue box, finding what looked to be a web address link.

"What's this?"

But Agent13 was still typing. A new message appeared.

FOLLOW THE LINK. NO TIME TO EXPLAIN.

A cold sweat ran down Tom's back. He stepped away from his computer.

He'd been watching more videos online. The lab in Belfast, where a dead man climbed out of his gurney and started walking around the room. The infected were all over the net, looking more and more demonic by the day. And they weren't the *only* demons. The demons in Tom's head ran rampant. He'd no pills. Felt more paranoid than ever.

Do I know this man? he mused. *I mean, REALLY know him?*

"Who are you?" he barked at the screen.

He typed the words back to Agent13.

Mere seconds passed before another line appeared:

TOM, IT'S AGENT13. NOT COMPROMISED. TRUST ME.

Tom ran a hand through his greasy hair.

He'd been cyber-chatting to 13 for years. They would talk for hours about everything. Not just truther stuff, but films they enjoyed, life and all the shit it threw at them.

Another message appeared:

NET GOING DOWN SOON. FOLLOW THE LINK OR WE'LL LOSE TOUCH.

Tom smacked a hand against his head.

He looked briefly at the link he was meant to follow. He couldn't focus on it. It was just squiggles and numbers and dots, dancing before his eyes.

"What to do? What to do?" he muttered.

The parrot imitated him, repeating the words back to him, "What to do? What to do?"

Tom sneered at the bird.

He moved back towards the keyboard, banging his reply out angrily on the keyboard. "Are you from the government?" he said as he typed, but he knew it was nonsense even as he said the words.

Seconds passed. The message on screen advised that Agent13 was typing.

TRUST ME

The same bloody message!

Tom growled, grabbing his hair with both hands. He was beyond frustration.

"What to do?" he said again and again to himself, the bird in the cage repeating his mantra.

HURRY, came another message.

Tom swore as he moved back to the computer.

He placed his hand on the mouse and hovered the cursor over the link. Its numbers and dots and squiggles were still dancing, making him dizzy.

He closed his eyes and clicked.

...

Ballynarry, Co. Armagh

The internet was fucked. Every last search engine, including AOL, failed to connect. YouTube was no longer accessible.

Colin leaned back in his chair. Rubbed his beard.

His eyes once again fell upon the characters written on the notebook page he'd found taped to the study wall. He'd tacked it to the corner of the monitor:

12/08

He remembered a conversation he'd had with Chris some time ago. Chris always struck Colin as a paranoid type, always going on about the government and the New World Order, all that American stuff that didn't make much sense to a guy like Colin, a guy who lived his life one day at a time. Chris would recite some date when the world was supposed to end. It was to do with some conspiracy or other.

Was this the date?

Colin looked back at the screen, and an idea struck him.

When he'd moved into Aunt Bell's house, he'd needed to get an internet connection put in. Aunt Bell didn't care for it. 'What's wrong with the television and radio?" she'd said to him. But Colin had experienced some problems getting connected and needed to ring a help desk. They gave him a long number with a few dots to type into the URL bar. Colin remembered it bringing him to his service provider's help page, where the technician could sort out his connection problems for him. All website addresses were coded like this, he'd learned.

He looked back at the numbers he'd found scribbled onto the page.

He clicked on explorer. It didn't connect, just as Colin expected.

He typed the numbers from the page into the URL bar, a full stop between the two dates:

http://12.08.

He pressed the RETURN key.

It didn't connect.

Colin leaned back in his chair, thinking.

Maybe he should put the year in. This year.

He was interrupted by Ciaran's voice from the other room.

Colin stood up, left the study and moved through the hallway.

He opened the kitchen door, finding Ciaran sitting on his makeshift wheelchair.

Vicky stood at the sink, staring out the window in front of her.

Colin followed her gaze.

Several figures stood in their garden, their bodies twisted like old scarecrows, their movements slow and laboured.

"They're here," Ciaran said.

PART FOUR:

THE LIVING AND
THE DEAD

ONE

The Chamber, Co. Armagh
30ᵗʰ July

Dr Miles Gallagher sat in front of his laptop, playing footage from the security cameras.

A crowd of dead people were pushing at the perimeter fence, surrounding The Chamber's Mahon Road base of operations. Their eyes held no emotion. Yet their hands grabbed the wire with aggression, their lips shaping cries of hunger and frustration.

The enemy was at the gate, Gallagher mused. And what a peculiar foe they were.

Gallagher turned away from the screen as several men entered the room.

An older man, the Colonel, stood po-faced at the front, watching as the others filed in. Some of the men sat in the chairs by each workstation, others moving to the back wall, preferring to stand. Once everyone was inside, the Colonel closed the door.

"Gentlemen, at The Chamber we've always worked on the premise that knowledge is power. It's been key to everything we do at this project: our surveillance work, investigative work, as well as our," he cleared his throat, looked to Gallagher, "interrogation work.

"Now I don't know a hell of a lot more than you about what's happening with this virus outbreak, but what I do know I want to share with you right now. Along with our options.

"Things aren't good as you know. Stormont's fallen. They tried everything to contain this thing. First with softer methods, then with more force. They tried quarantine," the Colonel continued. "Locked people in their homes. Sealed up hospitals and community centres. Opened death camps." He waved his hand. "None of it worked, gentlemen. This island is fucked beyond repair. And that leaves you and me with two options: we either stay or we go."

The Colonel looked around the room, expecting a challenge.

Gallagher, the trace of a smile across his long, pale face, followed the Colonel's gaze, finding only nervous eyes looking back.

"We've got seven golden tickets, gentlemen, and a people carrier cleared to go to RAF Aldergrove. There's talk of a chopper lined up to take you to London. We can't confirm or deny that, but God knows it's better than hanging around here, waiting for the fence to give way."

Still no one spoke.

"This hat," said the Colonel, reaching for the military cap on the table beside him, "holds a piece of folded paper for every man in this room, including myself and the good doctor." He looked over at Gallagher, who nodded in agreement. "The rules are simple, gentlemen. We draw from the hat. If you get an 'X', you stay. If the paper has a tick, you go." The Colonel looked again to Gallagher. "So let's begin."

The next few minutes were tense, each man passing along a regimented line to dip their hands in the hat and lift a piece of paper. The Colonel nodded as they passed.

As each man opened their paper, revealing mostly 'X' shapes in red pen, Gallagher could see hopelessness spread across their faces. It seemed like they knew they were in attendance of each other's funerals, standing over these old, knackered computer monitors like gravestones, hands hanging by their sides.

One man pulled a lucky strike, raising his fist in the air and blurting out, "Oh, thank Christ!" But he soon quietened down when the others glared at him with resentment and envy.

The next winner knew not to be so jubilant.

"Final draw," the Colonel announced quietly as the last hand dipped into his cap. He watched the young soldier as he opened the paper, his face saying it all. The Colonel smiled weakly. "Those with the appropriate papers should gather one small bag and assemble by the mess hall in the main campus at 21.30 tomorrow evening," he said. "In the rather unlikely event that someone wishes to give up a golden ticket, you can find me in my quarters. I will be only too happy to arrange a swap. As you were, gentlemen."

The soldiers filed out of the room, conversation muted and uncomfortable as they left. Gallagher stared down at his own piece of paper and the little red cross in its centre. He carefully folded it then dropped it into a nearby paper bin, before he too made for the door.

The Colonel stopped him.

"Doctor Gallagher," he said in a low voice. "A word, if you please."

Gallagher followed the Colonel to a quiet corner of the room.

The Colonel looked to make sure none of the others were in earshot.

"Take this," he said and then slid something into the doctor's lab coat. "We're both getting out of here."

Gallagher said nothing.

The Colonel walked towards the door before turning, then nodding.

Gallagher nodded back.

He reached in his pocket finding a piece of paper with a green tick marked on one side.

Gallagher smiled.

He was just about to leave when he spotted a man sitting at the back of the room. It was Charlie Saville. He was one of the engineers. Not someone used to the horrors of the frontline by any stretch of the imagination.

Charlie was a big man, fond of his food, always one for having a laugh in the mess hall with some of the other lads. He was popular with just about everyone, always a smile on his face or a joke to tell. Yet now, Charlie looked broken. He sat in his small chair like an overgrown schoolchild, face in his hands.

Gallagher approached.

"Come now, Charles," he said. "You're in the army. No room for tears among soldiers." He placed a hand on the big man's shoulder.

Charlie looked up at him. His eyes were like plugholes, deep set in his generously-sized face.

"Sorry," he said.

"Quite alright," Gallagher said.

He lifted his hand from the other man's shoulder, pulling up a chair beside him.

"You see, the human condition doesn't prepare us for this sort of thing," Gallagher continued, smiling. "Sudden death we're much better with. Something we can't plan or prepare for. When a man first joins the army, that's what he fears the most. The bullet or the mine. An attack from insurgents.

"Those are fears that we learn to control, to submerge within ourselves, only to arise mere moments from the end. If we're unlucky. But *this*," and here Gallagher lifted the ticket that sat beside Charlie, holding it in the air between them, "this is something alien to men like us. And altogether more brutal."

Charlie sat in his chair, sniffing back tears.

He reached into his shirt pocket, produced his wallet. He unclipped the button, sliding a photograph out, offered it to Gallagher.

Gallagher looked down at it, expecting to hear about the man's wife, his family. But the picture looked more like something Charlie had cut out of a magazine. It was a young girl. She was pretty, maybe someone famous.

"I carry this around with me," Charlie began. "Sometimes, when the other lads are telling me about a deployment to Iraq or Afghanistan, and they're all miserable and drunk and showing me pictures of their wives and babies, I show them this. And they laugh." Charlie's eyes narrowed. "Do you know why they laugh?"

Gallagher didn't.

"They laugh because they know I could never get a girl like that. Because I'm a born loser. Big Charlie, the guy you go to when you want a drink or a game of cards or to hack into some new porn site on the computer. That's all I mean to them. That's all I've meant to *anyone*." He threw the picture down, folding his arms and leaning back in his chair.

Gallagher sat for a moment, staring at Charlie intently.

He didn't feel pity for the man. Gallagher didn't *do* pity. He was a man for whom feelings and emotions and needs were useless, mere distractions from work.

He lived by routine – a routine that involved eating at a certain time, drinking at another. Using the toilet, having sex – these were necessary evils. They had a time and place to meet the basic needs of his body, to serve the human shell he found himself inhabiting. But deep down, Gallagher resented all of these things.

He didn't like his own humanity, but he liked to study that of others. He liked to explore what made people tick and what made them *not* tick. And he enjoyed studying Charlie.

Gallagher reached into his pocket and produced the piece of paper the Colonel gave him. Carefully, he took Charlie's huge palm, placed his golden ticket into it, and then closed Charlie's fingers over.

He smiled as Charlie looked up, confusion in his face.

"Perhaps you were born a loser," Gallagher said in a low voice. "But you won't die one."

TWO

31ˢᵗ July

The Colonel sat up from his bed, looking towards the picture on the wall.

It was the picture of a sunrise. Painted by his grandfather, a veteran from the Great War. This was a talented man, a creative man, who had left his family to be gunned down in the damp, muddy trenches of France.

The Colonel suddenly felt a sneeze come on, the blast spreading across the glass front of the picture. He was just about to wipe it away with his handkerchief when he noticed something that made him pause: there was a little blood amongst the droplets. Not much, just a few speckles.

He washed his face in the sink. He stared at the mirror, his eyes wide open as if frozen.

There was a tickle in his throat, a cough, wheezier than expected.

The Colonel laughed to himself, thinking back on how his mother used to call him a hypochondriac and how he hadn't understood what that meant, thinking it had something to do with the lies he would tell her to bunk off school. The Colonel, now a man in his sixties, wondered why the hell that thought had come to him now. But they said your life flashed before your eyes before death, didn't they?

The soap slipped out of his hands and into the sink.

The tap continued to flow, the soap's lather happily blowing more bubbles as the water got hotter and the steam rose up to create a thin veneer over his reflection in the mirror.

A tear surprised him, running down his cheek. He thought it was sweat, at first. But when he wiped the steam from the mirror, the Colonel found his eyes were glassy.

A lump gathered in his throat, and he wanted to cough it up, expel it like some sort of demon.

…

Later, the Colonel was fully dressed, washed and shaved, sitting on the edge of his perfectly made bed.

He had worked through his denial swiftly, as men like him ought to, men who had tasted the very worst of what life had to offer, who had lived dangerously, who had killed.

He unfolded the little piece of paper with the green tick. He had made it himself and made sure it ended up in his own palm. He had fixed the raffle and felt no shame about that. This was no time for altruism; this was the time for survival. He reckoned that anyone else in the room would have done the same, were they in charge.

He held a picture of his family in his hand. It showed his wife, his daughter, her husband and their children. He wondered if he would ever get to see them again. He wondered if they were at home in Birmingham or exiled somewhere else.

There were reports that the flu had now spread to Europe. They were unconfirmed, of course, but wasn't everything now? Nothing was certain anymore. Just rumours – and rumours of rumours. Who could be sure that the aircraft he'd been informed of was even going to leave RAF Aldergrove? Maybe it had already left.

There was a knock at his door.

"Who is it?" His voice came out higher and more strained than he planned.

"Gallagher."

"Good. Come in."

The door opened, revealing the project's longstanding doctor. The Colonel nodded simply and gestured that the other man take the only seat in the room while he remained sitting on the edge of the bed.

"I came as quick as I could."

The Colonel laughed. "Really no need. We both know how this thing pans out. It's not like there's a cure, is there? An antibiotic you can give me to make it pass?"

"No, there's not."

The Colonel studied the doctor's face, finding no emotional investment.

"I've contacted RAF Aldergrove," he said. "I've advised them that I'm not going tonight, that I've been infected by the virus and am to be quarantined at once."

"Of course." Gallagher's voice remained calm, matter-of fact. It was like they were talking about incomplete paperwork or some new procedure to be implemented.

The Colonel sighed. "Good, that's settled, then."

Gallagher nodded, smiled.

Jesus, give me something, the Colonel mused.

"What's it like outside?" he asked.

"We've strengthened the perimeter," Gallagher said. "But they're surrounding us in fairly heavy numbers. Some of the men are not dealing with the threat so well. There've been a number of suicides."

The Colonel shook his head. "Well things are perhaps even *worse* at Aldergrove, Gallagher. I think they've lost any structure they had. I've asked them to send a replacement down to relieve me of my command and, rather surprisingly, they've found someone willing to make the trip, despite the obvious hazards. He's to arrive within the next twenty-four hours."

Gallagher nodded. "I'll have an interview room set up for your quarantine, sir," he said. He went to say something else about the quarantine arrangements, then hesitated. "May I ask who the replacement is for the project?"

"Major Connor Jackson. I believe you used to work together, back in the heyday of the Chamber?"

Gallagher brightened. "Yes indeed."

"Well, no doubt you would have a lot to catch up on, if you weren't leaving for Aldergrove."

"I'm staying, sir."

The Colonel was taken aback. "Staying? Why the hell would you do a thing like that?"

"You say yourself that Aldergove has regressed, sir," Gallagher explained. "But I'd made my mind up to stay before any of this news. You see, I may not be the most conventional of soldiers. You and I both know that. But I'm still a soldier, and a *good* soldier never leaves their post until the job is done."

The Colonel's face reddened. He dipped his eyes to the cap in his hands, looking at the crest. He would never have thought that a man like Gallagher could ever better him when it came to moral fibre. For a moment he was silent, perhaps a little more of his life flashing before him, his conscience having a last ditch attempt at weighing up the good against the bad.

"I know how things will turn out for me, Gallagher," he said. "And I want you to allow me to regress as nature sees fit."

"I understand, sir."

"No doubt you do," the Colonel said. "I'm not a stupid man," he continued. "I know what this will mean for me." He pointed a finger to the picture above his bed. "Got my grey matter from him up there, I'm told." He smiled, eyes moistening.

"I know what some people in here think of me. I've heard them talk of me in, shall we say, less-than-savoury terms, but I won't have anyone think of me as a coward. I'm going to see this damn virus through, for worse as well as better. So, you use me as you see fit, doctor," the Colonel said, "especially if you can find out more about what makes those dead bastards tick."

Gallagher didn't as much as blink. The Colonel found himself wondering if the doctor had *ever* blinked in his whole damn life. Did he *need* to blink, or was he, as many would surmise, merely a machine? Some kind of android or robot.

His voice remained characteristically steady and measured when he spoke. "Quite, sir."

The Colonel placed both hands on his knees, his sweaty palms immediately darkening the fabric.

"So this Connor Jackson," he said finally to Gallagher. "The officer to replace me. Tell me more about him."

THREE

5th August

"Willis here. Go ahead, base."

Pzzzt. Landing area's been breached. We're trying to clean it up, but you'll have to hold back until we clear you some space. Pzzt.

The pilot was returning from his daily round. Surveillance of their immediate locality, checking for signs of life. But as time went on and more people fell to the virus, the dead began to heavily outnumber the living. He'd thought the strong, high fences would be enough to hold them back. But he'd thought wrong. The hundred or so bodies at the fences soon became two hundred.

Then a thousand.

As he continued his approach and got a bird's eye view of what the camp was dealing with, Willis had the urge to turn back.

And go where?

Pzzt. Base to Wessex. Willis, did you copy that last message? Pzzt.

Willis swallowed hard.

He looked to Davis, his co-pilot, sitting beside him. The man seemed every bit as nervous as Willis felt.

"W-we copy, base. Keep us posted."

Willis hung a left, initiating a circle of the camp. Despite his fears, he dipped lower to get a better look at what they were up against.

This close, it looked less like a mass of bodies. He could tell one apart from another. There were men and woman of all ages. Children. All wearing different clothes; all sporting different hairstyles.

These were people, Willis was reminded. They once had lives and families. Folks who loved them, folks who cared, who sent them birthday cards once a year and thought about them coming over at Christmas.

Willis tried not to think of his own family as he looked at the dead: his two boys, now grown up and married, his estranged wife. It was difficult not to wonder what fate had befallen them, whether they were quarantined in their own homes, or like the poor bastards down there.

Life was fast becoming a battle that looked impossible to win.

The dead seemed to be evolving, becoming more conscious. While united in their desire to break down the fencing and get to the base, it was tempting to think they were also in competition with each other. See who could make it through first, who could make the *first* kill, the *most* kills.

The pilot's eye was drawn to the fence. One section was beginning to give, near the landing area.

Willis spotted some soldiers moving towards the breached fence. Unlike the dead, these men looked exactly alike, wearing the same yellow plastic suits.

A few others hung back from the main offensive. From what he could make out, Willis reckoned they were carrying long strips of metal and welding equipment to reinforce the fence.

The main group moved en masse towards the breached fence, setting up position about fifteen metres from it. They aimed their rifles in unison and held their position.

Willis held tight above the action, noticing how some of the dead below had clocked him and were now looking up.

The whole scene reminded him of some of his later days in the army, providing support to the police and army during riots in Belfast. People then hadn't acted a lot differently from the dead he watched now. They mutilated their own territory with abandonment, burning cars and attacking the military Land Rovers that flanked them.

The fence gave way.

The first line of soldiers opened fire as the dead began to claw through the gaps, the hail of gunfire doing little to dissuade the heavy numbers pouring through.

From his vantage position in the sky, Willis was beginning to think that the dead might have compromised the base beyond rescue.

He looked to his co-pilot.

The younger man stared back, and Willis could almost read his face: *Let's go*, it said. *Let's just leave.* And Willis was certainly tempted.

But then another idea struck him.

Pulling back on the stick, Willis returned to the other side of the fence to face the back of the attacking crowd of dead. He then pushed forward on the stick, bringing the Wessex down towards the ground.

"What the hell are you doing?" Davis protested.

"Trust me," Willis said.

He reached the ground level, pulling back just before the Wessex struck dirt.

"Good girl," he whispered to the dashboard. "Hold steady."

She'd been his favourite helicopter to fly throughout his career. Although retired, the early days of the virus saw all of the newer vehicles freed up for more important work. The Chamber was left with the job of securing this old Westland Wessex, and Willis had had little difficulty in doing so, regardless of the legality. Like many other intangible constructs that society built up, property rights fell by the wayside when things got bad.

Of course in his short time with The Chamber, Willis had learned that this was a project well used to operating outside of the law. The law was for the likes of those poor bastards down below, the masses, the subordinates. The Chamber knew no such boundaries.

"Come on," Willis urged. "You can see us! Come on!"

He was almost level with the dead, now. Close enough to see the whites of their eyes, as the old saying went.

Those at the back of the crowd were turning towards him. Some believed their senses were dulled with the virus. But they could certainly *feel* the vibrations coming off the Wessex's propellers, the gust of wind that beat upon their drawn faces.

Slowly but surely, the dead at the rear of the crowd became curious. They began to move towards the helicopter. Soon, the dead at the front began to follow, losing interest in the destructive hail of bullets in favour of the more interesting vibrations from the helicopter.

Willis backed away as they came towards him, careful not to allow them too close, lest the circulating air force them off their feet. He continued to inch back as they approached.

"Base, you're clear to mend the fence. I'm drawing the crowd away. It should get lighter up front."

Pzzt. Roger that. Pzzt.

The bodies moved closer to the windscreen, some falling back with the force of wind from the propellers. Willis pulled back, gently encouraging the poor bastards to follow him.

He could see the soldiers behind the fence moving in to carry out the reinforcement work. Willis held the helicopter steady.

The work was done swiftly, the welders pulling back, replaced again by men with guns.

Pzzt. Base to Wessex. You're clear to land. Nice work on drawing those fuckers away. Pzzt.

Willis looked to the co-pilot and exhaled.

"Roger that, base," he said.

…

The two pilots moved through the outer buildings of the Mahon Road Army camp, finding a staircase leading down towards an underground part of the complex.

The closeness of the air hit him as they descended the stairs. It was the distinct aroma of sweaty men. They had been afforded some freedom from this smell in the helicopter. Now it seemed stronger than ever.

They reached the bottom of the staircase, moving along a short corridor.

They entered the control room.

This was the main base of operations for The Chamber and where most of the soldiers now assembled. One wall was covered with monitors. A line of computers faced the monitors, several men sitting at them. The computers were older models yet still seemed to work okay. In fact, *everything* was dated down here, as if in descending the staircase, Willis and Davis had stepped back in time.

Everything was dirty, too. Sleeping bags and old clothes littered the floor. Cans of beer and ashtrays surrounded each workstation. It seemed wrong: these were soldiers; they should be disciplined, organised.

A fifty-something veteran, Wills hailed from the old school. He'd joined the army over thirty years before, with a half-baked desire for action and excitement, clueless as to what else he could do with his life. A stint in the Falklands War had him rethinking his choice of career; his time in Northern Ireland left him completely disillusioned. But he stuck with it, nonetheless, perhaps spurred on by friends and family back home in Manchester who saw him as something of a hero.

But Willis didn't feel like a hero. And in all the time he'd spent in the army, he'd never met one. War was no place for heroes.

His own role had rarely involved being in the thick of it, action-wise. He always felt protected inside his metal bird, but the people he transported weren't as fortunate.

He would drop them off close to whatever mission or riot or assignment they were tasked with. The sounds of the fight would surround him, muted due to the ever-spinning blades of his aircraft.

Willis would see the looks of those men as they sat in the back of the helicopter, some of them younger than his own two boys back home. He would smell their fear, damp and heavy like rain clouds. And then he would release them, only to return some hours or days later, often to find the same men on stretchers, their own lust for action brutally realised. To Willis, that was the worst part of his job – seeing their eyes again, sometimes living, sometimes dead as they were placed back in the helicopter, looking towards him as if to say, *you brought me here and left me to die.*

And now, there was nothing but death around him. The dead filled the world like ghosts, haunting him. Reminding him of all the men he'd carried to hell and back.

Willis entered the control room, loosening the catch of his helmet and pulled it off. He ran one hand through his thick, grey hair.

One of the men looked up and nodded as he entered. Willis guessed it was the soldier he'd been talking to on the comms. None of the others so much as acknowledged him, never mind bothering to ask how today's recon went. It didn't matter. Nothing mattered when you were drinking and carrying on like most of this lot.

Another man entered from the other side of the room. His name was Connor Jackson. He was meant to be the Commanding Officer of The Chamber yet seemed every bit as dishevelled as his subordinates.

Major Jackson had replaced the Colonel after the old man fell ill. The Colonel was no angel, by any stretch of the imagination, but he'd a certain candour about him that endeared Willis. Jackson was just a lethargic and drunken old bastard. An evil bastard at that.

This wasn't Jackson's first time in this complex. He'd been CO here before, back in the bad old days, when The Chamber acted as the British government's post-internment interrogation facility.

On transferring to The Chamber's team in June, Willis had made it his business to find out as much as he could about what went on. He accessed files without clearance. Read things not meant for his eyes. Even after thirty odd years of service, taking in deployment in both Northern Ireland and the Falklands, what he read in those files shocked him to his very core.

And Jackson's name was prominent.

His most notorious work involved the interrogation of an IRA operative by the name of Pat Flynn. Flynn was privy to information The Chamber needed. When Flynn refused to talk, even resisting Gallagher's most excruciating powers of persuasion, Jackson had murdered the man's young son in cold blood.

Willis found a chair at the back of the room and sat himself down.

Jackson looked to the front wall of the control room, where a large wall screen was mounted. It was playing footage from the various surveillance cameras The Chamber had hidden around Belfast and surrounding areas.

"What's going on, Private?" Jackson said to one of the men, pointing to the screen.

But the Private was lost in the bottle, a shambles of his former self. He offered nothing sensible in reply.

Jackson pulled up a chair beside another man, started drinking.

The soldier next to the Major announced merrily that he was taking bets on a number of situations playing out on screen.

Willis looked to the screen, watching a man with a cricket bat tackle a crowd of dead in Castlecourt Shopping Centre. Those men sober enough to make sense of the screen were jeering along, waving makeshift betting slips.

"What are these?" the Major asked, ignoring the revelry and pointing to the screens, retrieving his glasses to get a better look.

"Surveillance cameras," replied one of the soldiers.

"Yes I can see that, Private," Jackson snapped. "But where are they watching and why?"

Dr Miles Gallagher entered the room, his yellow plastic suit covered in blood. He spent most of his time in The Chamber's interrogation rooms, where he'd set up a makeshift research lab. Willis shivered, wondering just what type of research the good doctor was involved in.

The men quieted somewhat as the doctor made his entrance.

Gallagher filled the Major in on the locations of the cameras and the work their footage related to: old cases that The Chamber had been working on prior to everything going south. One of the cameras focused on an apartment block in Finaghy, just south of Belfast.

Willis remembered reading about the case.

Brigita Fico, an illegal immigrant working within a prostitution ring in Belfast. Her flat was under surveillance by The Chamber as part of their contract with the Home Office. Brigita was quite the stunner, and Willis wondered, as he read, how someone so beautiful could get caught up in something so ugly.

"Good God," Jackson said. "Did you see that?"

Willis looked back to the screen.

They homed in on one of the bedrooms in the Fico flat.

"There's someone moving inside there," Jackson said.

"Probably one of the dead, sir," Gallagher countered.

"No, look closer," Jackson countered.

Willis watched as a small shadow appeared in the room, scurrying across the floor to retrieve something unrecognisable. The image was captured, refocused and enlarged.

It looked like a child.

Gallagher looked up, more interested now. "A survivor?"

"Has to be," Jackson said. "Moving too fast to be one of the dead."

Willis quietly lifted his smart phone, tipping its screen subtly at his desk to film the footage playing onscreen. He held the phone steady, praying that nobody would turn around and question him, that everyone's eyes would remain glued to the screen.

An expectant silence fell upon the room.

"We have to find out more," Jackson said, finally. "Where's Willis?" He looked around the room. "Could have sworn I just saw him…"

Willis pulled his phone down just as Jackson's eyes fell upon him.

"Ah, there you are. Gonna need you in the air again, soldier."

"Yes sir," Willis said, sliding the phone into his pocket.

"I want you to check out that apartment block in Finaghy," Jackson continued. "Preliminary surveillance run. I want to know how many infected are in and around the building, if there are any more survivors there, and what the best way to enter the building might be. Clear?"

"Clear, sir," Willis replied.

"And maintain full radio contact throughout the run."

"Roger that, sir."

Willis pulled himself to his feet, looking around the room for Davis, his co-pilot.

His mind returned to the phone, now hidden in his pocket. He'd check the footage later when he was on his own. He hoped it would be clear enough. But right now, he needed to get back in the air and check that building out. A survivor within a quarantined flat: the possibilities such could present were immeasurable.

He smiled to himself as he made his way back through the building.

This was big.

Tom was going to love it.

FOUR

Waringstown, Co. Down

The long wooden box sat at the back of his wardrobe, and Martin hadn't as much as touched it in twenty years. Dust seemed ingrained into the wood now, its once vivid blue having given way to a dull grey. Its lock showed signs of rust; the hinges browned at the edges.

Martin pulled the box out, lifting it from the wardrobe and setting it on the bed.

His back was straining, perhaps more due to his age than how heavy the object was. He straightened, rubbing his spine.

For a minute, Martin simply stood looking at the box. It brought back a number of memories – days that he was glad had passed, dangerous days in active service in strange lands.

A single parent, Martin had often left his daughter in the care of friends, colleagues and neighbours. Sometimes those people wouldn't speak English as their first language, and a thought crossed Martin's mind.

Is that why she went for the dummy?

A man whose sparingly-used voice was less obtuse than the German or French or Algerian that her ears would have heard so much as a child.

Martin fumbled in his pocket, finding the bunch of keys that he always carried. He thumbed along the key ring until he found the smallest key then used it to open the padlock on the wooden box.

He opened the lid to uncover an old double-barrelled shotgun.

It was his unit's gift to him as he left active service: *Something to remember us by*, they'd said.

How could he forget?

There was movement out in the hall.

"Daddy?"

It was Lize.

He took another look at the gun.

"Just a minute," he said.

"No, Daddy, come quick."

Martin made his way through to the landing. Her bedroom door was open, and she stood by the window, looking out.

"What's wrong? What is it?"

"Down there," she said.

Martin joined her by the window. Lize pointed down onto the road in front of the house, where a single figure stood.

"Isn't that Mr Gracy?" she asked.

If it were Gracy, Martin surmised, then Gracy was dead.

They'd encountered the dead already, of course. And each time, Martin was insistent that the survivors lie perfectly still and quiet until they moved on. But today he was angry. Today he wanted to show them what they would get if they kept coming here and threatening his family.

"Stay here," he said to Lize.

"Daddy, where are you going?"

"Where's Jamie?"

"Don't know. Maybe downstairs with Shaun?"

"Well, you just stay here."

"Daddy?"

Martin returned to the wooden box in his bedroom. He lifted the gun from the case, wiping it down with a handkerchief from his bedside table drawer. He found a box of ammo underneath it. There were only two cartridges left inside. He inserted both into the gun and snapped it closed.

Lize was at the door.

"Daddy?" she said. "Where are you going with *that*?"

"I told you to stay in the room."

He pushed past her, descending the stairs. He found Shaun and Jamie in the living room.

"Jamie," Martin said, "Go upstairs to your mother."

Shaun looked up at him, went to say something, but Martin ignored him and moved through to the kitchen.

The front door was boarded up, so the side door leading into the garage remained the only way outside.

Martin entered the garage, locking the door behind him, sealing his family into the house.

He sat the shotgun against the wall, unlocked the garage door and pulled it open.

Martin retrieved the gun and ducked under the partially opened door. Moved out into the yard, towards the front of the house.

He found Jack Gracy standing in the middle of the road, his head twisted, eyes fixed on some unknown spot across the fields. He almost looked alive, and for a moment, Martin doubted himself.

"Jack?"

Gracy seemed to notice him, turning.

"Jack, are you okay?"

But Jack was *far* from okay. As he turned his head, Martin noticed a slice of skin hanging from his face like dried up wallpaper. His lips were partially removed, as if one side of his face had been burned. His eyes were grey, the pupils invisible.

Martin wasted no time in dealing with Gracy. He raised the shotgun, took aim, then pulled the hammer back and fired. The blast took most of Gracy's head away. The dead man spun on his feet, falling. His body lay twitching on the ground.

Martin moved cautiously towards the corpse before a scream from the house startled him.

He turned sharply, finding Lize at the upstairs window, screaming and pointing.

"Get away from there," he shouted at her.

"Daddy, there's more of them!"

Martin turned quickly, finding an empty road stretching out to fields on either side. The sun was behind the trees, shadows cloaking the road.

Where are they?!

He heard a shuffle from his right. Something moved in the shade of the trees. More commotion, this time on his left.

"Show yourselves, you bastards!" Martin growled.

His shotgun moved from left to right, trying to lock in on a target. A light wind unsettled some branches and Martin pointed the gun in their direction, eyes searching.

"Daddy, get back inside!" came Lize's voice from the window again.

He started to step backwards, gun still primed, eyes still busy searching.

Something stepped out from the shade, and Martin fired immediately, his shaking hands upsetting his normally good aim to clip the thing's shoulder. It fell back with the impact, lying for some moments before getting up again. Its arm was hanging by sinews, blood rushing from the wound.

"Jesus Christ," Martin muttered, just as yet another one stepped into view to his left.

He raised the gun, before realising it was empty. He brought his aim down.

Several other bodies were closing in on him from the right, their infernal sniffs and grunts loud and obnoxious.

Martin swore loudly.

Damn stupid coming out like this! What was he thinking?!

He turned tail and ran back towards the garage, stooping under the partially opened door. He rested the gun against the wall. Closed the door down quickly. Locked it, his jittering hands struggling with the mechanism, then checking twice to make sure it was tight.

Martin lifted his gun again, moved through the garage, into the kitchen, pausing to lock the door leading to the garage from the inside. He stared at the locked door, decided to lean a chair from the table against the door handle.

He moved past Shaun, taking Jamie by the hand and leading him upstairs to Lize. The child started to weep, running to the arms of his mother, Lize's own eyes damp as she embraced him.

"Close the blinds," Martin said to Lize, moving to his own bedroom where he did the same. He came back into the hallway. "We need to be quiet. They'll move on if they forget we're here. They always do."

"What's happening?" It was Shaun, coming up the stairs, his voice loud in the enforced silence.

"Shut him up!" Martin half-whispered to Lize.

He was on the floor now, beckoning to everyone else to do likewise and lie low. Both hands still clutched the rifle.

"Shaun, there's more of them out there," Lize cried.

Shaun moved to the window, looking down upon the road at the front of the house.

Martin looked to Lize, his face incredulous and panicked, "Tell him to get out of sight!"

Lize left Jamie and went to Shaun, tugging on his arm. "Get down! Daddy says to get down!"

Shaun shook his wife's hand away. How dare she treat him like that in front of the boy? How dare she talk down to him, talk to him like he was a –

He remembered a family day out, when Jamie was very little. They'd gone to the park. Fed the ducks, played on the swings – did all the things a child liked to do in front of his parents and grandpa. Shaun went to buy some ice cream for them all. He'd come out to see Martin talking to Lize.

"Why did you have to marry that –?" he'd been saying.

That what? That dummy? That spastic?

And the worst of it was Lize just accepted it. Let that bastard talk like that about her husband.

Shaun's inner pop psychologist wasn't stretched to guess the reasons why, of course – entering this world by taking the life of her mother was bound to take its toll on a girl. The doctors called it a miracle birth but for Lize, it was more of a curse.

Maybe that's why she'd had the affair.

They still hadn't talked about it. Yet in the heat of this moment, the image of the photo he found in Lize's travel bag came back to him. The words scribbled in the card, with the Eiffel Tower on the front, now ingrained within Shaun's memory:

Love always…

Alan

And then it suddenly clicked as to why Shaun had recognised the dead man walking in that lab footage they'd been playing, over and over again before the TV shut down. It was the man from the picture. The man his wife was having an affair with… he was sure of it!

Lize went to tug his arm but Shaun shook her off.

"Alan," he said to her. "The man you were seeing behind my back. Where did you meet him?"

Her face creased in disbelief. "*What?*"

"Where did you meet him!" He was shouting now. He watched as Jamie leaned in closer to his mum.

"What does any of that matter now?" Lize protested. "Shaun, please. You're scaring the child. And you're shouting! And those things –"

"Your Alan is one of *those things*," Shaun cut in. "He was on that video footage. He attacked the doctor, and they cut his head –"

"Don't," Lize cut in. "Please, Shaun. Not now."

"Why not?! What was it about him? Go on, I want to know."

Martin rose to his feet, faced Shaun. "Shut up," he said. "Shut up, or I swear to God I will *shut you up*."

Shaun stared at him. "Have a go then, old man. See how far it gets you."

Lize looked at Shaun incredulously. "Why are you doing this?" she asked him. "*Why?*"

Why indeed? Shaun mused.

Was it because this was the end, their swan song, and they needed to talk this thing out? Or maybe he'd just had enough: all that pent up rage due to blow any day. Being locked up with a cunt like Martin for weeks only sped up the process.

Martin went to grab Shaun, but the younger man pushed him away.

He went to follow through, but Martin's gaze moved to the window, his attention suddenly drawn away from Shaun's angry glare.

Shaun looked to Lize and Jamie, both of them looking similarly spooked.

"What is it?" he asked, shaking the older man by the collar. "Tell me!"

Martin turned, looked him square in the face.

"I think they've broken into the house," he said.

FIVE

"The kitchen," Lize said.

Martin looked to Shaun. There was fear in the other man's eyes.

He pulled away from Shaun, went to move, but Shaun grabbed him again.

Martin looked up.

"I can help," Shaun said to him.

Martin seemed to think on that for a while and then nodded.

Shaun released him.

Martin unsheathed the knife from his belt. Checked the blade. Handed it to Shaun.

He grabbed the gun.

Both men went to go down the stairs, but Martin hesitated, looked at the gun before setting it against the wall.

"What are you doing? You're going to need that!" Shaun said.

"Empty," Martin replied, his voice raised.

They descended the stairs, Shaun letting Martin go first, despite being unarmed.

They reached the hallway.

Martin reached for the living room door. Nodded to Shaun then opened it.

Shaun was first through the door, his knife ready. In the corner he noticed Fred, the dog barking angrily at the dining room door.

Martin followed him in, the older man's eyes searching the room.

He called to Fred, and the dog wagged his tail enthusiastically but continued barking.

Shaun grabbed Fred by the collar, pulling him back. "Go on," he said. "Get out of here." But the dog wasn't for moving, struggling back towards the door.

"Leave him," Martin said.

The old man's eyes were drawn to the fireplace, finding a brass poker discarded in the ashes. He grabbed it, weighing it up in his hands. Looked to Shaun, then to the dining room door, and nodded.

Shaun reached for the door handle, pulling it open.

He stepped back, looked through the doorway.

The kitchen was jammed full of the dead. Through the dense crowd and plague of flies filling the air like smoke, Shaun noticed the back door hanging off its hinges.

"Fuck!" the younger man said.

He turned the knife in his hands, wondering just what the hell he was going to do with it.

Fred acted first, leaping into the crowd, snarling.

Martin was next.

As one of the dead struggled to make sense of the vicious dog, the older man grabbed it by the collar, pulling it through the door with one hand and then bringing the poker down across its head with the other.

It reacted, eyes alert, reaching for Martin, but the old man was quick, turning the poker skilfully then ramming it through the dead thing's open mouth, pinning it against the dining room wall. He held it there, the creature's arms flailing, trying to grab hold of its attacker.

"Do something!" Martin yelled at Shaun.

Shaun stepped forward, taking the knife and jamming it into the dead man's left eye. Through gritted teeth, he watched the thing scream as he twisted the blade deeper, blood and flesh spitting out from the wound, Martin still holding the creature firm with the poker. Finally, its hands fell by its side, and Martin released it, allowing the body to fall to the floor.

Another two were on them immediately, lunging from the kitchen, arms reaching aimlessly.

Shaun wasn't ready for them. His knife was on the floor, still buried in the first cadaver's eye. He grabbed his attacker by the shoulders, fought to keep its snapping jaws from his face.

Martin stepped back, busting his attacker's head wide open with his first swing then finishing the job with his second.

Shaun called out for help, all the while struggling to keep his attacker's rotten teeth at arm's length.

Martin brought the poker down heavy on the thing's head, splitting it like an overripe melon, blood soaking the younger man as he turned his face away.

The blood was in his eyes. Shaun couldn't see.

Silence rang as ever in his head.

His sense of smell was all he had now, the fetid breath of his attacker replaced by the overpowering stench of the whole damn pack.

Shaun was terrified, heart almost exploding from his chest.

Both arms shot out, trying to make sense of his surroundings. He staggered about like an old drunk, eyes still smarting, squeezed tight against the contaminating blood. He struggled against the onslaught of flies, swarming around his face, nose and mouth. He tried to catch his breath despite the obnoxious invasion clogging his airways.

Tears ran down his face, diluting the blood. Shaun opened one eye, just in time to dodge the affections of a rather scantly-clad girl, lipstick and blood spread across her face like jam.

She reached again for him, baring her teeth, the perfectly aligned veneers chomping down.

But Martin brought her flirtations to an end, swinging the brass poker down hard on her once pretty head, spilling her brains against the dining room wall.

The old man grabbed Shaun, shook him.

"Get it together!" he yelled. "I need you!"

Shaun nodded.

He looked back to the kitchen spotting Fred ripping at the throat of a felled cadaver, his tail wagging.

But still they came, driving once more through the dining room doorway. And still Martin battled, smashing through their mass with his poker, spreading blood and bile and brain alike, steadying himself and then striking again.

"I've no weapon!" Shaun yelled, but that wasn't enough for a man like Martin.

"Your fists," came his reply.

Shaun clenched his teeth, stepped forward, belting the nearest of the pack, following through with a left hook, sweeping the thing from its feet.

Martin finished the job, spearing the felled cadaver with the poker.

The older man was tiring, his hands shaking with exhaustion, sweat lashing off his face. But this was no time to stop. They needed to beat their way through to the back door, secure it. Despite the odds stacked heavily against them.

Just when Shaun thought all was lost, a hand fell against his shoulder. He looked around, finding Lize.

"Get out of the way!" she screamed.

Both men moved.

Fred looked up at her voice, spotted the gun then made himself scarce.

Lize fired, her first blast ripping into the chest of an approaching dead man. Her second shot, equally as cavalier as the first, took the head off the next cadaver, spreading it across his undead mates.

She looked to her father, smiled.

"I found another box of shells in the spare room," she said.

Martin patted her back. "Let *us* finish it," he said, looking to Shaun.

Lize stepped back obediently.

Martin rushed the remaining dead, his poker swinging. Fred followed suit, reappearing from whatever hiding place he'd found, tugging at one of the dead men's legs, another tripping over him, sprawling across the kitchen floor.

Their numbers were seriously depleted.

Shaun spotted the first one he'd felled, unsheathed his knife from its eye then jumped into the action, slicing a confused looking woman's throat with his first swing, finishing her with his second.

They were winning.

But then he saw Jamie.

His son was somehow in the kitchen.

His mother reached for the boy, screaming, but Jamie was too quick, heading for the back door, trying to push it closed.

Martin went to help secure it, but a sudden grab from one of the few remaining dead connected, the damn thing's mouth curling around the boy's hand.

"No!" Shaun screamed.

SIX

6th August

The three remaining survivors at Martin's house sat around the kitchen table. Not a single word had been spoken for over an hour. Each of them had cried, sometimes on their own, sometimes together, the hollow sounds of their sobs all but mirroring the low moans from outside.

The dead were brutally persistent, still pushing and beating and crying against the back door even now, despite the heartache they had already caused.

Inside, the corpses of their slain brothers and sisters remained on the floor where they'd fallen. After twenty-four hours in their company, the place reeked of their infection, but none of the survivors had the stomach to move them.

Shaun slammed his fist on the table.

"Fuck!" he yelled, fresh tears breaking from his eyes.

He still couldn't believe it. Jamie – *his only son, for Christ's sake* – had been quarantined. It was too dangerous for him to remain among them. He could turn at any time, day or night, so they'd been left with no choice but to lock the boy in the garage. They were to leave him to die in there alone. And that didn't seem right.

He was still alive. Shaun could hear him crying even now.

It wasn't fair.

Sure, the risks to all of their lives were obvious, but Jamie seemed somehow exempt to Shaun. Immune, even. But when the dead broke into the house and Jamie – *his little soldier* – tried to help repel them…

No. Still not fair.

Shaun weighed everything up in terms of effort. People who tried hard should survive.

He'd made the effort with his own life. Achieved despite his deafness. Learned to speak, read; all in a language that made no sense to him, a language that was intangible, relayed without sound.

He had made the effort with Jamie too. Taken him out of a falling city, retreated to the countryside. Shaun had even put aside his difficulties with Martin to ensure the boy's safety.

Surely that was enough!

He looked to Lize.

His wife wore a strained look. It reminded Shaun of her face when going through labour, giving birth to Jamie. He remembered holding her hand, the silent screams he saw her make, the sweat like mist across her skin.

The shape of his little boy's mouth as he made his first cry…

"This isn't right!" Shaun protested.

He grabbed the handle of the door leading to the garage, twisting it.

"Don't be a fool!" Martin yelled, rising up from his seat. He went to stop Shaun, tried to prise the younger man's hands from the door handle as he reasoned with him, "Think about your wife, for God's sake!"

Shaun was only able to catch bits of what Martin was saying, reading his lips while both men struggled with the door. But he caught enough to become enraged. He wouldn't let that bastard lecture him on looking after his wife.

How dare he?

Something snapped within Shaun.

His head crashed upon Martin's nose, the break of bone tangible, the jerk of the older man's body as he fell back onto the kitchen floor. Shaun then leapt upon Martin, punching and spitting and digging into him.

White heat seared across his eyes.

He felt another hand grab his shoulder, trying to pull him away from his prey, but Shaun lashed out at it too, his right fist unknowingly striking Lize across her cheek, sending her across the room.

Lize tripped on one of the bodies, fell back against the edge of the kitchen table then tumbled to the floor. Her own body shook briefly – like she was having some sort of fit – and then was still. Blood pooled quickly from the back of her head.

Shaun froze.

Fred was first over, until that point cowering in the corner, barking as the two men struggled with each other. He sniffed Lize's face, licking it once, twice before a short whimper escaped his mouth and he wandered away, head down and tail between his legs.

Martin was next across the floor. He scurried almost animal-like, grabbed Lize into his arms. Rocked her to and fro, all the while keening.

Things seemed to slow down for Shaun.

Everything else was forgotten: the dead outside, the virus, Jamie.

Shaun wouldn't remember Fred wandering over to him, sliding his head into his hands, seeking comfort and reassurance. Neither would he remember stroking the dog absently, tears running down his face and falling into the dog's fur.

He'd only remember Lize, her body still and beautiful. Yet lost to him.

…

At some stage, Shaun opened the garage door and took Jamie out, just like he'd been trying to do before. Only this time Martin didn't try to stop him. Both men knew there would be no use in that. They knew there was no use in *anything* now.

They sat on the floor at opposite sides of the room. Shaun with his infected son, cradled in his arms, sleeping. Martin with his ever-loyal dog nestled in against his shoulder. The kitchen floor divided them like No Man's Land, the bodies of the dead still lying where they'd been felled.

Lize's body lay amongst them.

Shaun's hand ran through Jamie's damp, warm hair. The boy's breathing was slow and laboured, in contrast to the panting of the parched dog by Martin's side.

The sun was valiantly fighting its way through a small gap in the wooden board covering the kitchen window. Several cadavers were prising their fingers through the gap, searching for weakness, still itching to get in.

"It isn't the deaf thing," Martin said. "You can't help that."

Shaun's eyes homed in on Martin's lips.

"It's Lize. I couldn't let go of her," Martin confided. "I couldn't hand her over, not after all that happened…"

The older man reached into his pocket, took something out, threw it over to Shaun.

It fell by Shaun's side. He picked it up.

It was a picture. Taken a long time ago. The colour was almost gone, like it had been sitting in the sun for some years. In the picture, Shaun could see Martin, a lot younger than he was now. The girl beside him looked exactly like Lize. Only Shaun knew it to be her mother.

Shaun threw the picture back. It landed on Martin's lap. The older man picked it up, stared at it quietly for a moment, and then smiled.

"It's impossible to let go of someone you love," he said. "Even when they're gone. You know that now."

Shaun looked down at the face of his son. He wiped the boy's forehead with an already sweat-soaked cloth.

"But when your daughter grows up to look and behave *exactly* like the woman you loved, the woman you lost…" Martin looked Shaun in the eye. "Sometimes it felt like you were sleeping with my wife, not my daughter."

For a moment, the two men sat in silence.

Then Martin stood up, the dog still close to him. He went to Lize, bent down to retrieve her body in his arms.

"The boy needs you," he said to Shaun. "Just like my daughter needs me."

Shaun nodded.

Martin left the room, Lize in his arms, the dog following.

Shaun returned his attention to Jamie. The boy's skin felt warm but not burning like before. He wasn't breathing anymore. Shaun held the boy up to his face, burying his head in the soft, damp flesh.

Silently, he cried.

SEVEN

The Chamber, Co. Armagh
7th August

Willis stood in the observation room, staring in through the one-way glass at Gallagher's makeshift research lab.. The doctor stood in the middle of the room, wearing his bloodstained plastic coveralls. Near him was the Colonel, or what was left of him; the rest of the older man was wrapped in clear, sealed bags and arranged on the nearby table. He was dead but, like the dead outside, still moving, his eyes staring at the doctor.

Major Jackson was strapped into a nearby chair, naked.

Gallagher proceeded to inject Jackson with something resembling blood.

Willis watched for another moment, swallowed hard, then pressed the red button on his side of the screen.

"Sir, you asked for me?" he said

Gallagher finished administering the injection before speaking.

"Ah, Willis," he said. "Thanks for joining us. You've been working on repairs to the helicopter, I hear. I hope that trouble you had from the last job didn't cause any long term damage?"

Willis recalled his recent approach of the apartment block in Finaghy, seeking out the young survivor located by The Chamber's surveillance cameras. Of how a man, now identified as ex-IRA operative Pat Flynn, had appeared from one of the apartment's windows and fired upon the helicopter, forcing Willis to take evasive action.

"Nothing serious, sir."

"Good," Gallagher said. "We've been monitoring the situation via the surveillance cameras. Flynn's no longer in the picture. The block was heavily invaded by the dead, and we feared we had lost not only Flynn, but also the Fico girl. Alas, two unidentified civilian survivors seem to now have her in their care. They're on the roof of the apartment block. I want you to go back there now."

Willis felt his heart skip. He'd watched with the others as they witnessed the miracle of the young Eastern European child, Brina Fico. She'd developed the virus, was quarantined, yet seemed to have somehow survived it. Although not a medically minded man by any stretch of the imagination, Willis knew what that meant: she was the key to survival. Humanity's last hope lay within the blood of that innocent little girl.

He wondered how he felt about that.

"I need the child," Gallagher continued. "The others are not important, but feel free to bring them if the girl won't come alone."

"And if they refuse?" Willis asked.

Gallagher looked again to Jackson. "I believe you weren't around to witness the full extent of what happened in the control room earlier," he said. "There was a disagreement between Major Jackson and I. The Major is a troubled man, Willis. Haunted by ghosts of the past, ghosts like our old friend Pat Flynn. But that life is gone now. We're in a new era, and nothing should hold us back from doing what must be done to ensure our survival." Gallagher replaced the spent needle on the table beside Jackson. "If the two civilians put up any resistance, you must kill them."

Willis was careful not to let the nervousness show in his voice as he addressed Gallagher: "Sir, permission to fly on my own, unaided by co-pilot Davis."

"And why would you request such a thing?" Gallagher asked.

"Fuel, sir. We're dangerously low. Even one man's weight can make the difference. Especially if I'm to return with all three survivors."

Gallagher mulled it over for a moment then nodded.

"Of course, Mr Willis," he said. "I trust you to know what's best. If you wish to fly alone, then that's fine with me." He smiled. "While in command, I would like to give you gentlemen as much autonomy as possible." He lifted a scalpel, turned his attentions to the Colonel. "Don't make me regret that," he added.

"Of course, sir," Willis said,

His eyes surveyed the lab once more before he left the observation room.

The doctor returned to his work at the table.

Jackson's eyes snapped open, the shamed officer immediately trying to pull free from his restraints.

"Ah," Gallagher smiled. "Just on cue."

…

He'd been infected.

But Major Connor Jackson was fighting back.

He tried to use his training. Mind over matter.

His body was jerking, his face grimacing as he resisted a virus that's sole aim was to consume him. To wipe his mind clean and replace the social conditioning that years as an army officer had ingrained in him.

Jackson fought against the virus because the life of a little girl, an innocent little girl who had already suffered enough, depended upon his fight. His eyes were closed, and his dissolving brain fought to hold the face of that little girl and the word *INNOCENT* in his mind, hoping that even when dead, even when reanimated as a monster, like the mutilated Colonel beside him, he might retain some sort of control.

God help him, he didn't want to do what the bad doctor *needed* him to do.

"For the greater good," Gallagher had said to him when challenged on his plans for the Fico girl. But what good could come from unleashing a monster on a child?

Jackson thought back to the gruesome day when his life had changed forever.

His daughter had been kidnapped by the IRA. Pat Flynn, well known IRA operative, was in his custody at The Chamber. As was Pat's son, Sean. When Flynn hadn't talked, Jackson was pushed to the edge, acting outside of his own character, doing something monstrous, something heinous, murdering the Flynn boy in cold blood.

INNOCENCE, Jackson said to himself now as he struggled against the virus. He said it again.

And again.

EIGHT

Willis passed the other soldiers in the control room.

Some of the men were working on the radio, surfing the airwaves. Arguing and fighting over connections and channels, every last one of them drunk as skunks.

Idiots, thought Willis as he passed.

The pilot retreated to the complex's toilets, checking first that the stalls were all empty.

He locked himself in one, retrieving the compact Blackberry from his pocket.

He connected to The Chamber's own server. It was weird to think that an old relic like The Chamber might have its own server farm. It had been installed years ago, communication deemed vital to The Chamber's work and, even though the connection wasn't great, the signal fading in and out, it had meant Willis could maintain contact with old Tom. He reckoned no one else in the complex had the know-how or motivation to spring him. Those fools out there were arguing over a damn radio, for God's sake. This was as secure a connection as Willis was going to find, yet he kept his comms brief all the same.

He logged into the makeshift user group. He'd set it up some time ago with Chrysler, another one of his contacts, in case of emergencies like this. For a moment,

Willis wondered again what had become of Chrysler. He sure could use the other man's expertise right now.

The pilot's own user name came up: AGENT13.

There was only one other user in the group: Uncle Tom.

Tom was a good friend. Trustworthy. Impulsive, but sharp.

Willis typed.

"Come on, Tom," he said. "Answer me, damn it."

…

Waringstown, Co. Down

"Tom, Tom, Tom," the bird shouted.

The old man's eyes popped open.

"What?" he said. "What's happening?"

He looked to the birdcage.

The parrot was chattering obsessively, acting very strange. It picked at its own wings, fluttering about in the cage like it was drunk.

"Damn bird," Tom growled. "I should just snap your fucking neck right now!"

He went to the window, looked out.

A group of dead filled the yard. He could hear them hacking up phlegm, gobs hanging from their lips like stringy glue.

"Fucking things!" Tom shouted out the window. He shook his fist.

Some of the dead looked up. A few moved to the door excitedly, beating the wood uselessly with their hands.

The computer started beeping, pulling Tom away from the window. He rushed over, slapping the keys. The screensaver gave way to the new user group's screen. It looked basic. Not like the chat screen he was used to.

"Come on, come on," Tom mouthed as he waited for the connection to kick in.

Jesus, it was patchy.

The screen loaded, Tom finding Agent13 waiting for him.

"Yes!" he beamed. "Still in the ring, boyo!"

Tom hadn't heard from 13 for a few days. He'd begun to fear the worst: that his old pal had succumbed to the flu like so many others. That he was left alone in this godforsaken world, with only his bird and the shuffling dead outside for company.

"Where you been, buddy?" Tom said as he typed.

He waited for 13's reply:

BUSY. DID YOU READ THE NOTES I SENT?

Tom scratched his head.

"What notes?" he typed.

MILES GALLAGHER, came the reply.

Tom swore loudly.

"Why are we still talking about this?" he complained. He typed it.

ALL RELEVANT, 13 replied.

"Why?" Tom typed back.

STILL OPERATIONAL. GALLAGHER IN CHARGE NOW.

Tom sighed, looked around the room, sifting through the many books and files that littered the floor, the desk, the bed. There were papers with words circled in red, underlined and punctuated with dramatic exclamation marks.

Tom sifted through the mess, retrieving the printout he was looking for, simply marked 'Gallagher'.

His eyes were tired.

"Dr Miles Gallagher," he read. "Decorated field medic. Worked the Gulf War. Particularly skilled in the art of interrogation. Ruthless, brutal, blah blah blah…"

Tom looked back to the screen, typed, "What do you need to know?"

CAN WE TRUST HIM?

Tom laughed.

"*Trust* him?! He's a fucking goon! Of course we can't *trust* him!" He was literally banging the keys as he typed.

Agent13's next reply bowled him over.

WITH GALLAGHER NOW.

"What?!" Tom bellowed at the screen.

He looked around, suddenly spooked.

"You fucking –" Tom rubbed his mouth. "No, don't speak!" he whispered to himself. "Don't speak, this fucker's infiltrated you. Played you like a fiddle."

He'd been right that 13 had been acting suspiciously last time. It hadn't just been the demons dancing in his head or the pills running out. It was his fucking gut trying to tell him something!

Tom went to the phone, picked it up. Rubbed his hand across the receiver, searching for bugs. "No," he said to himself. "They couldn't have got in here. You would have seen them. Get a grip, for fuck's sake! It's all online. All online."

He went to the computer lead, ready to pull it from the wall, but stopped himself.

13 had written more:

BEEN WORKING UNDERCOVER SINCE I HAD MY EYES OPENED. YOU CAN TRUST ME.

"Fuck!" Tom shouted, his fists clenched and raised, his eyes ready to pop. "What to do, what to do?" he ranted.

"What to do?" chirped the bird hoarsely.

"Fuck up, bird!" Tom yelled.

Another message on screen. It read:

TOM? YOU STILL THERE?

"Yes," Tom said. "Still here."

He cried out in frustration. The noise filled the room. He desperately needed to trust 13. He'd no other choice. There was nobody else out there.

NEED TO KNOW YOUR GUT INSTINCT ON GALLAGHER, came 13.

"Okay," Tom said, resigned to helping. He reached for the paper again. "Gut instinct. What's my gut instinct?" He scanned the text. It was all in there. "Interrogation, surveillance, covert operations. For God's sake, man, he's up to his eyes in shit!" He went to the keyboard. "Can't trust him," he said, typing.

OKAY, came 13's reply.

"Is it? What's okay about it?" Tom barked. "The whole fucking world's gone to hell, and you're sleeping with the goons! There's nothing okay about *that*!"

ONE MORE THING, 13 typed.

A media player file attachment appeared on screen.

Tom clicked in.

The video started to play. It was footage taken with a phone or digital camera. Tom saw a few goons sitting around what looked like some sort of control room. They were watching a large screen at the front of the room.

On the soldiers' screen, Tom could make out the image of a small girl running around her bedroom. The windows of the bedroom were covered by metal sheets, as if the room had been sealed from the inside.

SURVIVOR, 13 typed. QUARANTINED BUT RECOVERED FROM THE FLU.

Tom's mouth dropped. "Oh, lordy," he said.

But there was more:

I'VE GOT A PLAN, AND I NEED YOU TO HELP ME.

"My help?" Tom muttered. "What the hell can I do?"

He heard a thud from across the room and turned to follow the noise. His eyes fell upon the birdcage, but he couldn't see the parrot anymore.

Tom stood up from the computer, crossed the room. He leaned in closer to the cage.

Inside, he found the parrot had fallen from its perch. It lay perfectly still on the cage's floor.

Tom rubbed his mouth. "Oh shit," he said.

NINE

Ballynarry, Co. Armagh

The steam from the bath filled the room. It was like mist, and Vicky wondered if she could get lost in it, taken to another world, away from this house and fucked-up countryside, where only death thrived.

She didn't think she could feel any worse than she did. There was already plenty to feel shit about, after all: the ever-increasing number of bodies outside, the ever-decreasing supply of food and water *inside* (not that *she* cared much about that: Vicky couldn't remember the last time she'd eaten). But the mind was a funny old thing. And today, Vicky had woken with a brand new feeling of woe that was totally unexpected.

Guilt.

At first, she'd mistaken it for grief. The two feelings were pretty similar, she realised: both seeming to rise up from the gut, filling her chest like acid. But then her head got in on the action, and Vicky had words and pictures to go with her feelings.

The radiant face of Sinead filled her mind.

When she thought about it, Vicky reckoned that this image was merely a front. That Sinead's sweet, innocent face represented a lot of people that Vicky had pissed on from great heights throughout the years.

People like her mother, whom Vicky hadn't talked to in years, still blaming the old woman for the things that bastard husband of hers had inflicted on them both.

People like Colin. God knew, Vicky had been a bitch to Colin even before their whole shambles of a marriage fell apart. She *thought* that she loved him, and she probably had, as much as a damaged shell like her could. But how *real* was that love? Was it more a case of her just needing the complete opposite of her father: a man she felt stronger than, a man that *she* could manipulate?

Vicky closed her eyes, tried to will the guilt away. But it dug its claws in. A heavy, soul-shattering presence that wasn't for budging.

It possessed her.

The feeling was unbearable. And the more it consumed her, the more Vicky hated herself.

She already hated everything and everyone around her.

What was there left to live for?

As if to remind her, scratching noises suddenly came from the other side of the bathroom's single window. The sound was infuriating. Dead fingernails against glass. It dug right through her skin, reached into her stomach and twisted. Vicky started to retch, but there was nothing inside her to come up.

She sobbed in frustration and pain.

As the water continued to rise up around her, its heat surprisingly numb against her flesh, Vicky's eyes were drawn once more to the razor. It sat innocently on the side of the bath, by the taps. She'd used it already. Each time she'd entered the bathroom, actually. But only to take the edge off, only to draw blood and let some of the pain spill out across her skin.

Once, she'd pressed it against the bigger vein on her wrist, intent on slicing long ways, on making the bleed count – *really count* – but she'd lost her nerve at the last second, dropping the blade to the floor like it was scalding hot.

This time would be different...

PART FIVE:

THE BLOOD OF
THE INNOCENT

ONE

Craigavon, Co. Armagh

Willis clocked the mass of dead, gathering like doped-out wolves below.

He was flying over Lisburn. The new city seemed completely overrun. There was little chance of any survivors down there at all, the dead filling the streets densely, as if parading.

Willis flew further south, passing Lurgan.

He headed for the No Man's Land known as Craigavon. Even before the flu, there had been little of interest in Craigavon. Locals called it Roundabout City; the place offered miles and miles of empty road, punctuated by a shopping centre, some leisure facilities and random pockets of run down housing.

The helicopter reached an area within Craigavon known as The Lakes. Here water sports were the order of the day.

A well-trodden path circled the water. The path looked damp, miserable. Still drying from the rain showers that had broken the blue skies earlier. This was a popular spot back in the day. Sunday walkers would come from neighbouring Portadown and Lurgan, often with their dogs in tow.

The water split, disturbed by frantic air from the helicopter's propellers.

Willis spotted more of the dead.

A large, fenced-off compound had been erected, home to one of the so-called Rescue Camps the authorities had built to contain the infected. But the infection had consumed the place and everyone in it. Willis had followed the story on his Blackberry, watching the footage on YouTube. It was hard to believe that society could do this kind of thing to its own people. But here it was, in front of his very eyes: a concentration camp for the infected, where now only bodies roamed.

The pilot carried on.

He flew away from Craigavon's centre, out into the sticks, where the roads and roundabouts gave way to fields and foliage and confused cattle.

He found a deserted patch of land close to an old farmhouse and some trees. Willis circled the house, searching for signs of life (or death). It seemed clear, so the pilot pushed down on the stick, taking the helicopter in for landing.

...

Willis killed the engine, waiting in the cockpit as the blades calmed.

He could feel the confused stares of the three passengers behind him. Brina Fico, with her two civilian guardians, just as Gallagher had described. They looked tired, scared. Their clothes were still soaked by the rain from earlier.

Willis had picked them up from the roof of an apartment block in Finaghy, just as Gallagher asked.

Brina Fico was six years old, and she was important to The Chamber. Daughter of an illegal immigrant, Brina's flat was under observation by The Chamber for the Home Office. In the new world, however, Brina was important for very different reasons. She'd been quarantined, locked in her own home like many others who'd developed the virus.

Yet, Brina survived.

Willis looked at her now.

She sat in the back of the helicopter, cradled in the arms of one of her guardians, a young woman with red hair and pale, freckled skin. Willis didn't know the woman's name. She was of no real importance to The Chamber, apart from the fact that she seemed able to comfort the child.

Beside the girl was the other guardian. An angry looking fucker with tattoos and narrow eyes set deep within a shorn head.

It was Tattoo who addressed the pilot first: "Why are we stopping?"

Willis ignored him, climbed out of the helicopter.

He took a moment to reflect on what he was doing: Willis had every confidence that Gallagher could create some sort of antibody from the girl, maybe even a cure.

So why not bring her to him?

He thought back to what Uncle Tom had said: *He's a goon. Of course you can't trust him.* Yet a part of Willis respected Miles Gallagher. In a way, the doctor wasn't so different from himself: a truth-seeker of sorts, working in the lab, unravelling the mysteries of the reanimated dead. Gallagher probably knew more about what made those things tick than anyone else alive.

Was it jealousy, then?

Knowledge was a drug. Willis knew that better than anyone. But this was bigger than that. They were fighting a war. Willis and others like him. Uncle Tom. Chrysler. Truthers throughout the world. And that little girl was part of the fight.

She was the prize.

So innocent...

In a way, little Brina was the epitome of the whole sorry mess Willis had been mixed up in over the years. The government, the army and now The Chamber. The young kids he'd carried to war, their lives destroyed because of the whims of others; powerful and evil forces; groups like Bilderberg, pulling the strings, playing one nation against another for personal gain, their own hands as clean as the three-piece designer suits they wore.

The *real* knowledge, the *real* power was with those fuckers. Willis knew that. They were probably watching him right now via satellite, holed up in some bunker, waiting for him to do their bidding.

Waiting for Gallagher to extract the makings of an antivirus from the girl.

And then they'd come out again, seize power and rebuild an empire.

On their terms.

But Willis could end it all now.

He held the prize. The power.

He drew his handgun and moved around to the side door of the helicopter.

TWO

"Get out," the pilot ordered.

"What?" snapped the young woman. Her name was Geri McConnell, and she'd had enough drama over the last number of weeks to do her a lifetime. "This is the rescue? Humanity's last stand is… *some old farmhouse?*"

"Come on! Hurry!" the pilot said, looking around nervously.

Geri noticed the gun in his hand.

"Look, what's going on?" she said. "You told us you were taking us to safety." She poked her head outside, looked around, "Nothing here but wide open space. Doesn't look too safe to me."

"Just get out!" the pilot insisted, "Or God help me…"

His gun hand was shaking. His eyes were wide, a crazy look that was particularly unwelcome. After everything that had gone down, Geri was hoping for a bit of sanity. For comfort, security. Wasn't too much for a girl to ask, was it?

The pilot waved the gun at her again.

"Please…" he begged. Still that crazed look in his eye.

But Geri had some crazy in her too. God knew, you couldn't survive this long *without* going mad. Geri was nearing breaking point, and this asshole was going to know about it.

"No," she said assertively. "No to whatever madness you're peddling. I'm staying right here."

She looked to the young man beside her for support. His name was Lark, and while he looked like a mean son-of-a-bitch, he was acting quite the opposite right now. The little girl, Brina, was hanging off his neck, having left Geri in order to pull herself up onto the tattooed man's knee.

"Please, you have to trust me…" the pilot said.

The gun was still there, but his voice softened. He pulled at the strap on his helmet, removing it, dropping it to the ground. He ran a shaking hand across his brow, wiping it free of sweat, and then rubbed his eyes.

Geri took a chance.

She jumped down from the helicopter.

"Look, you're not going to shoot me…" she said and reached for the man's gun.

But the pilot grabbed her hand, turning it against her back, and pushed her to the ground.

It was then that Lark flipped.

In his head, he was no longer in this helicopter, parked somewhere North of Craigavon centre. Instead, Lark found himself in southern Afghanistan, a small village within Helmand Province. He wasn't looking at Geri and the pilot anymore. Rather, Lark watched a British soldier smack a young Afghan girl across the face, then pin her to the ground, three others looking on, waiting their turn.

Lark was one of them.

"Take your fucking hands off her!" he yelled now, leaping down from the helicopter and grabbing the pilot.

Lark pulled the older man away from Geri, throwing him to the ground.

He hit the man repeatedly.

He was still hitting the pilot when he felt Geri pulling at his shirt.

"Leave it!" she was shouting.

Lark jumped up, moved away.

He noticed his shirt was spattered in fresh blood.

"Fuck," he muttered to himself.

Geri stooped over the pilot's body, brushing her long red hair to one side as she searched the man's face for any sign of life. She prodded him with a finger, stepped back.

"You've killed him!" she said, turning again to Lark.

"He was touching you. No one fucking touches you!"

"Jesus, would you *listen* to yourself?!" Geri screamed. "What's wrong with you?"

The little girl was still in the helicopter, a panicked look across her face. Geri reached for her, lifted her down.

"Can you fly this thing?" she said to Lark, nodding towards the helicopter. "Because what we need right now is someone who can fly this thing. Not some mad man tearing into people like a fucking animal!"

That stung him. Lark felt a wall of rage rise up from his insides. He wanted to scream in Geri's face, to grab her –

To hit her? Pin her down?

He made for the nearby house. Anything to get away.

"Hey, where are you going?" she called after him.

"Leave me alone! Stay away from me!"

Lark reached the building. It was a small two-storey farmhouse. He pushed the door, entered.

Inside, the place was a mess. Spent cans of beer littered the floor. An overbearing smell of urine greeted him, mixing with other smells such as tobacco and sweat. A single bloody handprint stained a nearby wall.

But Lark didn't care: the place could be jam-packed with those dead fucks, and he *still* wouldn't care.

He fell onto the sofa.

"FUCK!" he shouted, wringing his hands.

A familiar scent filled his nostrils, mixing with the other smells.

Marijuana.

Lark's eyes widened. He rubbed his mouth, looked to a nearby ashtray where some spent roaches lay.

Christ, he needed a hit. Something stronger than weed, of course, but you had to start somewhere…

He reached for the longest of the roaches, pulled the lighter from his jeans pocket and sparked it up. He sucked the smoke in hungrily.

Lark hadn't scored in quite a while, and it was beginning to show. He was shivering all over. His bones were sore, his head wired. Geri was right: he was getting on like some kind of lunatic.

Lark took another drag. Bloody thing was spent already. He flicked it to the floor, leaned back in the sofa.

He heard the door open.

Geri came in, the child behind her. They sat down beside him.

Geri's face creased as the room's smells filled her nostrils.

"Dope?" she asked.

Lark didn't answer, his eyes staring dead ahead.

Look," she said. "What happened to you?"

He looked at her quizzically. "What do you mean?"

"To make you *like this*. Something must have happened…"

The tattooed man looked away. He noticed a calendar hanging on the wall. June, it said. There was the picture of a beach; the sand reminded Lark, once again, of his time in Afghanistan. He was taken back to that village in

Helmand, where the sky seemed so blue it felt like you could drown in it.

He had been only nineteen at the time. Sent to a foreign land where he couldn't speak the language. Where nothing was familiar. Where everyone looked dangerous and different and fucking scary, staring at Lark with hate and fear in their dark eyes.

But he hadn't touched that Afghan girl.

He'd watched as the others raped her one by one, on the dusty floor of her single-roomed home. They'd laughed at him when he wouldn't take her, called him a faggot. And he'd walked out with them and left her there, bleeding on the floor.

But he hadn't touched her. Surely that meant something!

Geri gestured to the child beside him now. "We have to look after her," she said to him. "She's important, somehow. I can feel it…"

The little girl looked up at him with her big doe eyes.

Lark laughed humourlessly. He was no family guy.

Sure, he had kids: two that he knew of. One in the States with her mum. The other he'd fathered with one of the most twisted bitches he'd ever had the misfortune to shag. She was in rehab, last time Lark heard. The kid was living with her grandmother in Carrick. A restraining order forbade Lark from seeing either of them.

"Do you hear me?" Geri pressed.

She moved a little closer. Touched him. Not in a big way, just her hand on his shoulder. But it surprised Lark. Ran through his skin like electricity.

"Look, I'm okay," he said to Geri.

He wanted to get up, move away. He suddenly felt very aware of himself.

Still she looked at him; still her hand remained on his shoulder.

"Seriously," he said. "I'm okay. It's just this –"

"What?" she said and her face was so close he could smell her. An unwashed smell, but still somehow fragrant.

"I don't want nobody touching you" Lark said, this time quietly. "Not him, not those dead things. Nobody."

His eyes blinked nervously as he talked.

He rubbed one hand across his brow, wiped it on his jeans.

"I know," Geri said, and when Lark looked up, he could see her eyes were moist.

The little girl broke in, hugging Lark's arm, but the tattooed man pushed her away.

"Lark!" Geri chastised.

"*What?* I don't even know her name!"

The little girl looked hurt, rejected. "Brina," she said, patting her own chest.

Lark and Geri exchanged looks.

"Brina," Geri said smiling. "What a pretty name." She ran a hand through the little girl's hair. "Can you understand us, sweetie?"

Brina looked confused for a moment but then nodded.

Geri smiled. "Well, Brina, we're going to look after you now. You don't need to worry about a thing."

Something outside disturbed them. A booming noise.

Lark got up, walked to the nearby window.

The helicopter was in flames, the pilot coming towards them, carrying the gun.

"Jesus Christ!" Lark exclaimed.

"What is it?" Geri said.

"The fucking pilot…"

"What!?" Geri went to the window, looked out. "Holy… Did *he* do that?" she said, looking at the burning helicopter. "Why would he *do* that?"

"Fucking nutter, that's why," Lark mumbled.

The tattooed man quickly scanned the room, finding an old walking stick on the living room floor. He retrieved it, went to the doorway and hid, waiting for the pilot to make his entrance.

Gunfire. Someone was shooting.

Lark swore again, venturing a peek outside the door.

He found the pilot now facing the burning helicopter, his gun hand primed.

A flock of dead emerged from the nearby trees. Some were heading for the flames that smothered the helicopter, their hands raised as if in worship. Others were heading for the pilot.

Lark swung his head to the right, following the tree line. More dead appeared, closing in on the farmhouse.

THREE

Lark shot a glance towards Geri and Brina.

"Stay here!" he ordered.

He stepped outside, closing the door behind him.

He veered towards the dead nearest to the house, raising the walking stick in his hands and swinging at the head of an older man wearing brown slacks tied with a rope. The handle of the stick connected with the dead man's jaw, shattering his mouth, spitting bone and teeth onto the muddy grass.

The dead man struggled to remain standing, but Lark struck again, this time bringing the stick crashing down on his skull, splitting it wide open. He hit the ground, but Lark attacked once more, the next blow sealing the deal.

Lark stepped back to avoid the lunges of a second dead man, this time tripping his attacker up before, once again, bringing the head of the stick down hard on the thing's rotten old head, piercing it like a ripe tomato.

Another one, this time a woman, came at him from his other side, managing to grab Lark's arm, but the tattooed man shook it off, twisting his body around in order to connect a left hook to the dead thing's jaw, flooring it with one blow. Then he was pounding again with the stick.

But there were too many of them.

Another one grabbed Lark, the tattooed man's stick falling from his grasp. Lark tried to pull away, but more of the fuckers were in his face, the nauseating smell of their rotten flesh overbearing.

"Ye bastards!" Lark screeched, closing his eyes, trying to shake them off.

And then there was shooting, Lark almost deafened as gunfire surrounded him. The bodies fell heavily around him, Lark managing to pull away as the shots continued. When he opened his eyes, Lark saw the pilot standing in front of him, gun in hand.

Lark could hear more of the dead pouring out from the woods behind him, their flu-ridden chorus loud and obnoxious in the still country air.

The pilot aimed the gun in Lark's direction. He squeezed the trigger.

Lark closed his eyes.

A click.

When Lark looked up, he found the pilot working at his gun, dropping an empty magazine, searching in his jacket for a fresh clip. He loaded the clip, chambered a round, and then turned the gun back on Lark. His teeth were gritted, his face still bloodied from Lark punching him earlier.

"Move, you idiot!" he said.

Lark moved, and the pilot offloaded several rounds into the crowd of dead behind him. Several of their number fell, but still more came, seeping out of the woods like a marooned army.

"Come on!" the pilot said, grabbing Lark and frog-marching him at gunpoint towards the nearby building.

FOUR

"Oh, this is great. Just GREAT!" Geri slumped dejectedly into the sofa. "Trapped in *another* fucking house."

The pilot ignored her, circling the downstairs rooms, latching the windows and doors.

He looked to Lark, said, "Check upstairs."

"Fuck off," the tattooed man replied. He was doubled over, his face pale, breathing heavily. Blood soaked his face and top. He looked like he was going to be sick.

The pilot waved the gun at Lark. "I'm warning you, punk, this is not the time or place…"

Lark exchanged a dirty look with Geri. Laughed then shuffled upstairs, still out of breath.

"Look, who are you?" Geri said to the pilot.

Still the older man ignored her.

Geri could see swelling around his nose and lips where Lark had punched him. He was still bleeding. He wiped a hand across his face, the bloody smear spreading like snail tracks across his sleeve.

"The woods," he muttered to himself as he looked out a nearby window. "Stupid to land here…"

He looked to Brina, frowned.

Brina frowned back, imitating him.

She didn't understand the words too well, but it was clear what was happening. They were trapped in the house. The dead surrounded them, creeping up against the windows, staring in with their stupid, vacant eyes.

They reminded Brina of Tony Farrell, one of the boys at her school. Like her, Tony wasn't local. He'd told Brina he lived in a caravan and travelled around. She hadn't understood him, but he'd drawn her a picture to explain. He was her best friend, but sometimes Tony looked a bit like those dead things. Like someone had switched him off inside.

"We can't let them hem us in. We have to get out of here," the pilot said.

"Says the man who torched the helicopter," Geri retorted.

"Upstairs bedroom window," Lark said, coming back down the stairs. "Drops down onto a garage. Leads out onto an open field. We could get a head start on them."

"Show me," the pilot said.

The two men disappeared up the stairs, leaving Brina and Geri alone.

From outside, the dead peered in at them, hands clawing uselessly at the windows, voices pained and hoarse like wounded animals.

Geri hooked her finger. "Double glazing, you pricks!" she yelled.

Brina felt trapped.

She thought of the flat back in Finaghy, where she'd been quarantined during the outbreak. Brina had been very sick, a merciless fever burning through her tiny body. Her mother was screaming, trying to escape, but the men in the yellow suits sealed them in.

And then she'd woken – bed sheets glued to her skin, the screams of her mother sharper, not unlike the noises made by the dead gathering outside the farmhouse now.

Mother had locked herself in the bathroom, but Brina wouldn't let her out…

A gunshot. Sounds of struggle.

"Stay here!" Geri shouted.

But Brina didn't want to stay. She couldn't face being alone again with those things.

She ran after Geri, following her up the stairs.

They entered the bedroom, finding Lark and the pilot on the floor, struggling for the gun.

Lark was on the receiving end this time, his eyes wide, his face puffed as the pilot's fists rained down.

Outside, Brina could still hear the dead, their voices louder, as if jeering on the two men fighting. She wanted to shout at them all, tell them to stop.

Her chest was bouncing, her gut churning like she needed to go to the toilet right away. She felt something in her chest, rising up within her, building in the back of her throat before erupting from her lips.

Her scream shattered every window in the house.

FIVE

For a man like Willis to experience something like this was incredible.

He'd been a truther for years now. He'd watched online footage of occultic rituals at Bohemian Grove, involving many of the world's so-called elite. But, while many truthers believed those rituals were mere theatre, Willis believed there was *actual* power involved, dark forces that could be tapped into. The dead rising was surely proof of that. And now this little girl, whose blood held a cure to whatever was happening around them, whose scream had just shattered every window in the farmhouse…

Willis looked to the other two survivors.

They were on the floor, still recovering.

He went to speak, to say something unrehearsed, to somehow capture what he'd just witnessed, but the ringing in his ears made his voice useless.

He couldn't see Brina.

Willis reached for the gun. He picked himself up and looked around for the little girl.

Where was she?

She'd maybe left the farmhouse during all the confusion.

Willis left the bedroom, descending the stairs to look for her. Stopped halfway down.

The full extent of their situation hit him on seeing the cadavers standing in the living room. He watched with horror as another, this one a middle-aged woman, dragged its body across the sharp edges of a devastated window. The broken glass tore at her clothes and skin, blood seeping onto the windowsill as the dead woman fought her way through. She spotted Willis, her arms reaching out towards him as she fell clumsily onto the floor.

Willis swore, heading back up the stairs towards the bedroom.

The other survivors were on their feet now, still looking confused.

"Where's Brina?" Geri said, rubbing her head.

"I can't find her," Willis said. "And those things have broken into the house. We need to leave."

He moved towards the bedroom window, pushed away some of the broken glass with his elbow, then clambered up and out onto the sloping roof.

He held onto the window ledge, securing himself as best he could.

He glanced down, noticing how the dead, perhaps attracted by the gunshot or struggles, or the little girl's scream, were gathering en masse behind the house.

"Damn it," Willis spat.

Still, there was no other way out.

He looked to the other survivors, shouted, "Hurry!"

The red-headed woman was next to crawl through the window.

The tattooed man remained in the bedroom. The dead filled the landing now, drawing closer. Tattoo was sweating it.

"Give me the gun," he shouted to Willis.

Willis retrieved the gun but hesitated; Tattoo was nothing but trouble. Unbalanced. Unpredictable. Willis could be done with him for good.

"For fuck's sake, man!" Tattoo protested.

The woman, halfway through the window, looked at Willis pleadingly.

"Help him!" she said.

Willis threw the gun into the bedroom. He watched as Tattoo lifted it, turned it on the encroaching dead, and fired.

SIX

The bedroom was small.

The dead were closing in, the smell of their crumbling flesh thick in the air, making Lark gag.

The tattooed man checked the gun. It was a HK USP. He flicked the safety, chambered a round and turned it on the dead. Lark fired in succession, punching holes in the filthy dead fucks as they filled the house's landing.

He looked back to Geri. The red-haired woman was still scrambling to get out through the window.

"For fuck's sake, MOVE!" Lark barked, then turned and fired another volley of shots into the throng.

But their numbers thickened, pouring through the doorway into the room.

Lark pressed his boot against the chest of the nearest of the pack, a young girl with pigtails and a blood-stained t-shirt that read NEW YORK CITY. He pushed the dead girl back with his foot then turned the gun on her, aiming for the head. The noise was deafening, the impact shattering bone, spreading the girl's pig-tailed hair and skull across the bedroom wall.

The tattooed man turned once more, this time finding Geri out of the bedroom, clinging onto the windowsill alongside the pilot.

Lark didn't waste any time, tucking the gun into the waistband of his jeans and following the others through the broken window. His hands and knees ripped against the sharp glass edges, the tattooed man wincing against the pain.

He joined the others hanging onto the windowsill, poised awkwardly on the sloping roof of the farmhouse.

"We need to move!" he shouted, "They'll be at our fingertips in seconds!"

"Down there," Willis said, looking towards an old garage just below the sloping roof.

Lark followed his gaze.

"Fuck it," he said, then let go of the sill.

Lark found himself slipping down the slated roof, the friction tearing more skin from his hands and elbows. His foot caught on the drain running along the roof and, as he was thrown down towards the garage, his ankle twisted.

Lark called out in pain as he landed hard on the garage roof. He remained on his back, looking towards the others, still wincing.

Geri was sliding down after him, her journey slightly more graceful. She slipped off the farmhouse roof, flying towards him.

Lark rolled to avoid her landing.

Together they looked back towards the sill, finding the pilot.

For a moment, Lark considered moving – splitting with Geri and leaving the old bastard hanging up there on the roof – but the pilot finally released his hands, slid down the farmhouse roof, landed with the others on the garage.

"Took your time, old man," Lark quipped.

The pilot said nothing, quickly picking himself up and looking over the edge of the garage.

The dead were mostly gathered around the house, following the main pack climbing through the broken windows. There were a few scattered around the garage, but not enough to present a problem.

"Is it clear?" Lark asked.

The pilot nodded. "More or less."

Lark went to move but winced against the pain in his ankle.

"What's wrong?" the pilot asked.

"Twisted my ankle!"

"Is it broke?"

"Not sure."

"Can you walk on it?"

Lark allowed the other man to help him to his feet. He took a few steps across the garage roof, smarting against the sharp pain.

"Okay," said the pilot. "We'll lower you down first. Best have that gun ready…"

"We need to find Brina!" Geri said.

The two men exchanged glances.

"We're not leaving without her," Geri protested.

"Maybe *she* left without *us*," Lark said.

The pilot frowned, glanced once again over the edge of the garage.

"Come on, help me," he said to Geri, grabbing one of Lark's arms.

The tattooed man was lowered down from the roof.

Geri and the pilot followed.

A spluttering cough from nearby had Lark raising his gun expectantly. But it seemed to be coming from behind the survivors.

Then came a scream. A little girl's scream.

SEVEN

"She's in the garage," Lark said. "That's why they aren't bothering us." He shook his head. "She's fucked. We have to go."

"No way," Geri said.

"She's as good as dead," Lark argued. "There's nothing we can do!"

Geri looked to the pilot in protest. The older man blew out some air.

"How did she do that?" he asked her. "The scream from before, I've never seen anything like that."

"Please," Geri said. "She's just a little girl. We need to help her."

The pilot rubbed his eyes. His face was starting to bruise heavily from Lark's beating. He looked tired, ready for giving up. Geri wondered what the girl, what any of them meant to this man. Why he had diverted the helicopter from its course then torched it. Why he was on the run from the army.

Could they trust him?

"What's your name?" Geri asked him.

"Willis."

"Well, Mr Willis, there *is* something special about that little girl. I knew it the moment I looked in her eyes, back in that apartment at Finaghy. But she's still just a child. A child with a name and –"

"I know her name," Willis broke in. "I know all about her. More than *you* know!"

He seemed angry all of a sudden.

He turned to Lark. "Give me the gun!" he barked. "Now!"

Reluctantly, Lark handed the HK over.

"Come on," Willis said to Geri.

…

The dead surrounded the garage, fighting each other to get through its open door.

Inside, Geri could make out the frame of an old tractor, half dismantled. On top of the tractor, Geri found Brina, her little arms wrapped tight around the steering wheel, her legs pulled up tight to avoid the probing hands of the hungry pack.

"In there," she said to Willis. "You have to help her!"

"Jesus Christ," Willis breathed, staring at the horde in front of him. There were a lot of the fuckers.

He looked to Geri. "I can't take them all," he said. "You'll need to help me."

Geri felt the blood freeze in her veins. Fear seized her, and for the briefest of moments she considered doing what Lark had suggested: turning and fleeing. Putting miles of green fields between herself and this garage full of dead things.

But Geri had fought them before.

She remembered sitting in a Land Rover, surrounded by the dead. Lark had showed her how to fire a Glock handgun, and she had fared alright for a beginner.

And then there was the apartment block in Finaghy, where, mere hours ago, a horde of the dead had chased them from the ground floor to the rooftop. Geri had protected Brina then, and she sure as hell could do the same now.

You're a survivor, she told herself. *Remember?*

Geri looked around the yard, her eyes falling upon an old hatchet buried in a nearby block of wood. She retrieved it then nodded to Willis.

"Okay," she said.

Willis aimed the gun, disposing with several stragglers flanking the garage.

Geri moved in from the right, edging towards the door.

The first of the dead to confront her reminded her of her cousin Michael for some reason. Lank hair fell over a long face. Big, nervous eyes stared back at her. Geri swung the axe at him, catching his neck. The young dead man struggled against the blade, blood spurting from his mouth and throat as his eyes rolled into the back of his head.

Geri pulled the axe free, using one long leg to kick him away as another of the dead homed in on her.

She disposed of this one with a blow between the eyes, splitting the thing's head wide open. She pulled the axe free then brought it down again and again, digging further into the man's face, tearing his flesh, blood soaking her vest and the bare skin of her arms, face and cleavage.

Geri screamed as she worked, her throat hoarse, mirroring the growling and rasping of the dead around her.

To her left, Willis continued to fire, dropping them like dominoes.

Another made a grab for her, but Geri turned the axe, slicing his arm off at the elbow. The poor bastard stumbled away, glaring at the bleeding stump she'd left him.

The next came towards her head-on. He was a big brute of a thing with thick curly hair and a meaty head. Geri buried the axe in his forehead. But this time, she struggled to pull the axe free.

Swearing, she let it go. Found some space and dodged through the remaining dead, heading for the tractor.

She climbed up to where Brina was, the little girl's hands still clinging tightly to the steering wheel.

Behind her, the sound of gunfire continued.

One of the dead made a grab for her leg but Geri kicked it in the head, spinning the bastard into the line of fire. The thing's head split against a piercing bullet.

Geri returned to Brina.

"Sweetie, it's me! Come on down, you're safe now."

But the little girl wouldn't move. Her eyes were closed tight, her face screwed up.

Geri prised her fingers from the steering wheel. "It's okay, pet," she said. "Come on, it's okay."

More gunfire. Geri heard the gun click on empty.

Finally, the child gave in, burrowing her head in Geri's chest.

Willis seemed to have freed Geri's axe, using it to finish the remaining stragglers off. They fell more easily now the herd was thinned.

Once done, Willis stopped and wiped his face.

He looked up to the tractor.

"She okay?" he asked.

"She's fine," Geri smiled.

She turned back to the girl. "It's okay," she soothed, holding Brina tight. "You're safe. I won't let anything happen to you."

EIGHT

They found Lark where they'd left him, holding a piece of rock threateningly above his head as they turned the corner.

"Watch it," the pilot said.

Lark lowered the rock, looked at the girl suspiciously. "Is she infect–" he began.

"She's fine," Geri cut in.

"Can you walk?" the pilot said to Lark.

Lark shook his head. "Ankle's fucked."

The pilot looked across the fields. "There's a road up that way. You'll be okay. It's not far."

They started across the fields, the little girl holding Geri's hand, Lark hobbling behind the others. The field was mostly clear, the majority of the dead drawn to the garage and house. But Lark was struggling.

"Hey," he called after them.

The pilot stopped, looked. "What now?"

"You're walking too fast," Lark said.

The tattooed man was sweating profusely. His face was still pale. The ankle was killing him and he wished, once more, that he had something to take the edge off. Hell, even a handful of painkillers would do. He stumbled a few more yards then stopped, out of breath.

The pilot shook his head.

His eye fell upon something on the ground nearby. He reached for it, overturning what looked to Lark to be a wheelbarrow. The pilot shook a little foliage out of the barrow then looked at Lark.

"You have *got* to be kidding me!" Lark spat.

But the older man wasn't smiling.

Lark swore angrily then limped over to the barrow and fell shamefully into its scoop.

The pilot handed him the gun.

Geri and the pilot took a handle each to drag the barrow across the dry-earthed fields.

They moved past some trees, Lark keeping his eyes open for any dead stragglers. He spotted one, standing in the middle of the field. As the wheelbarrow creaked past, Lark could make the dead thing out more clearly: an overweight hick wearing soiled jeans and a body warmer. Probably a farmer.

Lark fired, the first bullet striking the dead man in the chest. His second shot found the old boy's head, dropping him like a sack of potatoes.

Willis looked at him disdainfully.

"What?" Lark protested.

"You didn't *need* to do that," the pilot said.

He took the gun from Lark.

"Just like *you* didn't need to torch the helicopter," Lark countered.

"Yeah," Geri said. "Pretty fucking stupid, that."

"You wouldn't understand," Willis said, sighing.

They cut across another field, reaching a fence leading onto a road. It was deserted. Sun-baked tarmac rolled off into the distance, one end heading north, the other heading south.

A couple of trees stood a hundred or so yards to the south.

From one of them, a rope swung gently, holding the body of what looked to be a young man. Flies surrounded the body, their faint buzz the only sound the survivors could hear. The man's eyes were open, glaring at them as they passed.

A solitary car was stalled by the side of the road.

Willis dropped his arm of the wheelbarrow then headed for the car. Within moments, he had it started, the car's engine revving boastfully.

He dipped his head out of the side window.

"Hurry!" he called to the others.

...

The roads were empty.

Country life in Ireland was slow at the best of times, rural folks moving at a pace that would frustrate the average Belfastian. Now, it was even slower.

Nature was retaking the roads, its savage laws overruling the tarmac Kingdom before it. A flock of birds circled a dead sheep. As they passed, Geri watched the birds swoop, tearing into the carcass with their beaks, stripping the bone of meat.

She looked away, sipped at the bottle of water in her hand.

They'd found the provisions in the back seat, several bottles stacked with some tinned food and cans of petrol. There was a box of cigarettes which Lark grabbed, sparking one up immediately. Seemed like whoever owned the car was planning a long trip.

She was reminded of the young man's body hanging from the tree beside the road. *Must have had second thoughts*, she mused.

Further down the road, Geri spotted a felled tree. It lay unattended, surprising them on a twist of the road, Willis having to brake aggressively to avoid it. As the car moved slowly around the blockage, Geri noticed the body of a man lying by a nearby stretch of hedge. His mouth was open, twisted into an eternal scream. It reminded Geri of the Edward Munch painting she'd pinned on her wall back when she was a student.

"Where are we going?" she asked the pilot.

He said nothing, keeping his eyes in front.

"Why did you torch the helicopter?"

Still nothing. It was as if he couldn't hear her.

"He's a nut job," Lark offered, exhaling smoke out the wound-down window in the back. "And he's driving. So leave him alone, for God's sake."

The pilot's eyes blinked, his lips upturned slightly, suggesting Lark's latest quip had amused him.

Geri was exasperated. "Look," she said. "You come in your helicopter, boasting of some marvellous army base we can all feel safe in. Then you point a gun at us. And blow the bloody chopper up! I need to know why."

"You wouldn't understand," Willis mumbled.

"Try me," Geri pressed.

"Okay, it's not *you* they're interested in." He glanced in his rear view mirror. "Or *him*. It's the little girl."

"Brina?"

Willis nodded.

"What's he talking about?" Lark said.

Geri looked to the back seat, her eyes finding Brina, sat beside Lark, staring out the window, oblivious to the conversation. The little girl turned and smiled. She looked calm, safe. Like this was all part of some family outing.

Weird fucking family, Geri mused.

"That apartment block in Finaghy was under surveillance," Willis continued. "Doesn't matter why. But they saw the girl; saw that she'd somehow survived the infection." He looked to Geri, his voice lower. "They want to run tests on her, see if she's really immune. And if she is, extract some sort of antivirus."

Geri looked at him, and in a quiet voice said, "Is that such a bad thing?"

Willis glanced sideways at her. "You don't know the people involved."

Geri sighed.

Why was everything so complicated?

She looked to Willis. "Look, we need to start trusting each other. It's the only way to survive."

Willis laughed. "Survival," he spat as if the word was dirty. "That's all you care about, isn't it?"

"Yes," Geri said. Her tone was confident, defiant.

"You sheep are so bloody predictable," he said. "I don't care about surviving. I just want to know the truth. Who did this to us? And why? It's the only thing that matters now, the only thing driving me."

Geri shook her head. "Maybe Lark's right," she said. "Maybe you are insane."

She looked out the window again. The car was turning, heading up some dirt track.

"You didn't answer when I asked where we were going," she said.

Willis smiled. "We're going to see a friend."

NINE

This had been the plan all along.

Find somewhere safe to land. Torch the helicopter (which was probably being tracked) then head via road to Tom's place. They could hole up there for a while, decide what to do next.

Tom had seemed reluctant at first to reveal his location but eventually relented. He was still paranoid about Willis' revelation about being a double agent.

Willis wondered just how the other man was faring in general. Mentally as well as physically. He'd got a few scares during his last couple of convos with Tom. Being cooped up could do things to a man, drive him insane.

It made Willis nervous.

He'd shared so much conversation with Tom online yet hadn't a clue what the other man would look or sound like.

Did they really know each other?

Willis figured Tom would be of similar age to himself. He was into the same music and films. Yet, all the pilot knew *for sure* was that he trusted Tom. And that trumped everything.

He reached for the phone in his pocket, hoping to mail Tom, give him a heads-up on their approach. But it wasn't there. He checked other pockets as he drove. Still no phone. He looked on the floor of the car.

"Shit," he murmured, eyes back on the road.

"What's wrong?" Geri said.

"Nothing," he said. "Nothing at all."

...

The Chamber, Co. Armagh

Gallagher stood in the toilets of The Chamber, the smart phone in his hand.

On the front of the phone was a picture of Willis. Younger looking. Standing beside a young woman and child.

The phone wasn't locked.

Gallagher tutted, opening the phone's photo file, flicking through some other shots.

He found a video, clicked into it. The video was from The Chamber, footage of Brina's appearance on the flat 23 surveillance camera.

Why had Willis recorded this?

It worried Gallagher.

The Chamber was built on secrecy. Nothing getting out remained key to the project's continued success. An operative could be severely disciplined for recording classified data on a portable device. It was against the project's confidentiality policy.

Gallagher checked Willis' call record next. Nothing for weeks.

He checked the online activity of the phone, noting a particular site visited recently. Gallagher clicked into it.

His face creased.

"What are you up to, Mr Willis?"

TEN

Ballynarry, Co. Armagh

The computer was still working, meaning a little juice was left in the generator. Colin knew he should be conserving the electricity for important stuff like cooking and heating water, but it hardly mattered to him now. And anyway, he'd heard Vicky running a bath earlier. Why couldn't *he* be reckless too?

God knew, he *used to be* reckless. Kicking against the pricks. Doing his own thing. But somehow, this whole 'world-ending' thing seemed to have made Colin boring.

He took another swig of the bourbon in his glass. It was the only drink left in the house, but he was actually starting to enjoy it.

Colin looked back at the blank computer screen.

He was bored. This place was like a prison. Those fucking things had surrounded the house, meaning he couldn't even step into the garden for a breath of fresh air.

There was still some food left. Enough for another week, maybe.

But after that…

They were going to die, and Colin knew it.

The three survivors had grown apart in the house. Each took a separate room and claimed it as their own. Vicky spent most of her time in the living room, sleeping or crying. Ciaran could be heard rolling around the kitchen on his makeshift wheelchair, retreating to the spare bedroom every now and then. But Colin remained in the study with the computer.

He'd become obsessed by the date on that fucking notebook page. He'd found books belonging to Chris, sifting through their pages to see if he could find the date tied into some theory or other. He found notes in margins, things his friend had scribbled to himself while reading and researching, but so far no date that matched.

Some of the authors Colin recognised from drunken conversations with Chris over the years. People like David Icke. There were others, his friend's library boasting books from writers as diverse as George Orwell and Jesse Ventura.

Wasn't Jesse a wrestler? Colin mused. *Or an actor?*

One thing was sure: Chris had been deadly serious about this shit.

Colin assumed it was all just a laugh. Something to talk about when drinking or smoking blow. But the more he read, the more he wondered if maybe there were some truth behind it all.

He found a ring binder belonging to Chris. It looked like his friend was working on his own book. The main focus of his research was outbreaks. Chris had made notes on everything from the Foot and Mouth Disease (linking it to some contagion named Picornvirus) to a variety of flu outbreaks: bird flu, swine flu, even the so-called Spanish flu from 1918. According to Chris, these outbreaks were all manmade. Worse still, Chris believed many of them were government or military sponsored.

But why?

It didn't matter. Colin found what he was looking for on the final page of his notes. Chris had been brainstorming titles for the proposed manuscript. Circled at the bottom of the page, underneath several scored out alternatives, was the following:

DOOMSDAY - 12/08/2016

It seemed to tie into Chris' theory that all this messing about with viral agents would end in a mass and uncontrollable pandemic. That the pandemic would spread throughout the world like wild fire. 12th August 2016 was the proposed date for this to happen.

Think you got your timing wrong, mate, Colin mused.

He went back to the screen, blew some air out.

He typed the date into the address bar:

http://12.08.2016

He pressed RETURN, waited.

Still no joy.

Colin had another thought, retyping the numbers, this time dividing them up differently:

http://12.08.20.16

He pressed RETURN again.

He tapped his fingers impatiently, waiting for the inevitable error message.

But this time something was happening...

Colin leaned in closer to the screen.

What looked like an old-school news group popped up.

A message appeared in the chat box, accredited to UNCLE TOM, the only user in the chat room.

It read:

CHRYSLER?

"Jesus," Colin said.

Chrysler? He must mean Chris.

Colin swallowed hard, his heart racing. His hands moved to the keyboard.

NOT CHRYSLER, he typed. CHRYSLER IS DEAD.

A pause and then a reply:

WHO ARE YOU?

Colin breathed out some air. "Who the hell are *you*?" he said to himself, but typed:

COLIN. OLD FRIEND OF CHRIS. WHO ARE YOU?

Another pause. The computer was churning, Colin worried it might give any minute.

Then came the message:

ALSO FRIEND OF CHRYSLER. HOW CAN I TRUST YOU?

"Charming," Colin said. "But the same goes for you, mate."

He typed something similar.

Another reply:

TELL ME SOMETHING ABOUT CHRYSLER.

Colin smiled. He typed:

CHRIS WAS GAY. LIVED WITH HIS PARTNER BEN.

The pause this time was longer.

BEN TEN? YOU KNOW BEN TOO?

"Jesus," Colin said. "Ben was into this shit too?" *And what was with all the silly names?* "So where the hell are you, anyway?" Colin wondered, typing the question.

He waited for the reply. It seemed like Uncle Tom wasn't so sure of Colin.

And then it came:

CLOSE. NEED YOUR HELP.

"How?" Colin said. He typed it.

Another pause, then:

FIND EVIDENCE.

"Evidence of what?" Colin said as he typed.

The reply came quickly.

THE FLU. CHRYSLER KNEW HOW IT STARTED.

ELEVEN

A coded file simply marked CHRYSLER contained all that Chris Lennon knew about the mutated flu virus. The same numbers that had been used to access the user group got Colin into the file, leaving the jaded survivor to wonder if his friend had, perhaps even subconsciously, *wanted* someone to get this information. To follow the clues he'd left, to seek out the truth. To both earn and be burdened with the terrible responsibility that Chris himself had felt.

This news was as shocking as it was big.

Reading through the papers, Colin couldn't help but wonder if heartbreak alone had led Chris to take his own life. Would the contents of these documents have been enough to push him over the edge, either way, to leave him with nothing but an empty feeling inside?

"Found it," Colin typed to Tom.

God help us all.

His heart was thumping in his chest. He waited with baited breath for Tom to come back to him. He wanted rid of this stuff. For it to be someone else's problem.

A sudden noise.

Colin swung round in his chair, listened more intently. It seemed to be coming from the hallway.

He glanced back at the screen, noticed Tom was writing back.

He sighed, walked to the door and opened it, looking out into the hallway.

There Colin found Ciaran, the young soldier using a baseball bat like an oar, guiding his wheeled office chair down towards the bathroom.

"What was that?" Colin asked.

"Don't know," the other survivor replied. "I think it came from there," he added, using the baseball bat to point towards the bathroom.

"Is Vicky still in there?"

Ciaran shrugged. "Looks like it."

Geez, Colin thought. *She's been in that bath for hours now. What the hell's she doing?*

Another noise, this one more frantic than before.

Both men looked down the hall once more.

The light from the bathroom spilled out into the hallway as what appeared to be Vicky, naked and wet, crept slowly towards them. As she moved closer, Colin could see that her wrists were sliced, diluted blood seeping from the wounds.

"Oh Christ…"

Colin's stomach seemed to shrink.

He moved to Vicky, grabbed hold of her. Tried to hold her arms above her head. He thought he'd seen it done on some patient on a hospital show.

But Vicky wasn't just *any* patient…

Her face leaned in close to Colin's neck and he felt her teeth sink through his skin. As Colin struggled to let go of her body, Vicky continued to feast on him, roughly chewing on the flesh, ripping it away in mouthfuls.

…

Ciaran backed off, using his bat to roll himself away from the other two survivors, now struggling on the hallway floor. He watched as Colin pushed Vicky away then tried to stand up, one hand vainly placed against his torn neck, blood gushing between his fingers.

Colin looked towards Ciaran, eyes full of longing.

"H-help me," he mouthed.

"I-I can't, man. You're bitten!"

Ciaran's one good arm continued to work the bat, rolling his chair back towards the kitchen.

He watched as Colin's eyes rolled back in his head and he lost his balance, crumbling against the wall next to him. A red stain followed his trail as he slid against the white plaster, falling to the floor.

Vicky stood watching, her stone-blue face displaying neither regret nor satisfaction for what she had just done. Her eyes turned to look at Ciaran. She began to follow him down the hall, her movements almost as awkward and strained as his.

Ciaran pushed open the kitchen door, sliding himself onto the tiled floor and then trying to close the door with the baseball bat.

But Vicky's hand reached through the crack in the door, struggling to get through.

The young soldier wheeled himself away, knowing he had neither the strength nor agility to navigate the door against her efforts. He watched from the far side of the room, his back against the kitchen sink, as she pushed the door further open, clambering through to face him.

Outside, the sound of the dead rose, its gruff, congested choir perhaps a welcome to their new sister. Vicky stopped, seeming to stare out the glass-fronted patio doors, no doubt seeing the pack poised and waiting in the garden. Then she looked back at Ciaran, her head twisted to one side.

TWELVE

There was nowhere for him to go.

Ciaran looked at the baseball bat, deciding it was useless. He dropped the damn thing, his twisted hand reaching instead for a nearby drawer. He opened the drawer, his hand searching amongst the various utensils, finding a blade. He retrieved the blade, brandishing it in front of him, as if that action alone might scare Vicky off.

Still she moved towards him, her hands grabbing for his hair.

Ciaran dodged her.

He stood to get up from his makeshift wheelchair, swinging the knife in his one good hand. But the blade dabbed uselessly without any gusto and soon left his hand, gliding briefly in the air before hitting the floor, sliding across its smoothly polished tiles.

Ciaran tumbled after it.

Vicky bent down, reaching for him.

Her face drew close. Her skin strangely fragrant, the distinct aroma of bath crème still fresh on her.

Ciaran struggled to get away but it was useless.

A sudden noise drew his one good eye. Ciaran looked to find Colin stumbling into the kitchen, his face pale, his neck and t-shirt drenched in blood.

Great, the young soldier thought. *Now there's two of them to feast on me.*

But the other man bent to the kitchen floor, retrieved the knife. He made for Vicky, brandishing the knife with both hands and swinging for her. The knife bit deep into Vicky's neck, her head jolting up in what appeared to be surprise or shock. Colin dug deeper, the knife eating further into her neck until Ciaran could see bone.

Vicky fell backwards, her body jittering on the floor as if she were having a fit.

Colin fell against the cooker, spent.

He looked to Ciaran, his mouth fighting to speak. "The… the computer," he said. And then his head dipped to one side, and his breathing slowed to a standstill, his body sliding to the floor beside Vicky.

It took Ciaran a long time to pull himself back onto the swivel chair. He tried numerous times; each unsuccessful attempt leaving him sprawled across the floor. Finally, he made it, positioning himself once again in the driver's seat of his makeshift wheelchair.

He sat for a minute, catching his breath.

On the floor, the two corpses lay apart, Vicky's body still shaking, her bright eyes turned away from Colin.

The computer, he remembered. Those were Colin's final words.

The young soldier pushed himself away from the cooker towards the kitchen door. He used the door as leverage, entering the hallway. He moved back along the hallway, into the study, where the computer was still running.

He noticed the screen with several messages listed. Some answered, others unanswered. This was a chat room. He would have used them all the time back in school. Colin must have been using it before the shit hit the fan.

But who the hell was he talking to?

Ciaran started by asking that question.

...

Waringstown, Co. Down

Tom slammed his bottle to the desk.

"What do you mean, who am I?! We've been talking for ages!"

He typed it.

The reply came quickly:

NOT COLIN. COLIN'S FRIEND, CIARAN.

"What's going on? Some kind of fucking party?!" Tom's hands were shaking. He was so close. *So fucking close.*

He typed:

WHERE'S COLIN?

The reply came almost immediately:

DEAD.

"Shit!" Tom said. "They've been breached."

He started to panic. "What to do, what to do, what to do," he muttered.

He waited for the familiar mantra to be repeated, but the bird was dead. He knew that.

"No time," Tom said. "No fucking time!"

He returned to the keyboard. Looked like this Ciaran bloke was his only hope.

He started to type.

A sound in the corner disturbed him.

Gingerly, Tom turned back towards the birdcage.

The bird was moving. Fluttering around the cage, falling, then picking itself up and flying again. Bloody thing looked doped. Its beak opened to speak, but instead of words it released a shrill squawk.

Tom had never heard it make that sound before.

"Christ almighty," he muttered to himself. Now the infection had breached *his* house.

He turned back to the computer.

THIRTEEN

The Chamber, Co. Armagh

"Go fuck yourself, Gallagher."

The doctor smiled.

"Now, now, Major," he tutted. "You're an officer. Where's your manners."

Gallagher reached for the nearby packet of surgical wipes, retrieving one to remove the gob of blood and mucus from his yellow plastic suit. He dumped the wipe into the nearby bin.

"Now, let's try that question again. I want to know how you're feeling right now. As the virus takes control of your body, how does it affect you?"

"And I told you to go fuck yourself," Jackson said.

"Indeed you did, sir. Of course repetition is a key behaviour of the dead. This is promising. You'll make a fine specimen."

"I'm going to rip your heart out."

"That's the spirit!" Gallagher rejoiced. "Come on, Major! Let's have more of that anger. I'm convinced it will speed up your transformation."

Jackson laughed bitterly. "Why me?" he said. "Why not one of those other monkeys out there, drinking themselves to death."

"Because I'm not a monster," Gallagher said. "I'm not going to murder an innocent man."

Jackson laughed again, this time harder. The laughing gave way to wheezing, more blood spilling from his lips.

"We both know *exactly* what you are, Gallagher," he spat. "You're the coldest bastard I've ever known. How a man can inflict as much misery as you have and still consider himself human, I'll never know."

The doctor shrugged. "I'm sure our old friend Patrick Flynn could say the very same about you, sir. And yet here you are, pious to the end."

He smiled, strolled across to the Colonel's torso. There was even less of the old man left now, Gallagher having removed the dead man's lower jaw. He'd then pulled each tooth in the top row, piling them like shillings in the Colonel's old hat, the same hat they'd drawn from during that farce of a lottery.

"Why can't you be like the Colonel?" Gallagher said to Jackson, all the while stroking the dead man's hair. "Such a gracious host."

Gallagher retrieved some lighter fluid from the table, sprinkling it like vinegar over the Colonel's head, humming as he worked.

Once done, he turned to Jackson again. "You see, Major, the actual virus is quite a complex beast," he said. "Can take one man within a matter of hours. Another over the course of several weeks. And once dead, there are differing reports of how long the infection takes to *subvert* a host, shall we say.

"Yet on subversion, the risen dead will act quite a *primitively*. A slave to instinct. Mostly presents a pack mentality, using whatever senses the virus feels moved to leave them." Gallagher fumbled in his pocket and produced a lighter. "Watch this," he said, winking at Jackson.

He sparked the lighter, bringing the flame close to the Colonel's eyes. The old man seemed excited by it, his eyes widening immediately, following the flame as Gallagher waved it from side to side. Gallagher then lit the old man's wiry hair, the Colonel screaming as if in delight as both hair and flesh went up.

"Primitive," Gallagher said again, noting the Colonel's excitement as he burned, "drawn to light and fire. Worshipping it, I would suggest, even though it might very well destroy them."

Gallagher lifted a nearby mug of coffee and tipped it over the dead officer's head, putting the flame out.

He turned again to Jackson. "You've all this ahead of you, Major. Aren't you just the tiniest bit curious as to how it will *feel*?"

"You're sick!" Jackson protested.

But Gallagher smiled. "On the contrary, sir," he said. "I feel fit as a fiddle. All this excitement, you see. Warms a man's heart, no?"

There was a sudden beeping noise.

Jackson followed the noise, noticing what looked to be a Blackberry on the table, next to the Colonel. Gallagher moved towards the Blackberry, picking it up. He worked at the phone's buttons, smiling as he read whatever message had just come through. It struck Jackson as odd that any network would be live at this stage of the game.

"What's your thoughts on conspiracy theories, Major?" Gallagher asked. "Seems our man Willis is a fan…"

There was a knock on the door.

Gallagher looked to the Major quizzically, as if the infected officer might know who was there.

"Please excuse me," he said, sliding the phone into the pocket of his lab coat.

He went to the door, opened it.

One of the soldiers stood at the other side.

"Can I help you, Private?" Gallagher asked, smiling.

"Er, there's a call for you, sir?"

"A call, you say."

"That's right, sir."

"A call from *whom*, Private?"

"Dunno, sir. They asked for you."

The Private strained to look past Gallagher towards Jackson and the Colonel.

The Colonel shrieked, causing the Private to jump.

Gallagher left the room, pulling the door closed behind him.

"Okay, take me to this call," Gallagher said to the Private.

The younger man led Gallagher back through to the control room, where several other soldiers sat poised around the radio they'd been working at. A faint hiss escaped the contraption, one of the men holding its mic.

He looked up as Gallagher approached.

"Sir, we've been broadcasting a distress call. This … er… gentleman responded. He claims to be from the government."

Gallagher smiled. "How exciting," he said.

He pressed the mic, said, "This is Dr Miles Gallagher at your service, acting CO of The Chamber. To whom am I speaking?"

FOURTEEN

Waringstown, Co. Armagh

The country held a certain anarchic quality that Lark could appreciate, a grassroots sense of order that appealed to someone who had felt frustrated and confined by rules all of his life. Nature did as it pleased all the time.

"This is it," Willis said.

The car pulled up to another farmhouse. It looked very much like the one they'd left less than an hour ago. It had a small front garden, clumsily fenced, a garden path running to a heavily locked door. Weeds rose up from the cracks in the paved garden path like snakes.

Several of the dead littered the front yard, their faces turned to look at the car as it ground to a halt. Willis checked his gun, prepared to take the hostiles out swiftly.

A dark shadow fell upon them.

Lark looked up to find a flock of birds circling the house, their cries high-pitched and shrill.

"Just hope he's okay," Willis said.

He reached for the car door, waited.

"Come on," Geri said to Brina as she reached for her own door. "Let Mr Willis go first. And stay close to me."

Lark's gaze fell upon the birds again, their flight taking a random dip, swooping close to the car.

"Hey," he said, his own door only semi-open, "Maybe we should wait a –"

Their attack was as fast as it was brutal. The first one was on Willis within seconds, claws digging into his back, beak pecking at his head. Willis went to shield his face, shaking the dead bird off, but more lit upon him, digging into his flesh hungrily.

Geri pulled Brina close but stood frozen to her spot.

"Fuck," Lark muttered to himself. And then to Geri, "GET BACK IN THE CAR!"

Still she didn't move, so he reached to grab her arm, tugging her back. Geri grabbed Brina with her, and Lark pulled them both into the car, then slammed the door behind him.

One of the birds collided with the glass, piercing it with its beak. It hung there trapped, the bloody thing's wings shaking like it was possessed. Its eyes were frosted over. It was dead.

"Don't look at it!" Lark shouted.

His own eyes were drawn to Willis outside, the pilot now completely covered by birds, their black feathers like some kind of elaborate cloak. At his feet, the grass ran thick and red with blood. His screams were masked only by the unholy squawks of the birds as they tore into him, shedding his flesh like lumps of meat.

A smaller flock circled the car.

They swooped, like the first bird, ramming the glass like tiny kamikazes, falling onto the bonnet and then taking flight to attack again. Spider web cracks were starting to form in the glass all around the survivors.

They were fucked.

Lark patted his head.

"Think!" he said to himself.

Geri stretched across the back seat, covering the child with her own body.

The image suddenly reminded Lark of Afghanistan, of that house where his army buddies had thrown a young girl on the floor and had their fun with her. Of later seeing the girl's mother bent over the body of her daughter. Those bastards had killed that poor girl. Raped her and left her to die, bleeding on the floor of her own home.

And then Lark was in battle. There was confusion, insurgents thick and heavy on them. But in the smoke and dust and noise, Lark aimed his rifle and fired not at the insurgents, but at three of his own men, giving those rapist cunts as taste of their own medicine.

Friendly fire, they'd called it.

He repeated the words now: "Friendly fire…"

Something clicked.

Lark reached his hands across the back seat of the car, finding a petrol can. He shook it to his ear, ensuring there was some fuel in it, then stretched forward, dousing the front seat of the car with the contents of the can, emptying it completely then dropping it into the driver's seat.

He found a second can, did the same thing.

He reached for his lighter, looked to Geri.

"What the hell are you –" she began.

"When I say go," Lark cut in, "I need you to grab the girl and sprint as fast as you can away from the car!"

"You're insane!"

"GO!" Lark cried, flicking the lighter and chucking it into the front seat.

The whole front of the car erupted into flames, scorching his face.

Geri grabbed Brina into her arms, pushed through the back car door. She moved swiftly across the yard towards a nearby outhouse.

Lark struggled from the burning vehicle, aware of the birds flocking around the front bonnet, pecking frantically at the hot windscreen, trying to get to the flames that would no doubt consume them. The few dead hanging around the house joined the frenzy, moving hungrily towards the car, bathing in its flames and then flailing around like possessed men.

Lark hobbled forward, the pain in his ankle sharper than ever. He was only metres from the car when it went up in an almighty roar, the windows blowing out, raw heat eating into the back of his head as he was thrown to the ground.

FIFTEEN

Lark rolled over, watching the birds dance in the fire, their shrill cries piercing the still country air. As the flames continued to build, roaring victoriously, the squawk of the birds began to wane.

Lark pulled himself from the ground, feeling the bite of glass in his neck and back of his head. His eyes stung. He was feeling dizzy, nauseous. His stomach gave, filling his mouth with warm, thick bile. Lark puked it onto the ground.

God, he felt fucking awful.

The tattooed man moved towards the charred corpse of Willis. The pilot had been fumbling for his handgun, now curled in his right hand uselessly. Lark prised it from the dead man's shredded fingers, wiping it onto his t-shirt. The hard plastic of the gun was warm in his hands, but it looked undamaged. Lark dropped the magazine, checked then reinserted it before chambering a round.

He looked around, then up at the house. At the first storey window he noticed a face poking through the space where a wooden board had fallen away.

"Hey!" Lark called.

The face disappeared.

Lark limped over to the heavy front door, finding it boarded up and locked tight. He banged the wood with his fist, to no avail.

Lark aimed the handgun at the wood, blew a hole through. He then fired on the exposed door's lock. Noticed several other bolts. Blew them away too, kicked the door in.

He entered the house. Coughed, spitting another gob of bile onto the floor of the hallway. "Okay, where are you, ye bastid?"

The house reeked. Flies hovered like thick smoke in the living room. There was shit everywhere. Bin bags piled high. Spent gas cylinders.

He could hear something coming from upstairs. More bird sounds.

Lark readied his gun, clambering up the stairs.

He found the first bedroom door open, an old man sitting inside by his computer. In the corner was a birdcage, a clearly dead bird squawking and fluttering around inside, as if drunk.

The old boy turned and looked at Lark. "Where's Agent13?" he asked.

"What the *fuck* are you on about?!"

"The group!" the old man shouted. "I've made contact with Chrysler's place. They've found data, important –" The old man stopped talking, looked Lark up and down. "You're infected," he said, but there was no fear or pity in his voice. Rather a sense that the infection would spoil things, ruin things for him and whatever bullshit quest he'd signed on for.

Geri and Brina entered the room, Geri's arm wrapped protectively around the child.

"I swear," Lark said to Geri, pointing to the old man, "I'm going to brain this cunt."

"Jesus," Geri said, "Would you calm yourself down?" She grabbed the handgun from Lark's grasp, shook her head. "You'll upset the child."

That seemed to stall him. He remembered what had happened the last time Brina got upset.

Lark stumbled over to the nearby bed and fell down upon it.

The old man turned to stare at Brina. His eyes widened. "It's her," he said, and for a moment Geri thought he was going to reach for the girl.

Geri fixed the old man with a defiant glance.

He backed off, returned to the computer screen.

"You're Tom," Geri said to him.

But the old man ignored her. He scratched his head, and Geri could have sworn that she saw something fall from his hair. She almost gagged. He was filthy. The string vest he wore looked like it had *never* been washed.

She tried again. "That's your name, isn't it? Uncle Tom, Willis told us —"

"Willis?" Tom said, suddenly interested. His eyes fell to Geri's chest, then back to her eyes. "That was his *real* name, wasn't it?"

"He spoke very highly of you. Said you were a good man, Tom. Very learned."

"He's dead now, isn't he?" Tom said.

"Yes," Geri replied.

She thought of the birds. Of the dead gathered by the door. She looked out the window. The few remaining cadavers still circled the car, infatuated with the dwindling flames. But how long would that keep them occupied?

"Tom," she said, "we need to lock the door up again."

"The memos," Tom said, ignoring her once more. "Chris had memos from the top boys involved on his file. Don't you know what this means?" He looked to

Geri. "The government are up to their necks in this shit." A line of spittle broke across his beard. "And we can prove it!"

Geri sighed heavily. Tom wasn't addressing her as an individual, instead using her as sounding board for whatever life he was leading online.

"Tom," she tried once more, trying to focus him away from his computer, back to reality, "The door…"

But a sudden beeping noise had the old man transfixed.

"This is it!" he beamed. "He's sent it through!"

SIXTEEN

Ballynarry, Co. Armagh

The documents in the file Ciaran found told a story which might have been quite unbelievable, had he not witnessed the outbreak – and the government's attempts to deal with it – first hand. Previously, he would have thought the file to be the stuff of kooky conspiracy theorists. Today, it was something to cling to, a reason for everything that was going on and, more importantly, someone to blame.

In this instance, it was a laboratory, hired by the UK government to create a new strain of the flu virus. It was to be a distraction to recent bad press on expenses and an illegal war, a way the government could prove its relevance to people against a backdrop of corruption and collusion.

The documents Ciaran found on the computer spelled it all out.

They were trying to create a pandemic, a viral outbreak that would prove deadly to some, yet treatable for most. The flu would cull the older and more vulnerable populace, viewed by some officials as a drain on state welfare. The government knew the remaining populace would turn to them for help, and they would handle the situation admirably, primed with the resources to do so: inoculations, anti-viral treatments, those yellow fucking surgical masks and glossy self-help guides.

But something went wrong.

God knows, something went very wrong.

And these documents, these memos fingered every last bastard to blame for that.

Ciaran scanned everything into the PC as instructed by the man called Uncle Tom. He wasn't sure if he could trust this guy, if the user group was legit, but he didn't have much choice. There was too much at stake. And there was no way he could hold onto this information himself, given his present state of health.

Ciaran uploaded the scanned documents to the group.

A reply came back almost immediately from the man he'd been talking to.

GOT IT.

Ciaran took a breath, grateful the generator hadn't given up before he'd uploaded the docs.

He could hear a sound at his door, a banging, and wondered if it was Colin, risen from the dead. Or if maybe Vicky had found some way to pull herself back onto her feet and get revenge.

Not that it mattered.

Ciaran thought about the growing number of dead outside. His own mangled body. The strong possibility that the stinging sensation in his neck was nothing to do with his fall onto the kitchen floor and more to do with Vicky's long, sharp fingernails.

Polish Ron came into his head. The girl he'd met in the pub on the day he'd enlisted. How they had both been gunned down simply because a man wearing stripes deemed it the right thing to do.

He thought about his mam too, hoping against reason that she was still somehow alive down in Newcastle.

But, even if she were, Ciaran wouldn't want her to see him like this.

He was finished.

He returned to the screen. There were no more messages. But Ciaran typed one himself:

POWER ALMOST GONE. SIGNING OFF. GOOD LUCK.

SEVENTEEN

Waringstown, Co. Down

Geri watched Tom as he beavered away on the print-outs, oblivious to her. He was muttering to himself, circling bits of text in red pen, his random swears a mixture of delight and anger.

She left the old man to it, attended to Lark. She was beginning to worry that the tattooed man's sweating and nausea wasn't just the result of the ever-increasing stress to his body. That old Tom might be right: Lark was infected.

His sneeze confirmed her suspicions. Geri winced as it soaked her face.

With shaking hands, she pulled a tissue from her pocket, wiped the bloody snot from her face.

"Lark?" she called, running her hand along his brow. It was red hot.

His eyes opened.

"Jesus, you're sick," Geri said.

Lark pulled himself up, spitting a bloody gob to the floor of the bedroom. "First time anyone's ever called me Jesus," he said, offering a smile.

Geri buried her face in his chest.

Lark gently placed his hands around her. "Careful now," he said. "I hear this shit's infectious."

Another beeping noise from the computer. Old Tom looked up from his papers, staring at the screen. He reached for his mouse, clicking on the user group icon.

There was a message from Agent13.

Tom looked to the other survivors, confusion etched across his face. "What the hell," he said. "Agent13 is dead, right?"

"If you mean that twat, Willis, then sure," Lark said. He looked to the cage in the corner where the dead parrot still squawked and fluttered like some broken toy. "Henpecked," he added.

Tom turned back to the screen, still baffled. "Well, who the hell's *this,* then?"

The answer to his question appeared on screen.

MY NAME IS MILES GALLAGHER AND I WANT TO HELP YOU.

EIGHTEEN

"Gallagher!" Tom spat. He pulled back from the screen. "Damn it, he's infiltrated the group."

"Who's Gallagher?" Geri asked.

Tom was shuffling through more papers piled under the computer desk. "He's a fucking goon, that's who he is!"

Geri looked to Lark.

The tattooed man shrugged. "I think that's paranoid geek speak for 'military'", he rasped.

Another message came:

HEAR THAT SOUND?

The three survivors were quiet, all straining their ears for some unknown noise. Eventually, a faint buzzing noise bled in from the sky. Geri looked to Lark, then to Tom. Even Brina got in on the action, raising her finger to the still-squawking dead bird in the cage, whispering, "Shhhh!"

"What is it?" Geri said, but Tom shushed her.

"It's a helicopter," Lark said.

Geri looked to Tom, then to the screen.

She pushed him aside, went to the keyboard. "What does this Gallagher want?" She said, typing the question.

The reply came within seconds:

I TOLD YOU. I WANT TO HELP.

"Bastard!" Tom cried. "No one needs your help, fucking goon!"

There were tears in the old man's eyes. Geri could only guess that the reality of losing his friend, before they'd even met, had caught up with him. Tom was mourning Willis, transferring his grief into anger and blame.

She looked to Lark. Watched as he picked up the handgun, released the magazine, checked for bullets. Her heart sank. She really couldn't deal with any more of that. The running, the shooting, the hiding.

She looked to Brina, sitting by the birdcage, making faces at the dead parrot.

She recalled what Willis had said: the military, this Gallagher person, they planned to runs tests on Brina. Draw an antivirus from her blood.

Geri didn't know how that would work, what would be involved.

A dull feeling of guilt crept into her chest.

Tom was back at the computer. He was accessing files, downloading the contents onto his USB pen. It looked like he was planning to leave.

"Ask him exactly *how* he intends to help us," Geri said.

"No way," Tom protested.

Geri went to the keyboard, pushing old Tom away again.

"I will, then," she said.

She typed quickly, asking Gallagher if he had sent the helicopter.

NO, came the reply.

"Well, who is it then?" she asked, typing.

BAD PEOPLE.

"Bad people?" Tom barked. "*You're* fucking bad people."

"Gotta give it to this Gallagher fella," Lark laughed. "He's got a sense of humour."

He sneezed again, his face grimacing with the pain. "Fuck me," he croaked, shaking his hand dry.

"Ewww," Brina said.

Lark smiled painfully at the child.

I CAN HELP YOU, came the next message on screen.

"How?" Geri asked.

PROTECT YOU, Gallagher replied, still using the Agent13 sign-in.

The helicopter sounded closer.

"Can't trust him," Tom warned.

"I'm not even sure we can trust *you*, old man," Lark said, his voice like gravel.

Geri looked over at the tattooed man, concern in her eyes.

She turned back to Tom. "Find out exactly how he plans to help us," she said.

Tom went to protest, but Geri cut in, "Please, just do it."

The old man blew some air out. Still petulant, he returned to the keyboard, started typing.

Geri went to Lark. Sat on the bed beside him. "What if he has the cure," she said. "Willis said they were working on some sort of antivirus. Maybe they can help you…"

Lark stared up at her, his eyes darker than she'd ever seen them. "Look, do what you got to do. But I'm staying here."

"No," she said. "I'm only going if you come too. I *need* you."

Lark shook his head. "I'm fucked," he said.

"Please," she protested but Lark raised a finger to her lips.

"Shhh," he said.

He looked into Geri's eyes. Moved his hand across her cheek. Ran his fingers through her hair.

He smiled at her.

It was a beautiful smile. A smile without malice or sarcasm.

A single tear ran down Geri's face.

Lark moved his hand, found the gun and pressed it into her grasp.

"If you have to go," he said. "Then go *now*."

The helicopter was getting closer, almost upon them.

NINETEEN

The helicopter landed in the yard, near the still burning car.

Three soldiers exited.

They were not from the Mahon Road Army Camp. They'd come from somewhere else, somewhere further away.

Their mission was simple: extract the child alive, kill the others.

They were dressed head-to-toe in yellow protective clothing. They carried breathing apparatus on their backs, masks on their faces. They were armed, each carrying a rifle, primed and ready for action, aimed forwards as they moved stealthily towards the farmhouse.

A couple of dead things seeped out of the nearby fields. They showed little interest in the soldiers, more interested in the dulling flames of the burned out car. But they were taken out anyway, perfectly aimed head shots enough to put them down for good.

The soldiers reached the farmhouse.

The first soldier nudged the front door with his boot, and the door gave easily. He moved through, searching first the stairs in front of him before sweeping the muzzle of his rifle across the hallway.

His colleague entered next, taking the stairs and ascending slowly towards the bedrooms.

The first soldier prised open the living room door, once again using his foot.

The living room was a mess. Empty gas cylinders. Black bin bags, stuffed full of waste, stacked against the wall. One of the bags was ripped open, a mixture of empty bottles, cans and cartons spread across the floor in front of the soldier.. The fireplace was overflowing with papers, blackened, mixing with the ash, like they'd been burned some time ago.

There were flies everywhere. Oddly, as the soldier watched, some of the flies fell to the floor as if somehow rendered unconscious…

The soldier heard a sound.

He swung the rifle around towards the kitchen area.

The cutlery drawer was open, knives and forks and spoons spilled everywhere.

A faint hissing noise could be heard from the cooker. Through the eyes of his breathing mask, the soldier noticed movement in the air, like the glimmer of sun on an oppressively hot summer's day.

He was grabbed from behind. Noticed the glint of a blade as it moved in front of his eyes. Then a painful heat, searing across his throat before the blood came, flowing quickly down the yellow plastic of his suit.

As the soldier stumbled, he caught sight of his attacker; a tall thin man with tattoos, holding a kitchen knife.

In desperation, the soldier aimed his rifle and fired.

…

The blast ripped through the farmhouse, flames lapping through the door and gaps in the boarded up windows. A pungent smell of gas filled the air. The sound of automatic fire could be heard. Then screaming, the shrill cries of men burning alive diabolically loud.

Geri wondered if Lark's voice was among those she heard.

She held the child Brina in her arms, covering her sweet little face. She was too innocent, too beautiful to witness this kind of thing, and yet already, she'd witnessed much worse.

They sat behind the old shed in the yard, where the generator was stored.

Old Tom cowered beside them, surrounded by bags filled with papers and discs and books that he absolutely refused to leave without. His birdcage was there too; Brina had been insistent on bringing the parrot, despite its clearly dead demeanour.

Nearby was a helicopter. It looked a lot more modern than the helicopter Willis had flown. Geri could see the pilot through its dark glass windows, wearing similar protective clothing and headgear as the soldiers.

She sat Brina to the ground and made for the helicopter.

She grabbed the door just as the pilot went to close it. She struggled, wedging her foot in the gap to keep the door open.

The pilot fumbled for his sidearm. But his movements were clumsy, restricted by the gear. Geri got there first, aiming her gun squarely at his chest. She really wanted to kill this bastard, and the pilot knew it: he raised his hands to the air immediately.

"You're going to fly this thing," Geri told him. "Take us out of here."

Tom climbed into the helicopter, still swamped by his bags. He helped the child up, gingerly dodging the birdcage as she swung it into the seat beside her.

"W-where are we going?" the pilot asked.

"Mahon Road Army camp," Tom said, reluctantly. "Belly of the fucking beast."

EPILOGUE

Waringstown, Co. Down

Lize's body lay on the bed. Her eyes stared back at Martin as he lay down beside her. He'd tied her hands and feet. Covered her mouth with tape.

Martin pulled her close.

She struggled against him, her teeth grinding noisily.

"Shhh…" he said, stroking her face. "There, now…"

He'd spent the last hour opening the doors again, unwrapping whatever security he'd once deemed necessary to protect the house. There was no need for it anymore. His time had come.

Jamie and Shaun lay in the bath, their bodies broken up to ensure they didn't rise again.

Only Martin remained, but he was nothing without his girl.

Lize…

Looking at her, Martin wondered once more if there was any semblance of life left in his daughter's still beautiful body. Fred had wagged his tail when the body had first moved, excited by Lize's smell, maybe, or the flickering of her eyes. But Martin knew deep down he was lying to himself. His little girl was dead. The only thing living within her was that damn virus.

It wouldn't do.

Martin could hear Fred barking, no doubt warding off the first of the intruders. Soon the dead would fill the house, their coarse sounds already coming from the hallway, the stairs, the landing.

Lize continued to fight against the bonds.

Martin wanted release too.

He could hear the helicopter again. He wondered briefly who would be in it and where they would be going. He had called and waved as it made its first pass. But it was no use. He had been ignored by the helicopter, no doubt viewed as little more than a madman, dancing and waving from his window. And looking again at the mess he'd made of his daughter, Martin couldn't argue with that.

This was where it would end.

The dead were at his bedroom door now.

Martin closed his eyes and waited.

…

Deep in the bowels of the Mahon Road Army Camp, Dr Miles Gallagher stood over the body of his former commanding officer. After a brief and futile struggle, Major Jackson had given into the infection.

Jackson's eyes looked empty, like he'd given up long ago. But his lips dragged back against his teeth, frozen in one final silent scream.

He'd suffered terribly, yet Gallagher had offered Jackson no pity, and certainly no respect.

He simply waited.

Waited for the infection to move to its next stage.

Subversion.

In the distance, he heard the sound of a helicopter.

Major Jackson's eyes began to flicker.

Gallagher smiled.

ACKNOWLEDGMENTS

As always, I want to thank everyone who has supported my writing over the years – especially all those who have taken the time to e-mail or say hello at an event. It means a lot. Big love to Moody's Survivors, the best horror fan group on the web!

Thanks also to Ryan Fitzsimmons, Simon Caulfield, David Lightfoot and The Brave Blue Mouse for all their help with research.

Special thanks to my agent, Gina Panettieri, and everyone at Snowbooks.

Finally, I'd like to thank Rebecca for her love, support and belief in what I do.

ABOUT THE AUTHOR

Belfast born, Wayne Simmons has been kicking around the horror scene for years. He penned reviews and interviews for several online zines before publication of his debut novel in 2008. Wayne's work has since been published in the UK, Germany and Spain.

Wayne currently lives in Wales with his ghoulfiend and a Jack Russel terrier called Dita.

Look out for Wayne at various genre and tattoo cons, or visit him online: http://www.waynesimmons.org